RADKO'S WAR

DAVID WHALE

OCTOSQUID

For Crazy:

Without your support, encouragement & love, this thing never would have happened. Best 'spoose' ever.

For my parents:

Thank you for the years of encouragement. You're a big part of the reason you're holding this book in your hands.

For my grade 6 teacher:

Who gave me advice I have never ceased to ignore: "There comes a time when you have to stop writing about spaceships and robots."

Let us therefore brace ourselves to our duty, and so bear ourselves that if the British Empire and its Commonwealth last for a thousand years, men will still say, "This was their finest hour."

Winston Churchill

For the third time in the last half hour, Lieutenant Commander Fin Radko stifled a yawn. He wasn't tired, so much as he was bored. And as far as Radko was concerned, bored was a very good thing to be. At that moment, on the exact opposite side of Echo Station to where he stood, the commanding officer of the HMCS Vimy Ridge, Commodore Len Edwards, played the political game and attended a cocktail reception in celebration of Commonwealth Day. Though Echo Station was one of the most distant outposts humanity had yet placed in the universe, the celebration had been well-attended. Radko supposed that when one was this far out from a centre of political influence, the people who considered themselves important enough for cocktail receptions probably made a concerted effort to attend every single one, if only to make sure they were seen attending every single one. It was a political game and one for which Radko had little patience. The alcohol was always free-flowing and rarely ever benefitted anyone. One would expect a couple of drinks to help people loosen up and thus be a good thing. The issue was, as ever, that very few attendees stopped at a couple, and many strayed into the territory of far too many. It was disheartening to see so many presumably respectable people — Commonwealth military and civilian alike — behaving like idiots as a result of their inability to turn down a free drink. Radko had mercifully been able to keep his own appearance at the party short. There were a few introductions, a little glad-handing with key people Commodore Edwards felt they needed to be friendly with, and of course a quick fly-by of the hors d'oeurves. Because however Radko felt about parties, the food was always head and shoulders above what he would ever see aboard ship. Regardless, he was more than happy to take Edwards's request to return to the ship as if it were an order, and thus not have to put himself through even more glad-handing and pretending to care about all the supposedly amusing anecdotes about people he didn't know – or even worse, their children. Being left in command of a docked ship, even a frigate like the Vimy Ridge, was a fairly pedestrian experience, but it was still far, far preferable to the alternative.

Walking the corridors of the old warship, Radko nodded to the maintenance crews as they scurried past, clearly with more on their to-do lists than he on his. Though she was one of the older active-service ships in the Commonwealth Navy, the Vimy Ridge wasn't particularly high-maintenance. Any space vessel, no matter how new or advanced, required substantial maintenance just to keep the vacuum of space at bay, let alone keep their massive nuclear-powered engines running and running safely. Originally designed by Cagliari Aerospace as a pursuit ship, the Vimy Ridge had five such engines as opposed to the standard four, the only

Commonwealth vessel outside of the Churchill Class aircraft carrier with more than four engines. It made her a fast ship, but it added another layer to the duties of the engineering and maintenance crews. As Executive Officer of the ship, making sure those crews were operating effectively was part of his job, though he leaned heavily on others — Radko knew the basics of how the engines and mechanical systems worked, but as he often said when asked, "the basics" in his mind were that the engines made the ship go. Anything beyond that, he left to people far more qualified than himself.

"Sir."

The young crewman standing guard at the entrance to the Command Deck saluted stiffly and Radko returned the gesture a little more fluidly before stepping through the hatch and onto the Command Deck.

The HMCS Vimy Ridge itself was shaped much like a sperm whale, albeit an enormous, armour-clad, five-hundred metre long sperm whale with five barrel-shaped engines in place of a tail.

As Radko entered Command, a glowing holographic cross-section of the ship was displayed in the centre of the room, above the sand table. While its military ancestors used actual sand and physical models to plan strategy and troop deployment, the modern sand table – an upgrade to the Vimy Ridge completed only a year ago – used advanced holographics and infrared technology to produce three-dimensional objects that the user could manipulate manually. Radko watched as the ship's logistics officer Lieutenant Owens reached up and rotated the holographic Vimy Ridge a few degrees to the right, stabbing a finger into one of the cargo holds and pulling out a detailed manifest that he then slid to one side, the window hovering just to his right.

"Mister Owens," said Radko, stepping up to the other side of the table, looking through the floating ship. "Status report?"

Five years older than Radko, but one rank lower in the chain of command, Owens was the Lieutenant Commander's unofficial right hand. Radko, having come into his position as the ship's second in command by way of Commonwealth Naval Intelligence — a misunderstood branch of the service to be sure — had not had a strong feel for the crew, nor they for him. Relatively new in the role, many aboard the Vimy Ridge still saw him as an intelligence officer, a "spook," and he had even heard whispers that one or two even thought he was there to spy on them. He had never been part of domestic intelligence, but of course large sections of his service history were blacked out to those of lower rank, so they would be unable to see it. Owens, on the other hand, had served in the logistics department on the Vimy Ridge for six years, working his way up to his current position as the ship's primary. Everyone knew him and most everyone liked him.

That's not to say Radko was disliked. Most crew members who had direct interaction with the XO found him a little stand-offish, but not aloof. One or two had even, much to their surprise, heard him tell a joke. They'd also admit it wasn't a very good joke, but gave him credit for trying.

"We've just received the shipment of dry goods we've been waiting for. The supply depot on Echo Station is waiting for re-stocks itself, so I wasn't able to get us everything on our list, but we certainly have enough for the trip to Duster's Range. I'm told we'll be able to take on additional supplies once we arrive," said

Owens. "Our magazine is at seventy percent capacity, which again is lower than I'd like."

"Just bad timing," said Radko. In addition to the Vimy Ridge, eight other Commonwealth Navy ships had docked at Echo Station for resupply and two others had left twenty four hours before the Vimy Ridge had arrived. "And our special cargo?"

Owens nodded.

"On board as of seventeen hundred hours, sir. The ATC Castle personnel are logged in and have been cleared for our non-critical comm networks."

There was a slight change in tone when Owens mentioned ATC Castle. Radko couldn't really blame the man. ATC Castle Incorporated, the amalgamated entity that was once the Allan-Torballa-Clarke Security Corporation and Castle Armories Limited, was a private military contractor upon which the Commonwealth had been leaning quite heavily for security operations over the past several years. Many officers regarded ATC Castle as mercenaries and Radko was inclined to agree, especially given that ATC Castle was based out of the American Free States - Galveston, Texas, AFS, to be specific – meaning that they were neither members of nor beholden to the laws of the Commonwealth. It made for some uncomfortable interactions.

Radko nodded.

"Have their commanding officer report to me as soon as he and his team are squared away. I want to set some ground rules."

It was Owens's turn to nod.

"Yessir," he said, then paused. "Commander, we've also been... asked to transport a squad of Rangers to Redfall."

"Asked?," said Radko, failing to keep the exasperation out of his voice.

"Told, sir. They're already on their way."

"Damn it."

"My thoughts exactly, sir. Should I contact Commodore Edwards and see if he can-."

Radko waved a hand dismissively.

"No, I'm sure he's having a bad enough time at the reception – no sense making it worse. Who's in charge of the Rangers?"

With a few quick hand gestures, Owens brought up a new holographic window displaying a Commonwealth Army personnel file. He turned it around so Radko could read it and slid it toward the XO.

"Lieutenant-Colonel Harlan Gray," said Owens.

"A Lieutenant-Colonel? Great. All right, just... just have them stand by at the airlock and have Colonel Gray report to my office."

"Yessir, Commander."

His office really wasn't much. A desk, a couple of chairs, a bookshelf and a couple of personal touches – Radko's favourite being a framed black and white photograph of the Canadian National Vimy Memorial in Pas-de-Calais, France, commemorating the lives lost in the World War I battle for which the ship had been named. One day, he wanted to see the memorial in person. Though he'd yet to see it himself, he'd seen photos of the memorial and seen his ancestor's name carved into the white stone, one casualty among more than ten thousand. The numbers were mind-boggling. The Commonwealth government would start hand-wringing and finger-pointing if they lost ten members of their military. Radko couldn't imagine the unholy shitstorm that would erupt in the council chambers if the modern Commonwealth Armed Forces lost ten thousand. And Vimy was just one battle in a long war. The butcher's bill for World War I dwarfed the current population of Luna.

As he moved toward his desk, he stopped momentarily and chuckled. Sitting on the desk, between his tablet and a stack of perfectly-squared hard copy files, was a steaming mug of tea. Radko sat and took a sip of the tea. Nice and strong. No milk, no sugar. Perfect. She was a quick learner.

Unbuttoning his red uniform coat, Radko swore as the top brass button came off in his fingers. He set it down on his desk just as a soft chime came from the door. The bulkheads, designed to keep everyone safe in the event of a hull breach, were too thick for anyone to hear him if he just called out for them to enter. He tapped the desk-mounted button which would cause a yellow light to blink on the outside of the hatch, letting his visitor know they were clear to enter.

The hatch opened, and stepping into the XO's office was Anna Cortez. She stood at attention and snapped off a crisp salute.

"At ease, Cadet."

Cortez relaxed a little, but not by much. She was nineteen years old, placed on the Vimy Ridge as part of a hands-on learning program at the Commonwealth Naval Academy. Originally assigned to Edwards, the Commodore invoked privilege of rank and after two weeks of having Cortez follow him everywhere, delegated responsibility for her training program on the Ridge to

Radko. At first, she'd been an annoyance, altogether too chipper and eager and young, but after a nice long sit-down discussion with her about her strengths and weaknesses and in which direction she'd like her career to head, Radko had found Cortez to be a great asset. She was skilled with gathering information and compiling reports, which took a significant amount of work off his desk.

Besides, she was interested in becoming a Naval Intelligence officer. Until he had been appointed XO of the Vimy Ridge, Radko himself had been an "intel monkey" on both the HMCS Queenston Heights and the HMCS Juno Beach. And since the Vimy Ridge had been without a dedicated intel officer since Yvette Daigle managed to get herself shot as part of a bizarre love triangle, Cortez was gaining more experience than the rest of the cadets in her program combined. She was still young and inexperienced, but in amongst that and the eagerness and the almost bouncy enthusiasm, there was a glimmer of what she could become if she kept her focus. What had started as a burden he didn't want had turned into something of a mission for Radko, helping turn this inexperienced, wide-eyed cadet into an officer. He knew she had the ability, so he'd been pushing her — probably harder than any of her classmates were being pushed by their placement supervisors. Most of them were probably fetching coffee.

He glanced at his steaming mug of tea, guiltily.

Most of them were probably just fetching coffee.

"Sir, I have the latest Soviet deployment reports, as requested," she said, smiling her bright smile.

Radko couldn't help but reciprocate. She was just one of those people.

"Thank you, cadet."

He took the proffered folder and flipped through it quickly, looking for any highlighted pages. One of the first things he'd taught Cortez to look for was ship deployment outside the Soviet norm. While the Commonwealth and the CCCP were not officially at war – and in fact were officially in peace negotiations – neither side really trusted the other. And much like the Commonwealth, the Soviets had patterns, they had patrol zones they liked to stick with and they had standard deployments along their borders with both the Commonwealth and the icarans. Changes in any of those patterns were worth noting and reporting. The first lesson Radko had learned as an intelligence officer trainee was that no alteration of pattern was too small to report, and so it was the first lesson he'd passed on to Cortez. Radko had little doubt that somewhere in Soviet-controlled space there was a Captain-Lieutenant reviewing Commonwealth ship movement, looking for the same red flags as he and Cortez. But today, nothing was flagged as an anomaly. He'd review them in more detail later to be certain Cortez hadn't missed anything, but it was unlikely. As much as many crew members disliked the young woman's unflappable cheerfulness, none questioned her attention to detail.

"Good to see the Bear isn't wandering."

"Absolutely, sir."

"Thoughts?"

The young woman looked a little flustered.

"Um. Sir?"

Leaning back in his chair, Radko just watched her. Strangely, he hadn't realised until that moment that she'd at some point adopted his habit of wearing the red uniform coat while on duty, as opposed to the simpler duty uniform most officers wore. Despite her initial confusion at his question, he could see her mind working behind her dark eyes. He'd seen that during their first serious discussion and it was the only reason he hadn't immediately dumped her off on Owens.

"The Soviets appear to be committed to the peace talks," she said after a moment. "Or at the very least, they want to appear that way. None of their vessels have deviated beyond normal patrol or deployment patterns and there have been no unusual supply runs to indicate imminent military buildup in any particular location."

"Good."

He set aside the file before continuing.

"We'll go over these with the Commodore in our morning briefing."

Cortez nodded.

"Have a seat, Cadet," he said, and had a sip of tea while she did so. "We've been directed to ferry a group of Rangers to Redfall, since it's on our way to Duster's Range. Edwards won't be happy, but there's not much we can do about it. Their commander – a Colonel Gray – will be along shortly and I'm going to make you their liaison with the crew. Normally I'd handle that myself, but I have my hands full with the ATC Castle operation. Understood?"

"Understood, Commander. I'll put in my best effort."

"Never doubted you would, Cortez."

She smiled again, but said nothing as the door chime sounded twice in rapid succession. Both stood and Radko re-buttoned his coat, aside from the now-missing top button, tapping the entry light. The hatch swung open and in stepped a stereotype. Even if he hadn't been dressed in the CASCAM MTP – Castle Armories Camouflage Multi-Terrain Pattern – battle dress uniform of the Commonwealth Army or wearing the yellow beret of the Commonwealth Rangers, it would be clear to anyone that the man was a soldier. Gray wasn't much taller than Radko, but he was much broader in the shoulders and chest, built, as Radko's grandmother would have said, like a brick shithouse. His jawline was comic book quality.

Radko shook the man's hand.

"Lieutenant Colonel Harlan Gray."

"Lieutenant Commander Fin Radko. This is my assistant, Cadet Anna Cortez. Welcome aboard the Vimy Ridge."

Gray nodded.

"My men and I don't need quarters. Myself and my operating team. Twelve in total. I'd like to set us up in cargo hold one. That should be enough space."

"I'm afraid cargo hold one is occupied-."

"Nothing's showing on your manifest."

Silently counting to three, Radko did his best not to be annoyed by the Colonel's interruption.

"The cargo has only just arrived. It's part of an ATC Castle arrangement," said Radko, then quickly holding up a hand to quell Gray's inevitable objection. "Not my call, Colonel, and I can assure you it doesn't sit any better with me than it does you. That being said, cargo hold three is currently empty, so you and your men are more than welcome to set up camp there."

"Understood. I'd like to speak with Commodore Edwards when he has a moment."

"He's at the reception over on the station right now, so odds are he won't be available until the morning. I trust that's acceptable?"

"Of course."

"Good," said Radko. "I'm making Cadet Cortez your liaison on the ship. If you need anything for the duration of your stay with us, she'll be able to help you."

Gray gave Cortez the barest of glances and Radko couldn't tell whether the old soldier didn't care about having a liaison or didn't approve of the selection.

"Understood."

And then he turned on his heel and left, closing the hatch behind him.

"Well that was pleasant," muttered Radko.

The winter season was coming early to Von Daniken's Landing. The first snowfall had come nearly two months ahead of schedule and the ferocious winter winds had already begun to buffet the small colony. It was time for the annual winter evacuation.

The site of protracted battles between the Commonwealth and its enemies over the past hundred years, the resource-rich planet of Von Daniken's Landing was a near-paradise in its summer months. Rich farming zones, several types of metal and mineral resources so close to the surface that miners rarely had to venture more than a few hundred feet below the surface, and large fresh-water lakes, completely potable, filled by underground springs. Even the tall, yellow grasses and forests of thirty foot tall pitcher plants had uses — the grasses were edible and tasted much like a salty spinach, and the durable fibres of the pitcher plants had been combined with traditional fibres to strengthen the combat uniforms of the Commonwealth Army. But no matter how beautiful the planet's flora during the summer months, no matter how rich in natural resources, Von Daniken's Landing was not an environment that was particularly friendly to humans. Setting aside the fact that half the wildlife and even half the plant life was carnivorous, the extreme nature of the winters required total evacuation of the colony for four months of the year. With winds gusting upwards of three hundred kilometres per hour and nighttime temperatures falling to minus one hundred and eighty degrees Celsius, even the Soviet Union, with whom the Commonwealth had fought several battles over ownership of the resource-rich planet, had never made an attempt to move in during the winter months.

The agricultural section of the colony had been shuttered since the first snowfall, with the rapid temperature drop having rendered it impossible to continue the harvest. The workers, as always, were now engaged in efforts to ready the colony for evacuation and prepare their product and their more sensitive equipment for transport. Once the ATC Castle ship hired for transport off-world arrived, Von Daniken's Landing would be devoid of human life until spring thaw made the planet habitable once more.

Everyone on the colony was busy with some preparation or other, with most having been through the run-up to winter at least once before. But for someone who was experiencing their first evacuation, it was both impressive to see the entire colony working toward that one single goal and disturbing to know that their reason for doing so was because failing to evacuate could mean freezing to death.

Nasrin Khaifa shivered slightly and she wasn't sure it was from the cold.

"Doctor?"

Khaifa forced herself to re-focus, turning to the medic.

"Yes, sorry," she said. "Make sure everything is protected from the temperatures, but easily accessible. We should be the last to pack up, just in case."

The medic nodded, which was something of a feat in itself. Though it was not unusual to find brill serving in the MediCorps, this particular brill — whom everyone on Von Daniken's Landing had taken to calling Brill, as the brill species did not use given names — was one of the more interesting specimens. Known throughout the galaxy for their skill with medical and medicinal research, the brill were deep sea dwelling creatures, usually under half a metre long. Though much more complex and far more intelligent, the closest creature most humans were acquainted with when first encountering the brill was the marine isopod. Unlike the marine ispod on Earth, the brill wanted to explore beyond the oceans of their homeworld and so designed and constructed crab-like robotic suits to allow them to move about outside their marine environment.

But in the case of Brill, it was taken one step further. Feeling that the humans would relate better to a more human shape versus the crab-like shape, Brill designed and constructed a humanoid exo-suit. Though far from being human-looking, the shape was right — two arms, two legs, a torso and a head. A large, blue, single "eye" was where the face would be, and this eye transmitted visual information straight into the cerebral cortex of the brill nestled within the exo-suit's chest. And that was why the nod was such a feat. Brill had spent an enormous amount of time studying human body language and had somehow mastered certain small things. Aside from the nod, Brill had developed a tendency to speak with its hands in an alarmingly natural way. And all of it was controlled by an isopod – more or less - in a mechanical chest cavity.

"Agreed," said Brill. "I will proceed."

Brill turned and headed back into the storage area of the MediCorps building and Khaifa watched him... it go. That was another aspect of the brill that humanity had found difficult to wrap their collective heads around — the brill were a hermaphroditic species, so terms like him and her were not applicable.

Khaifa wrapped her heavy grey sweater tighter around her body. She had to admit that despite her initial anger at having been posted to Von Daniken's Landing, she'd rather enjoyed it for the most part. After all, she kept telling herself, she joined the Commonwealth MediCorps in search of adventure after having spent the bulk of her post-medical school career in civilian hospitals on or near Earth. It was just that she was never supposed to be on this planet.

The door to the MediCorp building – or the hospital, as Khaifa preferred to call it – opened, admitting both a cold gust of wind and a member of the colony's small garrison. Shivering, Khaifa forced a smile while wishing her sweater was thicker.

"Sergeant," she said.

She had to look up to make eye contact with the six-foot, two-inch tall Freyja Sigurdsson. The woman with the pale blue eyes offered an equally forced smile as she unwrapped her scarf and unzipped her parka.

"Doctor Khaifa, what's the status of medical?"

"Oh, we're fine. We've moved some of our liquid medicines to the insulated travel containers to protect against freezing –– just in case – but I've ordered my teams to keep everything easily accessible," said Khaifa. "I want to make sure the hospital is fully stocked and operational right up until the moment we load the shuttles."

Sigurdsson glanced around the medical shelter, nodding.

"Good thinking. I've just been out on the Northern perimeter. Temperature is dropping like a bastard out there. Fifteen degrees since this morning. Not even the terror birds are out anymore."

The terror birds were one of the first things Khaifa learned about on Von Daniken's landing. Their actual name was Latin, of course, and very difficult to pronounce, but their resemblance to an extinct type of giant predatory bird of Earth's Cenozoic period earned them the same nickname: terror birds. Three to four metres tall and, though flightless, capable of running speeds in the range of sixty kilometres per hour, they were the apex predator of at least this area of Von Daniken's Landing. The terror birds were very well insulated against the planet's harsh winters, so if even they had taken shelter, it was clear that this winter would be early and brutal.

"Anyway," said Sigurdsson. "In case I don't see you again before evac, I wanted to thank you. I know you didn't want to be here, but you did good work. It was nice to have a real doctor around, not just medics."

Khaifa felt herself blush. She knew she'd been... somewhat difficult when she'd first arrived on-site. Her posting was supposed to have been to a MediCorps mobile treatment ship, the MCV Seraphim, but through an administrative foul-up of epic proportions, she'd been assigned to Von Daniken's Landing instead. She'd been furious –– and terrified. She knew she hadn't even attempted to hide the former and was fairly sure she'd been unsuccessful at hiding the latter.

"Thank you, Sergeant, I do appreciate it. And thank you and your men – from all of us – for keeping us safe."

Sigurdsson nodded.

"We've got three more days until pick-up," she said. "Might want to start putting on some more layers – we're bound to start feeling the chill soon."

"Start feeling the chill?"

As Sigurdsson turned and headed back outside, Khaifa was fairly sure she'd seen the woman smirk.

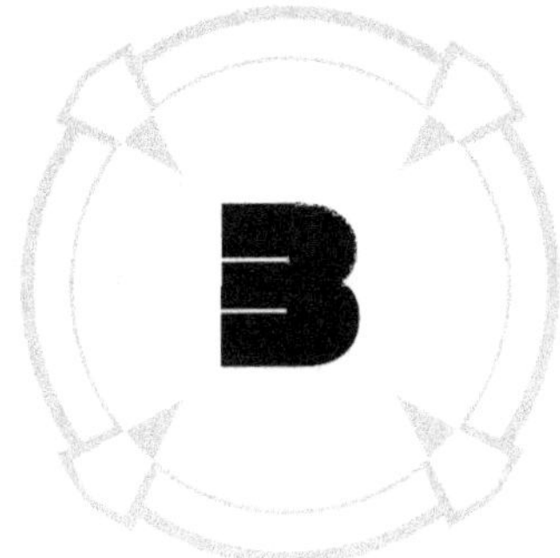

Cargo hold one was under guard. Two ATC Castle operators stood outside the hatch, one on each side, armed with Caliburn submachine guns. Radko wasn't thrilled about having SMGs aboard the Vimy Ridge, given that there was no shattergun conversion kit for the Caliburn. The majority of sidearms and rifles used by the Commonwealth Navy had readily available and easily deployed conversions as a matter of safety. The principle of the shattergun was to fire projectiles lined with deep grooves at much lower velocities than standard firearms. While still potentially lethal to living creatures, the projectiles would shatter upon impact with a bulkhead and thus avoid causing a hull breach and, potentially, the explosive decompression of the ship. The last thing Radko needed was for some trigger-happy mercenary to start shooting through bulkheads.

"Where's your team leader?"

"Inside, sir," said the female operator.

"All right. Open it – I need to have a word."

"I'm sorry, sir, this is a secure area. No one is allowed to enter," said the male operator.

Radko just stared at the man for a moment.

"What's your name?," he said finally.

"Gruen, sir."

"Mister Gruen, I know your team would much rather be on an ATC Castle ship and you know my people would much rather have you there as well. Let's just try to make this as easy as possible for everyone, all right?"

The man nodded, but looked slightly confused.

"And by that I mean how about we don't make assumptions about your ability to restrict my movements aboard my own ship. Unless you'd like to walk to Duster's Range?"

There was a brief pause then Gruen had a quick, whispered exchange with someone over his comm unit. Then the hatch popped open and Radko was waved inside by another ATC Castle operator – this one looking too young to know what he was doing. The young man stepped aside to allow Radko to enter.

The cargo hold was dominated by a large container about two and a half metres square, a biometrically-locked door set in one side and a metre tall window the length of each side set at eye level. Standing beside the container, his Caliburn SMG looking like a toy in his hands, was a mountain of a man. A Maori, judging by his ta moko — his facial tattoos — the man looked toward Radko and shouldered his weapon, extending a meaty hand.

"Lieutenant Commander Fin Radko," said Radko as they shook hands.

"Tangaroa. Sorry about my men outside. Both ATC Castle trained. No experience with the Commonwealth military."

"And you?"

"Royal 414th New Zealand Regiment. Fifteen years."

"Well, I'm glad one of you has some experience. How's the cargo?"

"No issues, Commander."

"Good," said Radko. "I want a report hourly. This..."

He waved a hand at the container.

"Makes me nervous."

Tangaroa grinned.

"You and me both, Commander."

"Glad we're on the same page, Tangaroa," he said, pausing slightly before continuing. "I wanted to give you the news in person. We've been asked to ferry some Commonwealth Rangers to Redfall – they're setting up in cargo hold three for the trip. Obviously, we can't have them coming in here. If they start to give you any trouble, come directly to me, understood?"

Tangaroa nodded.

"Yessir."

"Good. Now, what I'd like to..."

Radko trailed off as a substantial vibration rippled through the deck plating beneath his feet. Tangaroa looked as concerned as Radko himself felt and before the Commander could demand a situation report from the Command Deck, the voice of Lieutenant Owens came crackling through his earpiece.

"Commander, we have a situation. Several explosions have been reported on the far side of Echo Station."

There was a pause, during which a muffled background conversations could be heard, though it was too far from the active comm to be understood.

"Sir," continued Owens. "We've just confirmed that it's the INS Ranvir."

"The Ranvir? All right, contact Captain Sengupta and let him know our fire and repair teams are at his-."

"No, sir, the Ranvir is gone. It just... holy shit. Holy shit holy shit."

"Owens? Owens what's going on up there?"

Radko was already out of cargo hold one and heading toward command at a run when Owens finally responded.

"Commander, Echo Station is under attack."

"Report!"

Everyone on the command deck turned to see Radko step quickly through the hatch and immediately head to the sand table. It now projected an image of Echo Station, the Vimy Ridge highlighted in its docking berth, angry red dots flashing at various points on the other side of the station.

"Sir," said Owens, visibly shaken. "The Ranvir and the HMCS Terra Nova are confirmed lost. Echo Station is reporting extensive damage and casualties and... and sir, their fire suppression systems are offline."

The entire command deck went deathly silent for a moment as Owens's words sunk in.

Radko swallowed heavily. Without fire suppression systems on a ship or station, a fire would eat up an entire oxygen supply. Anyone who wasn't burned to death would asphyxiate. It was the nightmare death of anyone involved in space travel.

"Who the hell hit us? Have you been able to identify the-."

The whole ship lurched as something nearby exploded.

Someone swore floridly.

"We don't know who it is," said Owens as Radko climbed the ladder to the second level mezzanine of command deck. "LiDAR didn't register them as vessels."

On the second command deck – the observation deck – Radko looked through the reinforced 360-degree window, across Echo Station's broad spine. There were debris clouds everywhere, explosions rippling through the station as well as many of the docked ships as whoever had attacked continued to press the assault. A trio of small craft streaked overhead, firing into the station's hull, the subsequent explosions causing the Vimy Ridge to rock in her berth.

Radko's thoughts went immediately back to cargo hold one, and the locked container under ATC Castle guard. The cargo, which technically belonged to the Soviets, that members of Commonwealth Intelligence had managed to acquire and which, by its nature, would paint an enormous bulls-eye on the HMCS Vimy Ridge for any and all Soviet warships should its presence be discovered.

"We need to get Edwards back here. Now."

"We haven't been able to reach the Commodore, or anyone else on that side of the station."

"What the hell is going on?"

It was the voice of Colonel Gray. Radko looked down over the mezzanine railing to see the Ranger stride into command.

"The station is under attack."

"The Soviets?"

"We don't know, but it seems logical. Do you have any personnel still on the station?"

"I have three men on-station."

"Tell them to find Commodore Edwards and get him back here," said Radko, not caring in the slightest that he did not have the authority to issue orders to the Rangers.

"Sir!," yelled Owens. "Echo Station's reactor is going into meltdown!"

"God damn it. Lieutenant Owens, give the order to disengage docking mag-clamps, activate all defensive batteries and send rail-gunners to their posts. Colonel, how many men do you have with you?"

"Nine, not counting the three on Echo."

"Gear up, just in case," said Radko. "Whoever these sons of bitches are, I want to…"

He trailed off as he saw Owens's jaw go slack as the man looked up through the observation dome. Gray, beside him, swore softly. Radko look up.

Hundreds of… ships? He couldn't even tell. There were hundreds, if not thousands of the things passing overhead, leaving the critically damaged station behind. They moved like starships, but they looked organic. They looked alive. Covered with what appeared to be layered armoured plates, the vessels were a sickly olive green on top, fading to a dull grey underbelly and could very easily have been mistaken for living creatures were it not for the glowing red thrusters to their aft and the projectiles and beam weapons they were using to tear Echo Station to shreds. Small, fighter-like craft banked and dove around larger, bulkier vessels, which in turn surrounded a group of ships that looked like massive, space-faring centipedes, but in place of legs hung rows and rows of docked fighters.

Radko had seen nothing like it.

He doubted any human had.

"Echo Station docking control not responding," said Owens after a moment.

"Blow the clamps. Emergency release, do it immediately and bring the ERA on-line," said Radko, and then louder: "And get the fucking batteries up and running! I want rail guns by the time the mags are off!"

"Aye sir!"

"Communications!"

"Petty Officer Allard was on Echo Station, sir," said Cortez.

Radko hadn't even seen the Cadet enter, but she'd clearly been there long enough to know the situation. Her face was ashen and it looked like she might have been shaking slightly. The news she brought was not good. Already working with a skeleton crew, the Vimy Ridge was now without its only communications officer.

"Cortez," he said. "You're now acting communications officer. Get in touch with whatever ships have survived this and enquire about plans to regroup. See if anyone has any more information than we do."

"Yes... yes Commander."

To her credit, she immediately sat down and got to work.

Owens looked up from the sand table – displaying the Vimy Ridge again, green circles flashing over the railgun and missile batteries.

"Weapon stations reporting green, Commander. Blowing mag clamps in three... two... one...," a soft thunk echoed through the ship, and a small green icon appeared hovering over the holographic ship. "Mag clamps disengaged – we're free-floating, sir."

"Pilot, get us away from the station!"

"Heading, sir?"

"Just get us to as safe a distance as we can manage without engaging the reactor," he said. "Cortez, report."

"We're... There's... no one else."

"What?"

"There's nothing but static, Commander. I'm not... I'm not even getting distress beacons."

Distress beacons were automatically triggered as soon as lifeboats were launched from any vessel. Their absence meant that either nothing was wrong, or no one had survived long enough to launch a boat.

"Commander!"

It was the LiDAR technician, Chief Petty Officer Normand Hamelin.

"I think one of their battleships – or whatever they are – is coming around the station."

"You think?"

"It's hard to read them on LiDAR, Commander. It's like they're not ships. They keep getting filtered out by the software, like organic space junk," said the CPO. "But I keep getting little bits and pieces, like shadows, like footprints in the sand – I can see them for a second before they get washed away."

"How far away?"

"They'll be on us in less than a minute."

"Pilot, tap into LiDAR and swing us around to face the incoming vessel. Gunnery command, ready forward batteries. Is the ERA on-line?"

There were acknowledgements all around, then silence as everyone did their jobs. The Ridge was a heavily-armoured ship as it was, and the ERA – electromagnetic reactive armour – would, hopefully, give them even more of a fighting chance. Radko stood, staring out the dome down the bow of the Vimy Ridge, a muscle on the left side of his jaw twitching as, out of the corner of his eye, he saw portions of Echo Station breaking apart.

"Commander," said Owens. "Estimating reactor explosion on Echo Station in five minutes."

"Time to contact, Hamelin?"

"Forty-four seconds."

"Gunnery chief. Missiles on my mark, rail guns to follow immediately upon missile impact."

It was an old-school strategy used during humanity's first space-born war. Use missiles to destroy the enemy's armour plating, then rail guns to shred what was left. The strategy had caused massive casualties and if done properly, could nearly gut a ship from stem to stern in a matter of seconds. Many crews had been killed in their entirety and many sailors had been suffocated in explosive decompression. It was a horrific tactic and one that had been outlawed in one of the oldest unbroken treaties signed between the Commonwealth and the Soviet Union governing acceptable behaviour in interstellar warfare. Under normal circumstances, Radko would never have ordered such an attack and under normal circumstances he felt someone would have spoken out against it even if he had — but their present circumstances were not normal and their present foe was very clearly not Soviet and thus not party to the treaty.

And then the target came into view. It was no larger than the Vimy Ridge, but broader, and like the other ships in the assault force, didn't look metallic. It bristled with slender spines that in any other situation Radko would assume were gun placements. The ship was a mottled green with an oval opening to the port of its upper half that glowed orange. As he watched, the glow became brighter.

"Fire!"

A second later, a swarm of missiles snaked out from the launchers in the Vimy Ridge's forward hull, slamming into the other ship with bright but brief explosions. The explosions were immediately followed by the fire of railguns. The hyper-accelerated flechettes – each one about the size of a desk – tore into the hull of the unknown vessel and into the glowing orange opening. Suddenly, there was a rupture, the orange glow leaking out from several spots of damage and a series of small explosions ripped along the spine of the vessel before the entire port side erupted in a bright, brief explosion that all but vaporized the ship's port hull.

There was no cheering from the crew. Radko himself stood stone-faced, trying not to let the fluttering of fear in his chest show through.

"Pilot, find us a place to hide and get us the hell out of here. We'll use the explosion of Echo Station as cover," said Radko.

After a few seconds of silence, the pilot confirmed.

"Cortez. Anything?"

The look on her face said it all, even before she shook her head. Eleven ships docked at Echo Station – two civilian and nine Commonwealth Navy – and the only one still flying, the only one still intact, was the Vimy Ridge. The station, the headquarters of the Third Fleet, was about to tear itself apart in the thermonuclear detonation of its compromised reactor. With concerted effort, Radko was able to think of it in terms of lost assets — the ships, the station — rather than lost lives, which would, based on standard crew sizes for the Commonwealth ships and usual staffing rosters on Echo Station, number in the thousands. The lost lives could be mourned later. Until the Vimy Ridge was safe and secure and the rest of the Third Fleet had been warned about the attack and what Radko could only assume was an invasion, thinking tactically rather than emotionally was the key.

He forced himself to stop clenching his fists and he cleared his throat.

"Contact the rest of the Third Fleet," he heard himself saying. "Broadcast on our emergency channels, code seventy-seven blue, request priority one responses."

He turned to the aft and watched as the receding Echo Station blossomed into a sphere of flame and then winked out of existence.

"And inform them that Echo Station, Strategic Operations, everything is gone. We need to know who we should be reporting to — who is the ranking officer in the Third Fleet — and what their orders are."

"Yessir," said Cortez, her voice remarkably steady despite the fear in her eyes and the shaking of her hands.

Radko took a deep breath that was much shakier than he'd hoped and climbed back down to the sand table level of Command. The normal buzz of the command deck had been completely silenced. No one spoke, with the exception of Cortez quietly sending out their emergency broadcast. Owens busied himself going through the damage reports that had started to roll in, updating the holographic Vimy Ridge with a damage overlay detailing required repairs. Three red crosses also popped up on the display, one in the engine room and two in the medical bay. Casualties. The holographic crosses weren't pulsating, so the inujries weren't severe, which was a great relief and so far, none of the mechanical damage seemed critical. Radko was relieved to see that the efficiency of Owens had not slipped in the slightest. It was likely just a coping mechanism, but it was what the Ridge needed right now. All things considered, they had been extraordinarily lucky.

"Mister Owens, when you've finished damage assessment, I want you to do two things. First, run a simulation with all the information we have on the attackers – I want you to try to figure out where they may have reasonably come from and where they appeared to be headed."

"I'll do my best sir, but tactics aren't my strong suit."

"No, no, you're right of course."

Putting a hand on the man's shoulder, Radko tried and failed to force a reassuring smile.

"Focus on the damage reports and getting repair teams deployed. Then I want to call a meeting here at the sand table. Senior officers... senior personnel, including Colonel Gray and the commander of the ATC Castle team, Tangaroa."

"Yessir."

"And send every bit of info we have from the attack to Commodore Edwards's office. We should have our hull-cam footage, but we were also linked into Echo Station security."

"We should have all their hull-cam footage, too," said Owens, nodding. "I'll have it for you in ten minutes, Commander."

"Sergeant?"

Sigurdsson took one last glance at the foam-lined gun case laid out on the workbench before her. She'd just finished what would be the last cleaning and tune-up of the rifle within for the season. Her beloved Trondheim Arms 32A OSR – Operational Support Rifle. A sniper rifle given a more politically correct name. Though an older model that hadn't been standard issue for a Commonwealth Army sniper in nearly a decade, Sigurdsson continued to carry one with her on every assignment because as low-tech as the rifle was by current standards, it had never once had a misfire. It wasn't the most advanced, it wasn't biggest, it wasn't the most powerful and it certainly wasn't the prettiest, but it was reliable. It was there when you needed it, every time.

She'd named it Vidar, after the mythological Norse god of revenge and silence.

With a soft sigh, she closed the case on Vidar and snapped the clasps in place.

"Yes?"

Private Kenwick looked even more uncomfortable than usual.

"Sergeant, the Southern Belle missed its last check-in and I haven't been able to reach her."

The Southern Belle was their ride off Von Daniken's Landing. She was supposed to be departing Echo Station in the morning to make her way to Von Daniken's Landing and begin the winter evacuation.

"The wind interfering with our comm gear?"

The Private shook his head.

"No Sergeant – everything is clear on our end. The winds aren't near bad enough yet to interfere. I bounced a signal to a buddy of mine on Erindale Station and we had no issues," he said, pausing briefly. "But there was something else, Sarge. I picked up a Third Fleet signal. It was heavily coded."

"Kenwick, the Third Fleet has a whole department of spooks working out of Echo. Probably just an intel thing."

"No, Sarge, that's just it. It was a full-bore packet. A data drop," he said, getting more animated by the second.

Picking up her parka, Sigurdsson held up a hand as she slipped it on.

"Slow, Private. And in English."

"Sorry, Sarge. It was... the transmission was a big chunk of info, I can tell that by the bandwidth it's eating. But it was a general broadcast. That means, Sarge, that whoever sent this wanted to get the info to the entire Third Fleet. This wasn't some intel package, it's a bulk info dump."

Sigurdsson frowned.

"Show me."

With a nod, Kenwick zipped up his coat and led Sigurdsson out into the blowing snow, across the compound, past the massive gates that separated the military installation of old Fort Hathaway from the civilian colony and into the comm centre. They kicked the snow from their boots, shook off their parkas and Kenwick sat down in front of an array of monitors. He switched on his IR keyboard and tapped in a few commands.

"Look, here," he tapped one of the screens, but the fact that Sigurdsson hadn't a clue what she was looking at must have shown in her face. "The bottom image is the bandwidth profile of a standard transmission. This one's actually our last set of personnel reports to CENTCOM. The top image, here? That's the profile for the Third Fleet transmission."

Even Sigurdsson could see that the amount of data being transmitted was significant.

"But it wasn't targeted to one specific recipient?"

Kenwick shook his head.

"Negative. This was a wide-form broadcast. And it went out within thirty minutes of my loss of contact with the Southern Belle."

"Can you find out what it says?"

"Sarge it's heavily coded..."

Glancing down at him, she noticed his reluctance to make eye contact.

"That wasn't a no."

"As much I'd love to tell you I can do it... fact is Sarge, this encryption was written by people a shit-tonne smarter than me. Best I can do is find the originator."

"You mean find out who sent it?"

"Not the individual, but transmissions are all ID stamped by the vessel or facility whose gear is being used to transmit. It's not easy to find, but I can do it."

"Then shut up and get to work, Private," she said, patting him on the shoulder. "And keep trying to reach the Belle."

Leaving Kenwick to his work, knowing he'd call her the moment he had identified the originator or reached the transport, Sigurdsson headed back outside into the wind and snow. For a moment, she just stood in the cold, watching the snow swirl around her ankles. There were times when she thought she might like to find a way to stay on Von Daniken's Landing for the winter, to see the planet in all its frozen glory without another single human being around. Just kilometer upon kilometer of snow and ice and air so crisp and sharp it felt like needles driving into exposed skin. In the end, she knew she'd never actually stay; she knew she couldn't, at least not without significantly better shelters and significantly better cold-weather gear. As good as the Commonwealth Army supplies were, they weren't up to taking on a VDL winter.

The snow had stopped falling for the time being, but the wind was still creating clouds of the stuff. She knew it would be worse in the main body of the colony –– here inside Fort Hathaway, the walls provided at least a little protection from the wind.

A little. But not much.

Her hair whipping in the wind, the Sergeant quickly headed over to the main guardhouse, built into the Fort's wall to the left of the gate.

"Corporal Henning."

The grizzled old soldier with the bushy beard stood as Sigurdsson entered. Henning had been put in charge of colonial security on Von Daniken's Landing by Sigurdsson's predecessor and she'd seen no reason to make a change. She knew he called her 'The Battleaxe' behind her back, but she didn't care – he was an excellent soldier. And the nickname was kind of cool.

"Sarge. Didn't 'spect to see you out here this time of day."

"Shit happens. Listen Henning, I want double patrols on the perimeter until evac," she said. "And give me two extra spotters on the walls."

Henning frowned, but nodded.

"We expecting company?"

"No. But it's unexpected company that's usually the problem, isn't it?"

Again, Henning nodded.

"I'll get the duty schedule updated and have the extra bodies in place within thirty, Sarge," he said. "Course, you and me both know the best eye for up on the wall is that one right there."

He pointed to her right eye.

"I have to deal with something Kenwick is working on, but yeah, slot me in for a second watch on the walls."

"Understood, Sarge. I'll get it done."

"If it wasn't the Soviets, it had to be the icarans," said Colonel Gray. "They've been nosing into our borders for months."

He leaned forward on the edge of the sand table.

"Frankly, the Army has been expecting an icaran incursion."

"That may be the case," said Radko as he strode into command. "But I don't think this is it. Owens, I've sent you some stills from the cam feeds."

With a quick nod, Owens brought up the still images, displaying them in floating holographic windows above the sand table. Each image showed an attacking vessel - two like the one they'd destroyed and one of the immense centipede-like fighter carriers.

"Unless the icarans have completely redesigned their entire fleet, we're looking at something new here."

A moment of silence followed as the gathered group examined the video stills.

"I also did some trajectory mapping. It's by no means perfect, but..."

He approached the control console for the sand table and entered a few commands. The holographic Vimy Ridge faded away and the angular lines of Echo Station materialized, then shrunk down to the size of a golf ball as a star map overlay appeared.

"Based on the hull-cam data from the station and from our own observation, it appear as though the attack came from here. Or at least through here. We have no way of knowing yet where it originated."

A grouping of red arrowheads appeared at the far end of the sand table and began a slow advancement toward the centre, where the representation of Echo Station hovered.

"That would have them traveling through the Queen Victoria's patrol zone," said Owens. "Cadet Cortez, has the Queen Vic responded to our seventy-seven blue?"

Cortez shook her head.

"No, sir. They haven't."

"Who has?," said Gray. "We need to start compiling everyone's information, build some kind of profile on these… whoever they are."

"We haven't had any responses, sir."

Everyone turned sharply to look at her and the young cadet swallowed heavily, clenching her hands into fists to stop their shaking.

"No ships or facilities have responded to our emergency broadcast," she said, her voice cracking slightly. "I've picked up no emergency beacons and there is no chatter on any communications channel assigned for use by the Third Fleet."

She met Radko's gaze and he immediately knew that she understood the same thing he did. There was always comm chatter.

Reports being filed, families being called, current events being discussed, armaments or replacement parts being requisitioned... there was always something flowing back and forth on the Third Fleet's channels. No chatter at all meant-

"There's no one out there, Commander," said Cortez.

No one spoke for several minutes as the news sunk in. The Third Fleet was no more. Thirty Commonwealth Naval vessels and their crews, one major deployment station and three supply stations. Not one of them had responded to a seventy-seven blue – an emergency broadcast to which every ship and facility operating under the banner of the Third Fleet of the Commonwealth was obligated by law to respond.

The Vimy Ridge was the Third Fleet.

The realization hit Radko hard. As did a second realization that he quickly pushed aside.

"We have other problems," he said quietly, activating the slow playback of his trajectory animatic. "If the... if the swarm of hostiles continues on the same heading as their departure from Echo Station, they'll be going through Soviet space before re-entering Commonwealth space – the heart of Commonwealth space."

A small blue sphere began flashing in the swarm's path.

Owens stood with his mouth agape.

Colonel Gray slowly removed his beret and swore softly.

It was Tangaroa who finally spoke.

"Earth."

"Yeah," said Radko. "Earth. And every station and colony in between."

He took a deep breath.

"We're going to make a run for the Second Fleet. We have to warn-."

"Whoa, wait, hold on a second," said Owens. "We can't just walk away from the Third Fleet, sir. We need to find out who's in command of the Fleet and see what orders they plan to issue."

"You heard the reports from Cadet Cortez," said Radko. "We all did. There have been no responses to our transmission. Our best course of action right now is to regroup with the larger fleet."

"Again, sir, we can't just walk away from the Third Fleet."

It took all of Radko's strength not to reach out and strangle the man. The kind of response that Owens had given was always a possibility, Radko knew, but it was one he hoped he would not have to face. With Owens openly questioning his decisions, his ability to keep the rest of the crew from losing their grip on the structure and discipline that came from having an intact chain of command aboard the Vimy Ridge would erode very quickly.

"Owens, there is no Third Fleet. There's us. There's the Vimy Ridge and there's that fucking swarm. With Commodore Edwards dead, chain of command puts me in charge of this ship. And with the rest of the fleet gone, that also makes me the ranking officer in the Third Fleet of the Commonwealth Navy."

"With all due respect, Commander, you've been XO here for less than six months," said Owens. "Lieutenant Colonel Gray is the ranking officer on the ship and he's got much more experience with situations like this."

The Colonel didn't take his eyes off Radko when he spoke.

"I'm not a naval officer. As ranking naval officer, the ship belongs to Lieutenant Commander Radko," he said, then finally turned to Owens. "And son, no one has experience with situations like this."

"Please, Colonel," said Owens.

"Sir," said Hamelin, the LiDAR technician. "We need someone with your experience in command of-."

"Shut the fuck up, son. You want democracy, you should have joined a civilian ship," said Gray. "You're members of the Commonwealth Armed Forces, you wear a uniform that commands respect. You walk in the footsteps of giants, of legends, of brave men and women who have laid down their lives to protect the people of our Commonwealth and the ideals that it stands for. By being where you are – on the command deck of a naval frigate – you have taken your place among the best. So fucking act like it."

He looked around the table at the gathered officers.

"Radko is in command. Anyone who doesn't like that idea can go find a lifeboat and get the fuck off this ship. And you make sure every single person you have serving under you in your departments knows that those are the only two options available. We've just been attacked by God knows what. We need to get our shit together and figure out what to do next – we can't get ourselves wrapped up in our own internal bullshit. Is that clear?"

When no one responded, Gray slammed an open palm down on the sand table, causing more than one of the assembled crew to jump.

"Is that fucking clear?"

This time, everyone responded affirmatively.

"Good," said the Colonel. "Commander Radko. You said you have a plan of action?"

"We need to connect with the Second Fleet," said Radko, trying not to miss a beat. "We need to figure out what's going on and the Second Fleet has the largest intel network in the Commonwealth."

"But Commander, the Second Fleet is stationed here," said Hamelin, pointing to an area beyond the far side of the starfield being projected by the sand table. Between the Vimy Ridge and the Second fleet was the swarm. "We'll have to go right through those... things."

"Yes, we will. But as of right now, we may be the only people aware of the shitstorm about to hit the Commonwealth. We can't just sit here and hide – we're going to the Second Fleet and from there we're going to make a plan with Second Fleet Command for our next move."

"And what about the hostiles?"

"We avoid them for now, until we know more. We fight them if and when we can. Colonel, we'll need your Rangers at our disposal. And Tangaroa, you're now being drafted into the Commonwealth Navy."

The massive Maori simply nodded.

"Understood," said Gray. "Two of my men are trained in anti-spacecraft weaponry if your gunnery teams need extra help."

"Thank you. We may-."

"Commander!"

All eyes turned to Cortez.

"I'm... I'm sorry to interrupt, sir. I'm getting something. A signal," she said. "It's very faint, but......"

"Put it on speaker."

The Cadet tapped a few commands into her console and the speakers in the command centre crackled with static.

"-my Ridge, do you copy? This is Sergeant Freyja Sigurdsson of the 48th Highland Regiment. Repeat, HMCS Vimy Ridge, do you copy? This is-."

The signal was faint and so riddled with static that Radko had to wave to the command deck crew to keep their noise to a minimum in order to hear the transmission.

"This is Lieutenant Commander Fin Radko of the HMCS Vimy Ridge, we copy."

"My comm tech picked up your alert. Not sure what it's about, but we haven't been able to reach Echo Station or the SS Southern Belle. Can you assist?"

Radko noticed Tangaroa shift uncomfortably and looked at the soldier questioningly while motioning Cortez to mute their end of the transmission.

"The Southern Belle is the ATC Castle ship that dropped us off. Was still docked at Echo when the attack happened."

Radko motioned for Cortez to reactive the microphones.

"Sergeant... Sigurdsson, was it? There has been an attack on Echo Station. The SS Southern Belle was one of the casualties."

There was pause.

"The Soviets?"

"Negative, Sergeant," said Radko. "We have thus far been unable to identify the attackers. They don't look like anything we've ever seen before."

"Sergeant, this is Lieutenant Colonel Harlan Gray of the 15th Commonwealth Ranger Regiment. Where is the 48th currently stationed?"

"We're on Von Daniken's Landing, Colonel. The Southern Belle was supposed to be our way off-planet."

Gray lowered his head and massaged the bridge of his nose. Radko frowned then snapped his fingers at Owens and pointed to the sand table, which still showed the assumed heading of the swarm. Owens understood immediately and after a moment a flashing yellow sphere appeared on the sand table to represent the position of Von Daniken's Landing.

It was directly in the projected path of the alien swarm.

"How many people do you have with you, Sergeant?"

"Thirty soldiers and roughly a hundred and twenty civilians," said Sigurdsson. "Sir, what the hell is going on?"

"Sergeant," said Radko with a heavy sigh. "As I recall, there's an old fort on Von Daniken's Landing from back when we fought the Soviets for control of the colony..."

"Yessir, Fort Hathaway. I'm there right now."

"Are its walls and gates still intact?"

Again there was silence.

"Sergeant, is Fort Hathway intact?"

"...yes it is."

"Get everyone inside and seal the gates. You are directly in the path we estimate this attacking swarm is going to take."

"Get your men on those walls, Sergeant," said Gray.

"Understood, Colonel," said Sigurdsson. "What exactly are we expecting?"

"That's the problem, Sigurdsson," said Radko. "We don't have a fucking clue. But I promise you, we will either send someone to extract your group or we'll come ourselves."

"Thank you, Commander."

As the call disconnected, Sigurdsson just stood for moment, letting it all sink in. Her immediate concern of course was that the winter evacuation of Von Daniken's Landing would be delayed. It was the logistics side of her training forcing that item to the forefront. In itself, the delay could be a serious issue, given how quickly and unpredictably the weather changed in the geographic area surrounding Fort Hathaway, the wider colony and the mines, and during her time in charge of the garrison Sigurdsson had more than once recommended an earlier evacuation date. However, while weather was going to be a concern, it was now far from the most critical. That Echo Station had been attacked and the Southern Belle lost had been shock enough – by unknown enemies, no less – but it was what Radko and Gray hadn't said that weighed on her mind.

"We're in some shit."

Kenwick slowly looked up.

"Sarge?"

"If they're telling us to go to ground, they're not expecting anyone to stop this... what did they call it?"

"A swarm."

"They're not expecting anyone to stop this swarm," she said. "Should be a dozen or more Commonwealth Navy ships between the Vimy Ridge and us. And they think we're going to be hit."

She swore softly and rubbed at her eyes.

"Stay on the radio, try to contact Erindale Station and Fort Tiberius. And keep a line free so we can talk to the Vimy Ridge again if we need to."

"Yes Sarge."

The young man got to work and Sigurdsson headed outside, back toward the guardhouse. She didn't even bother zipping up her coat.

"Henning," she said as she stepped inside. "Call everyone back. All patrols are to return to Fort Hathaway immediately."

The old soldier looked up, the confusion evident on his face.

"Sarge? We just sent out-."

"Everyone back. Now. And all civilians are to be brought inside the fort's walls."

Henning stood, confusion replaced by concern.

"Understood, Sarge, but what the hell is going on?"

"Credible info about an impending attack."

"Soviets?"

"I fucking wish. Get everyone back here, Master Corporal," she said as she stepped up to the gun rack and grabbed a Trondheim Arms 33A1. It was the workhorse of the Commonwealth Army, a lightweight bullpup design assault rifle. If she couldn't use Vidar, the 33A1 was her next choice. She slapped in a mag and clipped two more to her tactical vest before turning back to Henning. "I want spotters on the walls at all times – I'll join them as soon as I get back. Have Franklin and Rupesh meet me on the civilian side of the gates."

"What do we tell the civilians?"

"Protection from a severe storm."

Henning quickly popped in his earpiece and began barking orders.

Slinging the rifle over her shoulder, Sigurdsson once more stepped out into a cold she no longer felt, jogging across the fort to the MediCorps building. Before she could pull open the door, her earpiece beeped softly and she tapped the activation stud.

"Go ahead."

"Sarge, it's Kenwick. The Vimy Ridge communications officer sent me the decryption key for the info packet they were broadcasting..."

"And?"

"Echo Station... is gone, Sarge. It's gone, along with every ship that was docked there. The station and ten goddamned ships."

Sigurdsson stood for a moment, snow swirling around her as she stared at the top of Fort Hathaway's walls. A strange feeling was creeping up her spine, a feeling she wasn't accustomed to and it took her a moment to identify it for what it was: fear. If Gray and Radko hadn't been able to identify the attacking force — and they were both experienced, high-ranking officers in their respective branches — then Sigurdsson felt confident that they were looking at something new. And 'new' meant that if this swarm did make planetfall, there would be none of the predictable tactics of the Soviets or the methodical advances of the icarans. She could prepare for a Soviet assault. She could set up her defenses to anticipate the moves of an icaran attack. But for the situation she now found herself facing, she had no playbook.

The unknown was what ended up killing soldiers like her.

"I'm looking at some stills," continued Kenwick. "But Sarge, I have no idea what these things are. They're not Soviet, they're not icaran... they don't even match udukiin design."

"That transmission is classified, Kenwick – is that clear? No one sees or hears any of it but you and me. No one else knows it exists without my express permission, understood?"

"Understood Sarge."

"Good."

She killed the connection, then stepped into the MediCorps bunker.

"Doctor Khaifa?"

One of the nurses pointed toward the rear of the building, where the administrative offices were located. As she headed in that direction, Sigurdsson tried to figure out how she could word her request, how best to get the doctor to go along with the plan.

The relationship between the civilian population of Von Daniken's Landing and their Commonwealth Army protectors had always been an uneasy one. Though the civilians knew they needed the soldiers – they weren't utter morons, despite what some of the soldiers might say – they still sometimes resented the military presence. Especially when the military tried to tell them what to do. Sigurdsson was going to need a respected, non-military voice backing her up.

"Doctor."

Sitting at one of the three desks in the admin office, Khaifa looked up and smiled.

"Sergeant. Twice in one day! To what do I owe...," she said, trailing off as she noticed the 33A1 hanging from Sigurdsson's shoulder. The woman's smile vanished. "Freyja...?"

After a moment's hesitation, Sigurdsson began to explain about a severe storm heading toward the colony, but then stopped.

"You know what, fuck it."

She needed this woman on her side and from what the people on the Vimy Ridge said, it didn't sound like she had a lot of time.

"Doctor, I need your help," said Sigurdsson. "It... looks like we may be facing an attack in the very near future and I need to bring the civilians into Fort Hathaway."

"An attack," said Khaifa, standing. Her face was etched with concern. "An attack from whom? I thought the Treaty of-."

"Doctor, it doesn't matter who. What matters is that if those civilians are outside these walls when the shit hits the fan, they're fucked. I can't defend an open colony, but I can defend walls. Here, we have defensive turrets and we have snipers. We have walls."

"I'm... I'm just not sure what you want me to do."

"Get the civilians inside the walls. If I issue an order, people will bitch and complain and drag their feet and get themselves killed. If it comes from you, they'll listen. You're MediCorps, you're essentially civilian. Besides, you've mended their broken bones, you've delivered their babies -- they trust you."

"Surely if you just tell them the truth..."

The Sergeant shook her head emphatically.

"Absolutely not. We may be able to colonize planets and fly through space, but we're still a bunch of selfish assholes. If people find out what's happening, they'll panic and gladly throw each other to the wolves to save their own skins," said Sigurdsson. "You know it's true. Our story is that we have a severe storm blowing in and we need everyone within the walls of Fort Hathaway for safety reasons."

She looked Khaifa square in the eye.

"Can you do this for me, Doctor?"

"Yeah. Yes. Okay."

"Good. Get your coat."

To her credit, the doctor immediately did so and followed Sigurdsson out of the MediCorps building and into the parade grounds of Fort Hathaway. Reinforced crates were stacked in the centre of the grounds, in preparation for loading onto the evacuation vessel. Even a civilian would be able to see an unusual amount of activity around the fort's guardhouse as Sigurdsson's people made plans for defending the walls of Fort Hathaway and she wondered just how long they'd be able to keep up the ruse of a storm being the reason for bringing everyone inside the walls. Hopefully long enough to get them all in and lock the doors.

They passed through the large metal gates, Sigurdsson nodding at a pair of soldiers guarding the path.

"I take it your people know what's really happening?," said Khaifa in whispered tones.

Sigurdsson nodded, but said nothing as they approached what passed for the colony's town square. Much like the colony itself, there wasn't much to it. In the centre was what the colonists referred to as Speaker's Corner – a four-foot high cement block with wooden steps fastened to one side. It was where the colonial administrators would make their announcements, but more frequently it was where the drunken colonists would air their grievances. And about half the time, those grievances were against the military presence.

Sigurdsson hung back as Khaifa climbed the step and cleared her throat.

"Excuse me, if I could have your attention please," she began, her voice carrying well despite the wind.

As word of mouth was quickly passed among the colonists and the people began to come out of their shelters and crowd around Speaker's Corner, Khaifa laid out the situation – the fabricated version. She told them about the major storm rolling in and she told them that for their own safety, each and every one of them needed to make their way inside Fort Hathaway. The storm was on its way and picking up speed, she added, so the move inside the fort needed to happen right away.

"This is an official MediCorps alert," she added.

MediCorps only rarely issued weather-related alerts, so the statement did exactly what she'd hoped it would. It got people's attention.

"Thank you," said Khaifa. "And please, start making your way inside the fort."

Stepping down from Speaker's Corner, she headed back over to Sigurdsson.

"Well done, Doctor," said the Sergeant.

"I don't like lying to these people."

"It needed to be done. It was the right thing to do, Doctor."

Before Khaifa could respond, Sigurdsson's earpiece crackled to life.

"Go ahead," she said, holding up a hand for Khaifa to stand by.

"Sarge," said Kenwick, his voice tinny through the earpiece. "I have Eisenhorn for you. Go ahead Corporal Eisenhorn."

"Sergeant, we got the order to pull back to the Fort, but Frenchie thinks she saw something touch down out near Big Rock," said Eisenhorn.

"What kind of something?"

"Not rightly sure, boss. Going in to check it out, then we'll try-.""

"Eisenhorn?"

"Check out... crash... survivors? ...take...... soon."

"Eisenhorn, please repeat – you're breaking up."

Silence.

"Kenwick, can you get him on a clean channel?"

"Negative, Sarge. There's some kind of interference. Been trying to clean it up, but it's pretty strong. Maybe we have a serious storm moving in after all."

"Yeah, maybe."

She cut the connection and turned to Khaifa. Privates Franklin and Rupesh had joined them.

"Private Franklin, assist Doctor Khaifa with moving the civilians inside the fort. Rupesh, gear up and get us ATVs. We've lost contact with Eisenhorn and Frenchie," she said. "We need to get them back here."

As Khiafa and Franklin turned to speak with a few civilians about the move and Rupesh headed off to the motor pool, Sigurdsson looked out across the snow-covered landscape and up into the slowly purpling sky. Maybe there really was a storm coming.

The question was what kind of storm?

"Hamelin," said Radko. "You said that those things barely registered on LiDAR."

"That's correct, sir. They just looked like the typical space debris that LiDAR has been designed to ignore."

"Can we... I don't know, recalibrate it somehow? Make our system sensitive enough to pick them up?"

Hamelin sighed, running a hand through his thinning hair.

"I can certainly try, Commander. But I'm not sure how we'd differentiate between the swarm and actual space junk. We could be tilting at windmills constantly."

"We need to find a way to separate them from everything else," said Owens. "We just don't know enough about the swarm, their vessels, their propulsion systems..."

"Is it reasonable to assume they're sentient?," said Radko after a moment's hesitation.

It was Colonel Gray who answered.

"The attack was too well-executed for it to be random. There was planning involved, so yes, I'd vote for sentience."

Owens nodded his agreement.

With a sigh, Radko locked eyes with Tangaroa and the larger man stood up a little straighter. Radko could tell they were thinking the same thing.

"Mister Owens," he said. "I'm appointing you as my XO until such time as we're assigned a new commanding officer."

Owens, along with everyone else, looked shocked.

"Sir? But I just-."

"I don't recall this being a question, Lieutenant. You have the command deck - I need to attend to a potential cargo issue with Tangaroa," he said, then turned to Gray. "Colonel, I'd like you to join us."

Gray narrowed his eyes in suspicion, but nodded his assent none the less.

"Cortez, see who else you can raise on the emerg channels and also monitor civilian bands - we might pick up some chatter there that could help us plan our route."

"Aye sir."

"Standing order is evade," said Radko, raising his voice for the entire command deck crew to hear. "Evade only. We don't engage until we have a better idea what we're up against."

After he received and returned salutes from the crew - his crew, now - Radko headed through the hatchway and into the central corridor, toward the elevators that would take him to the cargo deck. Tangaroa and Gray had fallen into step beside him.

"That girl you have on communications seems a little shaky," said Gray.

"She's a cadet. Nineteen years old. And we just witnessed the death of over a thousand people, Colonel. I think we're all a little shaky."

The Colonel nodded, but didn't say anything. Instead, he glanced at Tangaroa and though Gray was not an easy man to read, it was clear he was suspicious about both their destination and the reasons for it. The trio stepped into the elevator in silence and kept that silence down to the cargo deck, where they exited the elevator and headed for cargo hold one.

The ATC Castle guards out front – Radko had already forgotten their names – stood a little straighter as they saw the trio approach, but Tangaroa waved them away and opened the door himself.

Inside, the hold looked just as Radko had remembered it – two more guards, plus the large container with the eye-level windows on all side.

"Wait outside," Tangaroa said to the two guards.

He waited until they'd left and closed the hatch behind them before speaking again.

"Commander. Not sure this is a good idea."

"Me either, but if it can help us..."

"What exactly is going on, Radko?," asked Gray.

Stepping up to the container, Radko looked through the glass at their cargo and sighed. There was no question he was going to find himself in serious trouble for this, but for the time being, survival trumped career prospects. Should the Commonwealth Navy determine that his decision was worthy of a court martial, then so be it. He'd face those charges and their consequences if and when they were laid. For now, he was more concerned about getting word to the Second Fleet about what had happened at Echo Station and what may already be happening elsewhere.

"Our assignment, before taking you and your Rangers on board for transport to Redfall, was to deliver this container to the ATC Castle R&D facility on Duster's Range as part of a development contract with Commonwealth Intelligence."

Frowning, Gray stepped up beside Radko and glanced inside the container.

"The fuck...?"

Inside the otherwise empty, sterile container was a woman. A Chinese woman who, completely naked and with her long hair trailing down her back, sat cross-legged on the container floor. Her eyes were closed and she gave no indication she was aware of the presence of the three men.

"Have you ever heard of Project Nightwatch, Colonel?"

Gray nodded slowly. The Union of Soviet Socialist Republics, lead of course by Russia and China, had begun a program that would attempt to create the perfect intelligence operative. Someone who could steal secrets directly from people's minds and carry out assassinations without ever picking up a weapon. The Anglicized version of the name was Project Nightwatch and for many years, it had been perceived as a major threat to the Commonwealth — so much so that every branch of the military had tried to design countermeasures against it. Had Nightwatch actually succeeded, the countermeasures that had been designed would have been useless, but as it turned out, they were unnecessary. The project had been an utter disaster, with at least one of the project overseers executed for treason when word had leaked to the Commonwealth about what had been going on. Reports were that a handful of test subjects had survived, but none had survived in a state warranting transportation under armed guard.

Those reports were, as Radko had very recently learned, wrong in at least one case.

"Her name is Nixon. At least, that's what she was identified as in the Soviet documents we intercepted. Some kind of Cold War joke, we assume," said Radko. "She is, to break it down to its most basic, a mind reader."

Gray slowly reached up and rubbed at his temples as things fell into place.

"This is why you were asking about sentience."

"If she can sense these things-."

"Then she can supplement our LiDAR to tell us what's a rock and what's a hostile."

"Exactly."

"If she doesn't just kill us all and escape," said Tangaroa.

"I'm hoping that if we explain the situation, she'll agree to help."

"If she can read minds, she already knows the situation," said Gray.

Tangaroa shook his head.

"Container's insulated. Gives off some kind of... I dunno what. Acts like radio interference for her brain stuff."

Beside the keypad that would open the container was a square green button with a radio icon printed on it in yellow. Radko pressed it.

"Nixon."

The woman's eyes slowly opened. They were, surprisingly, a very pale blue.

"My name is Radko, Lieutenant Commander. Acting commanding officer of the HMCS Vimy Ridge."

Though she stared at him, she gave no indication of having understood any of it.

"Nixon, the Commonwealth has been attacked and-."

"Quon Li-Chen," said the woman softly.

"I'm sorry?"

"My name is Quon Li-Chen."

The three men exchanged glances. Radko took his thumb off the comm button.

"I'm going to open the door."

"That could be dangerous, Commander," said Gray.

"Because we're not already halfway to fucked, Colonel?"

The Colonel couldn't help but chuckle.

"Can't argue with that logic," he said, unholstering his weapon. "But one wrong move and I double-tap her in the forehead. Understood?"

"Understood."

As Gray and Tangaroa took up position for clear shots, Radko tapped in the security code he technically wasn't supposed to know. Though ATC Castle was good at some things and even great at others, designing code-locks wasn't among them. With a hiss, the door unsealed and Radko swung it aside.

"Miss Quon."

The woman – Quon Li-Chen – looked up at him curiously then slowly stood, making no effort to hide her nakedness. And Radko made a concerted effort not to notice it.

"Gallant gesture," said Quon quietly.

"Excuse me?"

He felt a strange sensation then, a pressure, like a tug on his mind and immediately knew what was happening. He hadn't thought it actually possible, but he knew it was happening none-theless. The woman stepped up very close to him, to the point where he could feel her breath.

"Miss Quon, get out of my mind."

And the tug suddenly stopped, Quon's brow furrowing slightly.

"The other two want to shoot me. You don't."

"No," he said, still slightly unsettled. "No, I want to ask-."

"For my help in tracking 'the swarm' as you call them. It's real, then, what I saw in your mind? The space station, the ships?"

"Yes."

"I'm not a LiDAR system, Fin."

He tried not to let it bother him that she was using his first name.

"Miss Quon, I am asking for your help. I'm sure you don't give two shits about the Commonwealth, but these things are also going through Soviet space as well, which means-."

"I don't care about the Commonwealth or the USSR," she said.

Though it wasn't the response he had expected, Radko pressed on.

"We are facing what appears to be a large-scale invasion. And by 'we' I don't mean the Commonwealth or the Soviets, or even the American Free States. I mean humanity. We're projecting-."

"I saw the projected path in your mind."

"Then you also no doubt know," he said through gritted teeth, trying very hard to control his rising anger. "That we are headed through the swarm, with your help or without it. I suspect our chances of survival, and therefore your chances of survival, are better with your assistance. I can get Tangaroa and Gray to give their word that neither they nor the soldiers under their command will harm or harass you if that's the concern."

Tilting her head slightly to the left, Quon stared for a moment, then almost imperceptibly shook her head.

"None of them can be trusted. But you," she said, slowly reaching up and placing her index finger on Radko's forehead. "I see you. I see you."

She dropped her hand and smiled, but there was no humour behind it.

"I will help you, Fin. But here is my condition: I will never reach Duster's Range. You will, prior to making rendezvous with your Second Fleet, give me a shuttle and enough fuel and supplies to leave Commonwealth space. And I will blissfully disappear."

Flicking a glance to Gray, Quon's smile broadened.

"Colonel Gray doesn't believe I'll hold up my end. He also thinks his wife is having an affair. What do you think, Fin?"

"He's a good looking guy, I don't see why she'd stray," he said, impressing himself that he'd been able to say it with a straight face.

"Cute."

"I think you'll do exactly what you promise."

"How can you be sure we can trust this woman, Radko?," said Gray.

Without breaking eye contact with Quon, Radko smiled.

"Because I don't need to be psychic to know that she knows this is the last card she has to play. We're her last chance to get away before she's locked away in an R&D facility for the rest of her life."

Quon's smile faded. Radko's did not.

"We'll get you something to wear."

He activated his comm unit.

"Owens, Radko. I need one of your people to find some clothing for a guest. Civilian clothing – no uniforms – so we'll likely have to borrow from the crew."

"Understood, Commander. What size should they be looking for?"

"No idea. The guest in question is in cargo hold one with Tangaroa, just send someone down."

"Yessir."

As the connection closed, Radko turned to Tangaroa.

"Stay with her for now. Once she's dressed, bring her and the rest of your team to the mess hall," he said, then turned to Gray. "Colonel, if you would assemble your men there as well. We'd better let everyone know what's going on."

"Agreed," said Gray, nodding. "I'll get them ready."

"Thanks. And Colonel," said Radko. "Thanks for the backup. Up on command deck."

Gray simply nodded again and headed out of cargo hold one.

"Nothing at all?"

"No, Commander," said Cortez quietly.

She and Radko were alone in his office, a moment of peace in what had – and would no doubt continue to be – a day of disaster. Too wired to sit, Radko paced while Cortez stood ramrod straight and watched him.

"Nothing," he said, more to himself than Cortez.

Cortez had had no luck in contacting anyone in the Second Fleet or in intercepting any chatter on either military or civilian lines. The only signal they'd been able to pick up since the swarm had swept through their sector had been the transmission from Von Daniken's Landing.

"There must be something interfering with our signal," said Radko.

"Sir, I...," she paused and took a deep, shaky breath. "Sir, what are we going to do?"

"Exactly what I said we were going to do. We'll meet up with the Second Fleet and..."

He trailed off, looking at Cortez for the first time and seeing that she was close to tears. As much of a shock as the attack and the destruction of Third Fleet had been to people like him and Lieutenant Colonel Gray, people who had many years of service under their belt, people who had been in combat situations – even dire combat situations –– before, the events must have been absolutely terrifying for Cortez. The memory of his very first combat experience was still a vivid one for Radko, even fifteen years later. The knot of fear in his gut, the cold sweat, the sudden feeling of weakness in his legs. And that been a well-planned engagement against the Soviet Navy and something he and his crew mates had prepared for over the course of two weeks. Cortez had been thrust into a new role and faced a surprise attack by an unknown enemy. She'd performed so well in the crisis that he'd almost forgotten that she was just a cadet, just a kid really. When she'd been forced to focus on doing a job, she'd been fine, but now that there was time to reflect...

"Cortez," said Radko, stopping his pacing to place a hand on each of her shoulders. "I'm not going to pretend that I have all the answers. Colonel Gray was right when he said no one has been in this situation before, so we just have to do what we think is best and keep moving forward. We have to keep thinking tactically, not emotionally. Understand?"

She nodded, but he could still see the tears welling up in her eyes.

"Your performance to this point has been nothing short of amazing, Cadet. You stepped up when I needed you and I'm not going to forget that," he said. "I can't promise you that this is going to get any easier, Anna. But whatever doubts you have about yourself and your ability to cope with what we're going through right now, I want you to know that given your performance thus far, I have none."

The left corner of her mouth twitched upward slightly and the ghost of a smile passed across her lips. It wasn't her usual room-brightening smile, but given the circumstances Radko would take whatever he could get.

"Thank you, Commander," she said softly. "I hope I can live up to that."

"You will."

There was a pause and Radko thought he may have seen a slight blush creeping into the young Cadet's cheeks.

"Are... you going to be okay, sir?"

With a small smile, Radko patted her on the shoulder.

"Of course. I'll be fine. Now why don't you go see if Lieutenant Owens needs any help preparing the briefing documents."

"Right away, sir," she said, snapping off a quick salute, then disappearing through the hatch.

As the hatch closed behind her, the smile vanished from Radko's face.

Of course he'd be okay. What choice did he have? He was, after all, the ranking officer in the Third Fleet of the Commonwealth Navy. A fleet of one ship, with a swarm of alien invaders between it and any reinforcements.

Of course he'd be okay.

Slumping against the bulkhead, Radko closed his eyes and sighed heavily.

His name was Jaeger. No one knew for sure where he'd come from, he'd just kind of shown up one day three seasons ago and stuck around. Certainly no one on the colony had ever claimed to be his rightful owner and no one could even tell you how everyone knew his name, but everyone did. The prevalent theory is that the large German Shepherd had been a stray on some other planet, had one day wandered onto a transport headed to Von Daniken's Landing and, finding the colony and colonists to his liking, decided to stay.

For the past three years, he'd made the annual winter trip from and spring trip to the colony just like everyone else.

And he loved going on patrol with Freyja Sigurdsson.

And, though she'd never admit it to anyone, she always felt a little happier when she and Jaeger were out walking the perimeter together making sure the colony was safe from threats both human and alien.

Jaeger was probably the only creature on the entire planet that Sigurdsson really connected with, not counting Nasrin Khaifa.

But wasn't that another fucking story, thought Sigurdsson as she watched Rupesh approaching with the requisitioned gear. Jaeger trotted along four paces ahead of him.

He was a good soldier, that one.

Rupesh wasn't too bad either.

"Sorry I took so long, Sergeant," said Rupesh. "I thought you might want this."

Stepping off the ATV, Rupesh unstrapped Vidar's case from the cargo rack. Sigurdsson smiled as she knelt down to give Jaeger some attention, scratching heartily behind his ears.

"Thank you, Private. I take it still no word from Eisenhorn or Frenchie?"

Rupesh shook his head.

"All right," she said, standing. "They were going to check something out over by Big Rock, so we'll head that way. You drive, I'll spot."

She zipped up her CASCAM parka and her combat vest over it, then put on the goggles Rupesh left dangling from the ATV handle bars. Within a few minutes, they were headed out across the plain, toward Big Rock.

The terrain around the colony was so uneven, Rupesh couldn't take the ATV to its top speeds for safety concerns, which meant that Jaeger, running along beside them, didn't have much trouble keeping up. The other effect of their necessarily cautious progress was that it took far longer than normal and far longer than Sigurdsson had hoped for them to reach the patrol zone to which Eisenhorn and Frenchie had been assigned. As the ATV rolled to a stop, Sigurdsson swung her leg over the back and pushed up her goggles, squinting into the snow and declining light.

"No sign of them at first glance," she said. "But that would have been too easy, eh?"

Rupesh chuckled and Sigurdsson unpacked her sniper rifle, Vidar. Thumbing off the caps at each end of the scope, she raised the rifle to her shoulder, using the scope like a telescope to scan the landscape. The snow was blowing too much across the plains for any tracks or footprints to last more than a few minutes. Though nothing the Sergeant had ever seen could rival the beauty of the Von Daniken's Landing plains in full summer bloom, fall quickly became winter and turned the plains into little more than a frozen wasteland. Where once long grasses and tree analogues swayed in the breeze, now there was just a seemingly endless landscape of snowdrifts and ice-covered rocks.

Though Sigurdsson had to admit, it was still a beautiful landscape in its own way. So white and crisp and most of it untouched by man or beast.

"Try comms again," she said, lowering Vidar. "I'll switch to infrared and see if I can pick up anything."

Pulling off her right glove, she reached up with her index finger and tapped her right temple. There was a momentary buzzing feeling as the contact node implanted in her finger connected with the one implanted in her skull and her vision shifted, the cybernetic enhancements to her right eye coming online. It had taken her months to get used to, but she switched from standard mode to infrared instinctively now, just as she did to the other several features the cybernetics –– an ATC Castle product – provided.

She could hear Rupesh repeating his message over and over into his comm unit, adjusting signal boost, trying again, as she raised Vidar back to her shoulder. Through the scope, a scope that she really wouldn't need if she switched from infrared to targeting functions, Sigurdsson scanned the area again.

"There," she said, pausing in her sweep. A pair of glowing red and yellow blotches against the dark blues of the cold snow. "Found them."

Looking up from the comm unit, Rupesh lifted his binoculars and looked in the same direction as Sigurdsson.

"I think I see them...," he said, then smiled slightly. "At least we know this camo works."

Despite the situation, Sigurdsson laughed. They'd all bitched and moaned when the Army had mandated the switch from their old winter camouflage gear to the CASCAM... something. She couldn't remember what stupid acronym they'd given it, but it was now the official camouflage of the Commonwealth Army. Multi-terrain, arid, temperate, urban and of course winter were all essentially the same pattern, just different colouration. And Rupesh was right, it seemed to work.

She tapped her temple again to deactivate the built-in optics.

"All right," she said, lowering Vidar and sliding it back into its case. "Let's go get them."

Rupesh nodded his agreement and the two hopped back onto their ATV and headed across the snowy landscape toward the spot where they'd sighted the missing soldiers. As always, Jaeger ran along behind them. The trip was short, but as they approached, Eisenhorn waved at them to stop the ATV and proceed on foot.

"What's going on?," said Sigurdsson as she, Rupesh and Jaeger met up with Eisenhorn and Frenchie – whose real name was Francesca De Los Apostoles Covadogna Contreras and had thus been shortened considerably. At first, it had really confused Sigurds-son, calling the Spaniard "Frenchie," but eventually she realized it was just so much easier than using her real name. The pair was up against a chest-high embankment of snow and ice-covered stone.

"Not rightly sure, Sarge," said Eisenhorn, his bushy brows knit in uncertainty.

It got Sigurdsson's attention. Eisenhorn, though he was gener-ally regarded as kind of an ass, wasn't prone to flights of fancy. He was straightforward, logical and a seasoned soldier who had spent seven seasons on Von Daniken's Landing and knew every single thing the planet could throw at him. He didn't suffer fools gladly and had no time to deal with anyone else's dramatics.

"We saw something make planetfall by Big Rock," he contin-ued, pointing toward the shadowy form of the distant, massive boulder the original colonists of Von Daniken's Landing had crea-tively decided to call Big Rock. As stupid as the name sounded, it was entirely appropriate — the boulder stood taller than the look-out tower on the walls of Fort Hathaway. "Thought it might have been a lifeboat or something, so we decided to check it out."

"Then we got your recall," said Frenchie. "So we were going to take a quick look and head back, just in case. But the closer we got, the weaker our radio signals got, until we had nothing at all."

"But I swear to God, Sarge, I seen movement."

Once again unpacking her trusty sniper rifle Vidar, Sigurdsson was about to step up beside Eisenhorn to have a look when she noticed that Jaeger was standing stock still beside the ATV, ears flat against his head, fur bristling down his spine, teeth bared slightly. A low, barely-audible growl escaped his lips.

Sigurdsson swore softly, then joined the others against the embankment, flipping out Vidar's bipod and setting it up on the top of the rocks.

"From where?," she asked, flipping off the lens covers and sighting through the scope.

"Two o'clock," said Eisenhorn. "Just past the West side of Big Rock."

Grunting an acknowledgement, Sigurdsson rotated herself to the right, focusing her scope first on the hazy shadow of Big Rock, then panning her field of vision slowly left. All she could see was more rock and snow. The only movement she saw was the occasional snow devil whipped up by the increasing gusts of wind, but the two soldiers had seen something and something had Jaeger spooked. One of those factors alone would have been enough for Sigurdsson to perform her due diligence, but both together, along with the warning passed down by the Vimy Ridge...

And there it was. Movement. Just a shadow of a shadow, but it was there.

She quickly activated her optics. First magnification to get even closer to the object in question than Vidar's scope would allow, then adding an image enhancement overlay. The visual stutter that accompanied the overlay activation had, back in her first few months with the implant, given her an immediate and splitting headache, but it was something to which Sigurdsson had become so accustomed, the tick barely registered any more.

"What the actual fuck..."

As the enhanced image stabilized, Sigurdsson drew in a sharp breath. What had appeared to be just shadows moving against the darkening sky had now become sharper through the grainy image enhancement filter. It wasn't just one thing moving. It was dozens. Maybe more.

And then, for just a moment, the snow clouds parted, allowing through a thin ribbon of sunlight that illuminated several of the objects and Sigurdsson felt a coldness in her stomach.

She jerked back from Vidar's scope and deactivated her optics.

"Back to the fort. Now."

"Sarge?," said Rupesh. "What is it?"

"It's an army," she said, packing away the rifle. "I've never seen anything like this, but it moves like an army on the march."

As the other lashed their gear to the ATVs, Sigurdsson knelt, trying to comfort the still on-edge Jaeger while she contacted Fort Hathaway.

"Kenwick, it's Sirgurdsson – copy?"

"I'm here, Sarge."

The signal was incredibly weak. She was having a hard time hearing him.

"Are all the civilians within the fort walls?"

"Negative. There are about two dozen arguing that they're perfectly safe in their homes."

"Tell Henning to get those people inside the walls – I don't give a shit what he has to do. And try to patch me through to that Lieutenant Commander aboard the Vimy Ridge."

"By now you all know the basics of what happened today," said Radko.

He stood at one end of the mess hall, Owens on his left, Gray and Tangaroa on his right. Cortez stood off to one side with Quon – who was now dressed in jeans and a tee shirt that was one size too small. She was drawing some stares from a handful of the crew members and Radko was beginning to wonder if it might have been a better idea to have her wait in his office and give her these details later. The hall was packed with the entire crew of the HMCS Vimy Ridge, from officers to maintenance technicians to the cooks and the plumbers. If they'd been running with a full crew, they would have had to have this meeting in two sessions, but as it was, everyone on the ship managed to squeeze in.

"Echo Station has been destroyed, along with every ship docked there. Our Commanding Officer, Commodore Len Edwards, was aboard Echo Station at the time of its loss. The Third Fleet has also been lost," he said, continuing on despite the gasps that followed the statement. Perhaps there should have been more to it than that, more of a statement about the loss of Edwards and the kind of man he was, and about the horrific loss of life that had been suffered with the destruction of the fleet. But those were all things that could be handled later. The crew would be back on their heels enough with the information he was delivering — having them shocked, scared and depressed would help no one. "As of this moment, the Vimy Ridge is the Third Fleet. Mister Owens?"

Clearing his throat, Owens stepped up to take the spot that Radko had vacated. He pressed a button on the small device he held and a large holographic projection appeared above his head, a slowly rotating representation of one of what he and Radko had begun referring to as the Swarm Battleship – the same type of craft the Vimy Ridge had successfully destroyed.

"This is a reconstruction of one of the craft that attacked Echo Station," he said. "It is very obviously not a vessel from the Soviet Navy, nor is it of icaran design."

"Udukiin?," asked an anonymous voice.

Owens shook his head.

"The udukiin design principle for everything – from architecture to space craft to cutlery is tied to the Book of Ur, their prophecies. There's just no room for variation -- at least, not enough variation for them to produce something like this. The kriasi don't have a space fleet and the krellin, while certainly having shown a willingness to attack us in the past, have been focused on recovering from their recent pandemic."

He paused, taking a breath and a sip of water.

"We have no records of any ship of this design ever before being sighted by human observers. It is our belief," he said, nodding toward Radko and Gray. "That we have been attacked by a previously unknown alien species."

As expected, a barely-contained murmur rippled through the mess hall as the crew expressed shock, fear and whatever other emotions ran through them.

"Why would they hit Echo Station?," asked one of the crew, dressed in the yellow jumpsuit of a mechanical repair technician.

"The same reason we've always assumed the Soviets had their eye on it," said Radko. "Aside from being home base to the Third Fleet, Echo Station is... Echo Station was strategically placed to make it an excellent staging ground for strikes into a number of possible hot zones – including both Soviet and icaran space – in addition to being a defensive wall on the Commonwealth border."

"With Echo gone," added Gray. "The flank of the Commonwealth is undefended."

Another murmur ran through the crew, but Radko held up his hand and everyone fell silent.

"The loss of Echo Station, those ships, all those lives... it's a tragedy," he said, standing up a little straighter. "But as I said in the beginning, we are now the Third Fleet. As of this moment, we may be the only living souls aware of what's about to carve a path through Commonwealth space. We've done some work to project the flightpath of the attacking force based on the data we have available. That flightpath leads right through the heart of the Commonwealth."

One of the gun crew commanders stood suddenly.

"Commander, do you mean Earth?"

Radko nodded slowly.

"I mean Earth. And every colony, facility and ship between here and Earth. We estimate that the destruction here at Echo Station cost us just over three thousand lives. But we could be looking at billions of lives," he said. "So here's what we're going to do. We're going to go full burn to the Second Fleet. In a straight line."

It was the first time he'd articulated that part of the plan, so Gray and Owens looked as shocked as the rest of the crew. Sensing objections about to be raised, he continued on.

"We're going straight through to the Second Fleet, through icaran space, through No Man's Land, through Soviet space. The Second Fleet, the First Fleet," he said, then waved toward Gray. "The Commonwealth Army... everyone needs to be warned and put on alert before it's too late. We can't warn people in time if we stand by all the political niceties and skirt around borders. We need to stop these sons of bitches before all the treaties become irrelevant."

Closing his eyes momentarily, Radko took a deep breath.

"Commodore Edwards once told me you should never swear in front of your crew. Showed you weren't in full control of your emotions, he said. I may be acting CO of this ship, but right now, I'm not talking to you as a senior officer. This is not going to be an easy mission; we have no frame of reference for what we're about to do and what we're about to face, because no human has had to face it. Ever. If we're going to pull this off, we're all going to make sacrifices. We could very well go days without sleep. If we get waylaid at all, we may run short of supplies – we were only carrying enough food and water for the trip to Duster's Range. And I can guarantee you we will face combat again. And some of us will die," he said. "So I'm here before you, just a fellow sailor. A fellow member of the Commonwealth Armed Forces, who took the

King's shilling and swore to defend the people of the Common-wealth from all enemies. And I'm asking you to help me do this."

There was a momentary silence before the gun crew chief who had asked about Earth stood.

"I'm with you, Sir."

"I'm with you," said another crew member as she stood.

Within moments, there were dozens standing, until the entire crew was on their feet, swearing to their duties.

"Thank you," said Radko. "Now let's get back to work -- we'll set out to rendezvous with the Second Fleet immediately. Dismissed."

As Radko left, Gray, Tangaroa and Owens with him, the crew began filing out and Cortez, looking relieved, glanced up at Quon.

"How did he know the crew would follow him?"

"He didn't," said Quon.

Cortez looked up at the woman, frowning.

"Well... what would he have done if they hadn't gone along with it?"

"He'd have shot one of them as an example to the rest."

The ride back to the colony was tense. Whatever it was marching toward them was picking up speed, because it seemed that no matter how fast the two ATVs went, Sigurdsson – facing rear to keep an eye on things – could still see the mass of shadows through the blowing snow. She had her left arm wrapped around Jaeger, who sat awkwardly in front of her, pressing his body against hers, while in her right hand she held her 33A1 at the ready, just in case. Though she wasn't sure how accurate her shots could be, bouncing along on the back of an ATV.

"Sarge," said Kenwick as Sigurdsson's earpiece crackled to life. "I've connected with Lieutenant Commander Radko of the Vimy Ridge. Patching you through now."

"Sergeant Sigurdsson," said Radko, his voice echoing like he was speaking to her through a tunnel. "What's the situation on Von Daniken's Landing?"

"Not good, Commander," she said, practically yelling over the sound of the wind and the ATV motor. "One of my patrol teams saw something make planetfall, so we checked it out. Sir, there's some kind of army marching on the colony. I reckon we have less than an hour before they're... fuck. Make that less than half an hour."

Switching image enhancement back on, she saw that her initial thought had been correct – the marching horde was even closer.

"An army? Can you describe what you're seeing, Sergeant? We've only encountered space-faring vessels, no ground forces."

"Sorry, Commander, visibility down here isn't great. Our winter is starting early. All I can tell you at this point is that there appear to be at least three sizes of ground units and they're moving really fucking fast, pardon my language," she said.

"Understood. We're on our way to rendezvous with the Second Fleet. Once we do, I will make sure that reinforcements and a way off-planet are sent to you immediately."

"I appreciate that, Sir."

"Were you able to get all the civilians inside your walls and seal those gates?"

"Not yet, Sir. I'm on my way back to Fort Hathaway now, but from what my people tell me, we have some... uncooperative civilians."

She was pretty sure she heard Radko curse under his breath.

"What a surprise," he said. "Sergeant... you have to protect those you can protect."

For a moment, Sigurdsson didn't say anything. She knew exactly what Radko was saying, or more accurately, what he intentionally wasn't saying. The good of the many was paramount. If she couldn't convince that stubborn minority to get themselves inside the fort, then she'd have to lock the gates and leave them to survive on their own.

And she would.

More often than not, her job of protecting the colonists on Von Daniken's Landing meant protecting them from themselves, but this time there was a bigger picture. She couldn't have endless discussions and try to make them see things her way. She couldn't solve this dispute through mediation or by letting someone sleep off their drunken rage in a holding cell at the barracks.

"I understand, Commander," she said, pausing briefly. "What's your ETA to the Second Fleet, sir?"

What she wanted to ask was how long before she'd have passage off planet. How long she'd have to hold off the advancing horde before reinforcements arrived. And she wasn't sure she was going to like the answer. While Sigurdsson was not particularly well-versed in stellar cartography or naval operations, she knew where Echo Station was... where it had been, and she knew where the Second Fleet was based. By her admittedly rough estimation, it would take the Vimy Ridge at least five days to reach the Second, then at least another twenty-four hours for a vessel to reach Von Daniken's Landing. And that was without getting into any scraps along the way.

"Two days," said Radko, and Sigurdsson frowned.

"Sorry, Commander, bad connection. Thought you said two days."

"I did, Sergeant. We're taking a shortcut."

She was about to ask what he meant when the colour-coded star map she'd often been forced to study popped into her head.

"The Soviets won't be happy."

"The Soviets are never happy," said Radko. "They're Soviets, that's their thing."

Despite the direness of the situation, Sigurdsson smiled. Even if he was Navy, she was starting to like this Radko guy.

Before she could reply, there was a sudden jolt and Sigurdsson, along with Jaeger, was tossed from the ATV, landing heavily on her left shoulder. She rolled up onto her knees, quickly raising the assault rifle to her shoulder, scanning the area. Jaeger was up and at her side, growling into the wind, but there were no hostiles in sight aside from the steadily approaching mass of shadow on the horizon. Lowering the rifle, Sigudrsson felt something grinding in her left shoulder, but ignored it. The ATV was upright, but the angle of the front wheels was all wrong.

"Sigurdsson? The hell just happened?"

It was Radko. The line to the Vimy Ridge was still open.

"Give me a second, Commander," she said. "Rupesh?"

"Yeah," he said, picking himself up off the ground. He'd been flung over the handlebars and there was an ugly gash on his head.

Eisenhorn and Frenchie had turned their vehicle around and pulled up beside the damaged ATV.

"Broken axle," said Frenchie. "Doesn't that just figure."

Sigurdsson muttered a curse, as did the other two. They'd been having problems with the axles on their ATVs for months, but their maintenance team thought they'd finally found a solution. Apparently it had been temporary.

"You three get back to the colony and get those stragglers into the fort," said Sigurdsson. "Jaeger and I will follow on foot."

There was room for three on one of the ATVs – it would be very cozy and might even feel vaguely like sexual harassment, but it was workable. Four was out of the question. Four plus a dog was an impossibility and Sigurdsson would be damned if she'd leave Jaeger on his own.

As the trio of soldiers drove away, Sigurdsson unpacked Vidar and slung it over her shoulder and began jogging back toward Forth Hathaway, Jaeger at her side, 33A1 clutched tightly to her chest.

"Making my way back to the fort on foot," she said into the open channel. It would reach Radko and Kenwick.

"Will you make it back in time?," said Radko.

"We're going to find out."

"Save your breath, Sergeant. We need you in that fort. That's an order."

"I don't take orders from the Navy," she said, grinning in spite of herself. But she followed the order nonetheless, increasing her speed from a jog to a flat-out run. Jaeger easily kept pace.

Though in excellent shape, better shape than most of the soldiers in her garrison, jogging for an extended period in temperatures of minus fifteen degrees Celsius, and dropping quickly, took its toll. She felt it in her legs first, a stiffness in the muscles that slowly became a dull ache. But before the dull ache became actual pain, she began to feel the burning in her lungs, her breath beginning to almost have a taste to it that told Sigurdsson she couldn't keep up her current pace for too much longer.

But she ignored it.

Her body and its complaints was just going to have to suck it up, because being sore and out of breath was better than being dead.

Loping along beside her, Jaeger appeared to be doing just fine and Sigurdsson was rather jealous but she was also happy. She knew the dog could have easily run ahead without her, but he'd decided to match her pace instead.

Though it seemed like an eternity, she finally reached the edge of the civilian colony, marked by a low concrete fence.

"Inside the perimeter fence," she said, as she dropped to one knee behind the fence and unslung Vidar. "Checking on the status of the horde, then I'll make my way to the fort."

She took a moment to control her breathing and give Jaeger a reassuring scratch behind the ears. Sigurdsson smiled.

"Thanks for sticking with me, buddy."

The big German Shepherd wagged his tail and tilted his head, pressing it into her hand.

"Don't worry, everything will be okay."

Raising the sniper rifle to her shoulder, she peered over the top of the fence. It took a moment to focus, but when she did, she swore. The horde was even closer than she'd anticipated and she could almost make out the lead ranks.

Activating her optics once more, she magnified then added the enhancement layer as well as the night vision layer. Three optic enhancements active at once was pushing it, but she'd deal with the headaches later. As the night vision kicked in, compensating for the failing natural light, the lead rank of the horde came into full focus.

"Mother of fuck..."

They were nothing she'd ever seen before.

Broad-toed digitigrade legs supporting a barrel-chested torso. Two sets of arms – one large, set midway up the torso and ending in oddly-shaped pods rather than hands, and one set closer to the neck, smaller and ending in what looked like a trio of tentacles.

The neck was long and the broad, flat head that instantly re-minded Sigurdsson of a manta ray was constantly in motion. She counted six eyes and from what she could tell, each moved independently.

After a moment of shock, Sigurdsson quickly activated the recording function in her cybernetic eye and transmitted a short video clip to Kenwick's station.

"Kenwick, I just uploaded a video file. Give it to all of our people and send a copy to Radko."

She glanced at her range-finder. The maximum effective distance of the 32A OSR was supposedly four thousand five hundred metres – four and a half kilometers. Sigurdsson had never made a shot that long herself, but a sniper from the 5th Commonwealth Rangers notched a confirmed kill with the 32A at three thousand, nine hundred and eighty-eight metres. According to her range-finder, the front rank of the horde was five and a quarter kilometers away and closing.

Staring through the scope at the alien, the manta-headed bastard, Sigurdsson settled her breathing, relaxed her muscles. The wind was going to play havoc with the shot, but she'd been on Von Daniken's Landing long enough to know how to compensate for it. The great unknown, of course, was where the thing kept its brain. Briefly, she switched on an infrared layer, but it was too much for the optics processor to handle – it immediately switched off again.

Five kilometers.

Educated guesswork would have to do.

Thus far, the only sentient species mankind had encountered that didn't have an actual head was the krellin. And every species with a head kept their brain inside it.

Her targeting reticle came to rest in the centre of the thing's broad head then she adjusted for range, temperature and wind.

Four thousand eight hundred metres. Bloody hell. They'd covered two hundred metres in under sixty seconds.

Taking a shallow breath, she slowly exhaled, squeezing the trigger as the breath was halfway out.

Through her scope, Sigurdsson watched the alien's head disappear is a spray of greenish yellow fluid and its body topple to the ground, sending a puff of snow into the air.

Her range-finder logged the kill at four thousand, seven hundred and seventy-six metres, which, as far as she could recall, would be a record. But she wasn't going to stick around to verify the kill, the distance or anything else. She was going to get behind some fucking walls.

"Radko, you still on the line?"

"Affirmative, Sergeant."

"We have made contact with the advancing army. You should be receiving a video file momentarily."

Switching off her optics, Sigurdsson snapped the bipod closed, slung Vidar over her shoulder again and picked up her assault rifle.

"Sergeant?"

She whirled around to see Eisenhorn standing behind her.

"I told you to get the civilians into the fort, Corporal!"

"They won't go, Sarge. The doctor is trying to convince them, but-."

"Doctor Khaifa?"

"Yeah..."

As she followed Eisenhorn up the hill toward one of the civilian housing units, Sigurdsson wasn't sure if the heat she was feeling in her chest was fear or anger. It was probably equal part of each and she had to force herself to relax her grip on the assault rifle. Putting herself in harm's way was one thing, it was her job, it was what she was trained for, but other people...

She barged through the door and, seeing Khaifa nearby, grabbed the doctor by the upper arm and dragged her outside.

"What the fuck are you doing?"

Khaifa looked at her, a mixed of shock and fear in her eyes.

"Freyja, you're hurting me."

Sigurdsson looked down at her hand, clamped around Khaifa's bicep as if she was seeing it for the first time. She immediately released the woman.

"Sorry. I'm sorry," she said softly. "But Nasrin, fucking hell. You should be inside the fort where it's safe."

"I couldn't just leave these people. What if you're right and someone attacks?"

"Someone is attacking, Nasrin. Echo Station wasn't just attacked, it was completely destroyed. The Commonwealth Third Fleet is now a single ship -- I've been in contact with them and they gave me the heads up. We're directly in the path of an invading force. And they're here," she said. "I've seen them. I just killed one."

Khaifa just stared for a moment, her deep brown eyes wide.

"Echo Station... Freyja...," she swallowed heavily. "My husband was on Echo Station."

For a moment, Sigurdsson had no idea what to say. Under normal circumstances, an 'I'm so sorry for your loss' would have been appropriate, but Khaifa and her estranged husband hadn't spoken in months. In fact, one night while more than a little drunk, Khaifa had confessed to Sigurdsson that she'd never even made her husband aware of the mix-up that had seen MediCorps assign her to Von Daniken's Landing. The Sergeant tried to convince herself that it was that fact, the strained husband-wife relationship that made her hesitant to say she was sorry, as opposed to her own complicated relationship with the doctor.

"Nasrin," she said quickly, trying with little success to conceal her impatience. "The horde will be here in minutes. We have to get inside the walls. Now."

Khaifa nodded vigorously and the two stepped back inside.

"Everyone," said Khaifa, her voice shaking. "Please follow me into Fort Hathway. For your own safety."

"We've already said we're not going. We're not going to abandon our homes just because the army is afraid of a storm," said a grizzled old settler. His name was Barnes, as Sigurdsson recalled, and he had a habit of belligerence toward the soldiers, especially when drunk. Which, again as she recalled, was fairly often.

A couple other voices joined his in protest.

There wasn't time to do this the polite way.

Sigurdsson fired two shots from her assault rifle into the ceiling and everyone, including Doctor Khaifa, ducked their heads in fear.

"This colony is about to be attacked. In the event of military action against Von Daniken's Landing, the garrison commander is entitled to invoke martial law," she said. "Consider it invoked.

Now get to the fucking fort. The next person to protest or slow our progress will be shot. Am I making myself clear?"

Nods of understanding all around.

"Move."

Eisenhorn led the way with the civilians, surprisingly quiet, filing out behind him. Sigurdsson and Frenchie, along with   Jaeger, brought up the rear.

"Would you really have shot them?," asked Frenchie.

Before Sigurdsson could respond, Frenchie's chest exploded in a spray of blood, bone and meaty chunks.

"This is apparently what we're up against," said Radko as Owens displayed a looped copy of Sigurdsson's video file in a holographic window above the sand table.

"At least we know we can fight them with weapon technology we already have," said Gray. "And as a side note, that Sergeant Sigurdsson is one hell of a shot."

"Let's hope the rest of her garrison can follow her example, or they won't last long enough for us to extract them," said Radko. Then turning to Owens, "Estimates on the number of hostiles they're going to be facing?"

Owens shook his head.

"The field of vision in this video is too narrow. From her audio transmissions, it sounds like she saw... what was the word she used?"

"A horde."

"A horde, right. But in the video, we see maybe five, six. Possibly seven, if this shadow in the back is another hostile unit."

"A swarm and a horde," said Gray. "Lovely."

"Okay," said Radko. "So where are we on making contact with the Second Fleet?"

"We'll be passing through icaran space in roughly forty-five minutes, Commander," said Owens, sliding aside the video loop and bringing up a star map superimposed with their planned route. "But thus far, we haven't had any response to our emergency broadcasts."

"They could be on radio silence," said Gray. "In our case, the Rangers have standing orders to maintain radio silence if it's believed the enemy could be listening in or manipulating transmissions."

Though he said nothing, Radko hoped the Colonel was right.

"All right. Once we enter icaran space, we need to be on high alert. You can bet they won't be-."

"Sir, I've got an icaran cruiser on LiDAR," said Hamelin.

"What's an icaran cruiser doing inside Commonwealth space?," said Gray.

The irony of the question was not lost on Radko.

"Give me a magnification window on the observation deck, Owens," he said, already climbing the ladder to the second command deck level, Gray following close behind. By the time they reached the large, curved windows, a one and a half metre by one and a half metre square hovered a centimetre from the surface of the window, its edges pulsating a pale blue. Radko tapped it to activate, then slid it slightly up and to the side, corresponding roughly to the positioning of the icaran vessel.

"Can you pick up any transmission," said Radko as he waited for the resolution of the magnified image to sharpen.

"No sir," said Cortez. "But it makes sense for them to run silent if they've intentionally crossed our border."

"Look," said Gray.

He was pointing to the now-sharp magnified image. It was definitely an icaran cruiser, but it was in several pieces. The propulsion section was entirely gone and Radko assumed the debris cloud surrounding the ship to be what remained of its engines. One of the weapons pods had been sheared off and was free-floating about a kilometre away, while the remaining weapons pod was so scorched as to be barely recognizable.

Radko turned, about to order a continuation of their course when Quon suddenly stepped up beside him.

"There are survivors on board that ship," she said.

"What?"

Glancing back at the image, he found it hard to believe that there would be any breathable atmosphere remaining. It had been shot to pieces.

"Eleven."

"Shit."

There was a lengthy pause before Radko spoke again.

"Colonel, do any of your men have experience with ship-to-ship extraction?"

"Yes," said Gray, nodding slowly. "Are you suggesting we bring those icarans aboard the Vimy Ridge, Commander?"

"I am, Colonel."

"They've entered into Commonwealth space illegally, Commander."

"Which is exactly what we're going to be doing to icaran space very shortly, Colonel, so it might be in our best interest to have a little bit of goodwill to drop off on our way through."

Though it was logical and more than enough reason to justify the action, it wasn't the most important factor as far as Radko was concerned. Being a naval officer, someone who lived most days aboard a space-faring vessel – a nuclear-powered ship with only bulkheads keeping him alive – simply allowing someone to asphyxiate in the vacuum of space was unthinkable. Friend or enemy, it wasn't an act he was willing to entertain. And he knew every single sailor on the Vimy Ridge would feel the same. Colonel Gray wouldn't understand. No matter how frequently he and his Rangers used ships to get from place to place, they were still a ground unit. They spent most of their time with their boots in the dirt, not thumping along on deckplates. They were used to breathing fresh air, not recycled, re-oxygenated air.

Finally, after a few moments of thought, Gray nodded his assent.

"All right, we'll extract the icarans."

"Thank you, Colonel. I'd like you to take Tangaroa with you," he said, continuing quickly to quell the inevitable objection. "It may help the process to have a neutral party, given the number of skirmishes the Commonwealth has had in recent history with the icarans."

"And ATC Castle is officially not involved in any of it."

"Officially."

"Except those bastards sell weapons and gear to everyone with a credit account."

"I'm not asking you to get in bed with ATC Castle, Colonel. We just need to use every resource we have at our disposal."

With a nod, Gray headed down to the main command deck. Radko could hear the man barking orders into his comm device as he disappeared down the corridor.

"You should have left them," said Quon. "This operation will slow you down."

Before he could respond, he felt the same tug on his mind that he'd felt when Quon had first read him in the cargo hold.

"Quon..."

The tug stopped.

"I see you have your reasons. I don't see them as valid, especially after the Queenston Heights-."

"You know exactly fuck all about what happened on the Queenston Heights, Miss Quon," he snapped. "You are here for one reason and one reason only, and that reason is not to provide commentary. I will hold up my end of our deal, but I promise you, the second you become more hindrance than help, I will shoot you myself."

There was no immediate reaction from the woman. She simply stared out into space, hands calmly clasped behind her back. Radko waited for several moments, expecting a response – any response – but then he chuffed and turned to head back down into the main command deck.

"I'm... sorry," said Quon.

Radko paused and turned back to the woman.

"I don't trust," she said.

He waited for her to continue, but nothing came.

"Don't trust what?"

"At all. Anyone. It was a full statement – I don't trust. It isn't something I do," she said, still not breaking her gaze from the observation dome. "Delving into one's mind is my way of discovering truth."

"Look, Miss Quon, I understand that you have trust issues. I get it. I really do. You escaped a Soviet science project only to be captured and shipped off to become an ATC Castle science project. But I am giving you a chance at freedom – a chance at freedom that will very likely net me a disciplinary hearing if not an outright court martial when all this is over – and I don't have time to be handing out hugs and painting pictures of fucking rainbows for everyone who's having difficulty with their current circumstances."

"That's a shame. I was looking forward to the fucking rainbows."

Sighing, Radko leant forward on the rail.

"My turn to apologise. That was... a little harsh. Sorry."

For the first time since she'd joined him in the dome, Quon turned to face him. Her eyes were narrowed, her head cocked slightly to one side.

"You are an odd man, Fin."

"Yes, I really am."

"Sir," called Owens from below. "The Colonel's shuttle is away. They'll be docking with the crippled icaran ship in just under three minutes."

"Thank you, Lieutenant."

"He doesn't understand why you made him your executive officer after he opposed your taking command," said Quon, low enough that only Radko could hear.

"He'll figure it out."

"You would be a very difficult opponent in a game of chess, wouldn't you, Fin?"

"What do you mean?"

"You see the whole board, all the pieces. You're setting up your pieces to fit the strategy you plan to execute," she said, a hint of admiration in her voice. "And if you have to sacrifice a pawn to..."

She stopped and turned sharply back to the view of space.

"Something's coming. There."

Radko slid the magnification window over to where she was pointing. Shapes were visible, but they were still too far away to get any kind of identification.

"Cortez, any signals coming in? Any chatter?"

"No, Commander."

"Hamelin – LiDAR?"

"No, sir. Nothing."

"Everything is very faint," said Quon. "But none of it is intelligible. They're not human, but they... feel different than those icarans."

"Owens, can we enhance this image any further?"

"Working on it, Commander..."

And a few seconds later, the image became even sharper. Everyone on command deck remained silent as the display solidified into an image of two swarm battleships surrounded by a wing of fighters.

"HMCS Vimy Ridge to Lieutenant Colonel Gray."

It was the impossibly young cadet Radko had, for some reason, assigned as his communications-slash-intelligence officer. Gray stood, waiting for the thunk of the airlock seal before responding.

"Vimy Ridge, this is Gray. We have airlock seal – preparing to board icaran vessel."

Hefting his assault rifle, he used hand signals to direct the team to their positions. They were all wearing armoured environmental suits, making their movements much slower than normal. It was a necessary evil. They had no idea how many compartments between the airlock and the surviving crew had been compromised.

His best Sergeant, the tall and handsome Edward Vossek popped the hatch and led the team into the icaran ship.

"Colonel, we have picked up incoming hostiles," said Cortez. "Estimated time to contact twenty minutes."

Bloody hell.

"Identity of hostiles, Cadet?"

This time it was Radko's voice that came through the comm unit.

"Two swarm battleships and what appears to be a fighter wing."

There was a long pause before Radko continued.

"Colonel, if you want to scrub the mission-."

"Never scrubbed a mission in my life, son. Not about to start now. Gray out. All right, ladies and gentlemen," he said through the open channel to his full team. "You heard them – we need to get this done quickly. Move out."

Tangaroa, who had taken up position with Gray, motioned for one of his people to stay behind with the shuttle and Gray shot him a questioning look.

"Former hot zone extraction pilot," said Tangaroa.

Gray simply nodded. Hot zone extractions were hairy and a lot of pilots were shot down during attempted extractions. If this one had lived long enough to actually leave the service and hook up with ATC Castle, she'd be just the kind of pilot they'd want at the controls if those swarm ships got a little too close. The trip back to the Vimy Ridge could get interesting.

Vossek had taken point, naturally falling into the position Gray had been assigning him almost since day one. Kwabena, the lanky Ghanaian, fell in beside him and the rest of the unit followed, Tangaroa and his two PMCs settling into the middle of the small group with Gray.

As much as he may have disliked the icaran military, Gray could admit that their ship designs and layouts were bordering on beautiful, all soft curves and none of the harsh angles so prevalent in Commonwealth vessels. This icaran ship was a mess, broken and twisted. Gray's group made their way cautiously, passing holes through which they could see stars – and even once seeing the Vimy Ridge – and passing icaran bodies and body parts floating in zero gravity.

"Sir," said Kwabena. "The hatch ahead is sealed."

"Test it."

With a nod, Kwabena knelt beside the hatch, drawing a small digital tool from his subload pouch. He placed it against the door and waited for a moment, then shook his head as he read the results.

"There is no atmosphere beyond, Colonel."

"Then they're either dead or wearing enviro suits," said the Colonel, stepping up to the hatch. "Everyone get ready."

He flattened himself against the bulkhead beside the door while his men arrayed themselves for clear shots. Gray pounded his fist on the hatch.

"This is Colonel Harlan Gray of the 15th Commonwealth Rangers! We are here to assist!"

There was no response.

"The hostiles who attacked your vessel are on their way back," he continued. "In two minutes, I'm leaving here with my men – it's up to you whether you're with us when we leave. If you want to die here, cowering in a cargo bay, that's your call."

There were another few moments of silence, but just as Gray was preparing to give the signal to wind it up and get back to the shuttle, he felt through the bulkhead the clunk of a locking mechanism being disengaged. The hatch slid back and up and Gray saw his men tense a second before he saw the reason why. Standing in the doorway was not an icaran naval officer, but a fully armoured and armed icaran commando. And behind him were ten more, just as well-equipped. The lead icaran turned and the Colonel looked up to see his reflection in the blank face plate of the towering icaran. Those face plates were one of the more disconcerting elements of facing the icaran military. Their helmets covered their entire head, no eye holes, just a blank face, or sometimes a design painted on it to personalize the equipment. Inside the helmet, Gray knew from having recovered one or two from the battlefield, was a full three-hundred and sixty degree holographic heads-up display. Targeting, range finders, armour status... Gray would kill to have that kind of technology in the hands of his Rangers. Rumour was that ATC Castle was working on something similar, but Gray didn't put a lot of stock in the promises of mercenaries.

"Identify," said the icaran. His words, filtered through the Commonwealth's translation matrix and piped through Gray's earpiece, were bland and stilted as the software cobbled together the phonetics to transform the oddly lyrical icaran tongue into the King's English.

"I'm Colonel Gray. And you are?"

He knew the icarans had similar translation capability. He knew this because the Commonwealth translation matrix was reverse-engineered from stolen icaran technology.

"Brigadier-General Locaris of the Venator ICA Commandos."

"Sir," called Kwabena. "The swarm ships will be in striking range in four minutes!"

Gray nodded and turned back to Locaris.

"We need to get to our shuttle on the double. I'm sure you understand that I'll need you to surrender your weapons to my men," said Gray.

The icaran hesitated for a moment, but handed his own bulky rifle to Gray. The rest of the ICA Commandos followed the Brigadier's lead, handing off weapons to the Rangers and ATC Castle PMCs.

"All batteries report ready, Commander."

"All right," said Radko. "Unmanned turrets on auto. Manned turrets, target those fighters and protect Colonel Gray's shuttle.

Missile batteries, target the battleships. Rail gunners, you are free to select your targets as you see fit. And everyone is free to fire at will – you have a standing order to fire."

"Commander," said Owens. "What are your orders regarding our nuclear warheads?"

"Our nuclear arsenal is not an option."

He continued when several of the crew looked at him in surprise. After all, he was taking their most powerful weapon out of the equation.

"Nuclear launch requires two activation keys," he said. "One of which Commodore Edwards wore around his neck at all times."

Owens nodded. Conventional weapons would have to do.

He activated the strategic operations layer of the sand table, all the charts, readouts and status indicators already present rising up to accommodate the star map of the area which materialized directly above the table's surface. The Vimy Ridge was displayed at the centre of the map, the remains of the icaran ship just off its port bow. The incoming swarm ships were on an approach vector directly ahead of the Commonwealth frigate.

"Commander," said Owens. "I'm not sure the Colonel is going to make it back before we have to engage."

"Shuttle is disengaging from the icaran ship," someone called out.

"Weapons free," said Radko as he quickly scaled the ladder to the observation dome again. Under normal combat circumstances, he'd be at the sand table working out strategy, but this fight was more about throwing everything they had at their attackers and hoping it was enough. Still...

"Owens, activate second level sand table."

A second later, the projector mounted at the apex of the observation dome flared to life, an exact duplicate of the sand table display below hovering four feet above the catwalk.

"Make sure our hull cameras are recording every second of this."

He glanced over at Quon, who hadn't moved an inch nor has she looked away from the approaching ships since first sensing their approach. Though she was hard to read, Radko's gut told him that she was uneasy, that she was nervous about what was coming. He couldn't say he felt any differently, given what he'd seen the swarm do. That the Vimy Ridge had destroyed one swarm battleship was the only comfort he had going into this fight.

The deck plates vibrated slightly beneath his feet as the first of the swarm fighters began their attack runs and then he could feel the rhythmic pounding of the Vimy Ridge's guns as his people began fighting back. The different feelings one could pick up through a ship's deck plates came to be something a sailor relied upon to learn even the smallest things about their ship. An old hand in maintenance, for example, could tell when an engine needed calibrating just by how the deck plates vibrated up on command deck. But Radko had never had a mind for mechanicals. For him, it was the guns. Steady, even firing was a good sign – focused crews, crews doing their jobs smoothly. Uneven firing meant sloppy crews or frightened crews or crews depleted by injury or death. Any of those scenarios could mean the difference between victory and defeat.

He watched a pair of fighters streak in and then he watched them vanish in yellowish balls of flame as the rail gunners entered the fray. The rail gunners always began their firing cycle later than the missile batteries and gun turrets due to the warm-up time necessary for their electromagnets, but the damage they could cause was far greater. Without wind resistance in space, the rail gun projectiles – just blunt metal cylinders – would travel at speeds upwards of Mach 20, hitting their target with more force than any weapon in the Commonwealth arsenal, save nuclear warheads.

Swarm fighters continued to scream by the observation dome – at least Radko imagined that they screamed. In reality, they made no sound at all in the vacuum of space, but it was amazing what the imagination would fill in after a lifetime of space combat movies and their larger-than-life sound effects. And just as his mind added in the sounds of the fighters, so too did it add in the resonant thump of an explosion as another enemy bloomed into a brief sphere of flame and then winked out of existence.

"Status?"

"We have four confirmed kills," said Owens, checking data streams in four different holographic windows as well as his tablet. "We're taking damage, but it's manageable. Minor casualties reported, only two requiring more than simple first aid."

Nodding, Radko turned back to the transparent dome and looked out toward the carcass of the icaran vessel. Gray's shuttle was almost exactly halfway home.

The shuttle rocked as it was hit by another strafing run and Gray heard something pop and start hissing. He braced himself even harder against the bulkhead, his right hand clamped tightly on the back of the pilot's chair. Logically, he knew he should be strapped in with his men, but he wanted to see everything that was going on around them.

"How much longer?"

"Sixty seconds," said the ATC Castle pilot. He had no idea what her name was, but Tangaroa was right about her being solid behind the stick.

"Colonel!"

Gray turned to see Vossek popping his restraints and grabbing a first aid kit. One of his more junior Rangers, Specialist Anders, was clutching his thigh just above a ragged bloody hole about the diameter of a shot glass.

"Shot came right through the shuttle and Anders," said Vossek as he knelt beside Anders and applied the self-tightening tourniquet. "We're leaking oxygen hardcore."

"We're almost clear, just patch up who and what you can."

The shuttle dove sharply, so sharply and so suddenly that Gray felt his magnetized boots almost let go of the deck plates. He had an answer to his question before he had a chance to ask it.

"Two bogies on our six," said the pilot, the strain evident in her voice as she put the shuttle into a climb just as steep as the dive. "Heading for home — if you aren't already strapped in, do it now."

Looking through the cockpit canopy, Gray saw the gaping maw of the Vimy Ridge shuttle bay approaching at remarkable speed.

"Aren't we coming in a little fast?"

"Yeah we are, so get strapped in or you might fly through the canopy when we stop."

Though Gray had been called many things and would admit that many of them were true, he had never been judged a stupid man. He immediately took his seat and strapped in, ordering

Vossek to cease first aid ministrations and do the same. He felt the landing gear extend and then felt the jolt and tearing of metal as they sheared off against the edge of the hangar and felt the grinding vibrations as the shuttle skidded across the metal plating. The bay doors must have closed then, because he heard the sound of the landing thrusters firing as the pilot tried to get the landing under control and then both felt and heard the impact as the small shipped slammed into something solid and came to a rest.

The air smelled of smoke and ozone and Gray's ears were ringing. A quick glance down the line told him his people were okay, aside from the injury to Anders. The icarans he didn't particularly care about. They seemed fine in their armour. After trying and failing to unclip his restraints — apparently damaged in the crash — he drew his survival knife and cut himself free, heading into the cockpit.

As he leaned over the pilot, he stopped and swore softly. There were pieces of the shuttle's instrument panel embedded in her face and neck and a three foot long piece of bulkhead had buckled inward, driving itself halfway through her torso just below the ribs. She was still breathing, but it was a low, shallow gurgle.

Gray put a hand on her shoulder.

"Thank you for getting us home."

The corner of her mouth twitched slightly, the closest she could likely manage to a smile, and then she died.

Radko had felt the sudden jolt through the deckplates and had been both relieved and alarmed when informed it was Gray's shuttle making a hard landing, but making it back to the ship. The relief was short-lived though as a second, heavier jolt rippled through the Vimy Ridge. This one was strong enough that Quon, unaccustomed to life aboard a space vessel, staggered slightly.

Though he maintained his balance, Radko's frown deepened.

"Owens, what was that?"

"A swarm fighter, Commander."

Potentially very bad news. The attacks from the fighters to that point had been fast, but their weapons had not been over-powered. The hull plate armour of the Vimy Ridge had held up better than expected against the alien technology and the ERA was doing just what it did against more traditional enemies – re-leasing such high voltages of electricity after the first layer was pierced that the projectile was vapourized before it could pene-trate the ship's hull. This new impact had felt significantly more powerful.

"Are they using secondary weapons?"

"No sir," said Owens. "I meant it was an actual swarm fighter. It was damaged by our guns and just rammed right into us. On purpose, I think."

"Shit. Damages?"

"Just getting the reports now...," said Owens. He swore under his breath as he looked up from his tablet. "We've lost a rail gun."

Closing his eyes momentarily, Radko took the news without comment. None was needed. Everyone on command deck knew how important their rail guns were going to be. Without the abil-ity to deploy their nuclear arsenal, it was the rail guns that would make or break Radko's entire endeavour. They simply could not afford to lose any more firepower.

Tapping on his tablet, Radko brought up the resource management screens for gunnery crews and saw Owens already re-allocating assets from the damaged gunnery station to those still functional.

At the bottom of the resource list were their nuclear warheads.

There had to be a way to deploy them without Edwards' activation key. A way to re-wire the arming mechanism. Even if they couldn't be launched as missiles, they could be armed and loaded onto a shuttle and flown on a collision course with the enemy — just like the swarm fighter had just done to them, though their shuttle would be carrying a much more destructive payload.

"Commander, the swarm battleships appear to be powering up weapons... as near as we can tell."

As Radko watched, the off-centre opening in each of the two ships began to glow brighter.

"Hit them with everything we can muster," he said. "Same pattern as last time – missiles first, followed by rail guns."

As the batteries opened fire, out of the corner of his eye Radko saw Quon spin around to face the rear of the observation dome.

"Commander!," said Hamelin. "There's a vessel off our port stern! I'm picking it up clearly on LiDAR, sir."

Which meant it couldn't be part of the swarm. Another icaran vessel? Radko slid the magnification layer along the dome to face the approaching ship as the Vimy Ridge lurched under the impact of the swarm battleship weapons.

"Armour plating holding!," he heard someone yell out.

As the new vessel came into focus, Radko sucked in a breath. The ship's massive olive drab hull bore an enormous red star and a gold CCCP, and a string of six-metre tall Cyrillic letters spelled out Леонид Горшков.

"Sir it's Soviet. It's-."

"It's the Leonid Gorshkov," said Radko.

The Leonid Gorshkov, the largest carrier in the Soviet Navy. Named after the founder of the new Union of Soviet Socialist Republics, the man who had single-handedly reinvented Communism and, somehow, managed to build an empire without falling into the trappings of power. He shared power, he delegated, brought the Chinese into his USSR, making them full and equal partners. And then, when the next generation of thinkers came along, he retired, presiding over elections.

He was, even by Commonwealth standards, an impressive mind and fair leader.

But as tended to happen with great figures in history, his legacy was corrupted and co-opted by those who came after. The man became a symbol and the symbol became a tool of politicians who would not be so open to power-sharing and delegating and would not be so willing to step aside so that new ideas and new leadership could step in.

Radko drew in a breath as the Gorshkov disgorged a wing of fighters from the launch bay that took up the majority of its bow, giving it the look of a basking shark with its gaping maw. He was about to give his turret gunners revised orders when he saw the Soviet fighters streak by and engage the swarm fighters, completely ignoring the Vimy Ridge. And then the Gorshkov's rail guns sprung to life, spitting projectiles at the nearest of the swarm battleships.

"Son of a bitch," said Radko. "Let them have their targets – revised orders are to target the second swarm battleship and fighters in our zone only!"

The orders were relayed and Radko watched with no small amount of satisfaction as each of the two battleships fell to the combined onslaught of Commonwealth and Soviet weaponry.

As the crew cheered, Radko watched the Soviet fighters return to the Leonid Gorshkov.

"The question is," said Quon. "What will they do now?"

"Sir," said Owens, calling up from below. "Colonel Gray is down in the shuttle bay with the icarans. He says they're asking to speak with the commanding officer."

"Tell the Colonel I'm on my way."

Before poor Frenchie's body had even hit the ground, Sigurdsson had spun around, dropped to one knee and fired off two quick bursts from her assault rifle. There was screaming behind her and she knew that the civilians would now be making a mad dash to the gates of Fort Hathaway. Through the blowing snow, she saw manta-shaped heads weaving back and forth.

The front rank of the horde had reached the perimeter fence of the colony.

The pod-like appendages attached to each creature began to glow internally and as they raised those pods, Sigurdsson realised they were weapons.

She ran to her left and dove behind the thick steel wall of a storage building that had been converted to a school for the handful of children on Von Daniken's Landing.

"Jaeger! Come!"

The dog ran to her and skidded to a stop beside her just as the horde began firing. Whatever their arm pods were shooting hit the ground and building with as much force as a high-calibre rifle round, if not more. Dirt, stone and snow exploded in clouds and

Sigurdsson flinched as it rained down on her, but didn't dare close her eyes. When there was a pause in firing -- whether to reload, recharge or just pick a new target she didn't know – the sergeant peeked out from behind cover to note enemy positions.

They were very close.

"Henning," she said into the open comm line. "Get those fucking turrets online!"

A response came through, but Sigurdsson didn't hear it. She was leaning out from behind the wall, firing bursts from her 33A1 into the advancing creatures. The bullets tore into two of the lead rank, the same greenish-yellow liquid spraying from the wounds as the pair fell heavily to the ground. Sigurdsson didn't wait to see if they stopped moving entirely – she ducked back behind cover just as one of the other aliens spotted her position and raised his pod-guns. Diving to the ground, she pulled Jaeger down with her, hugging him close to her body as she began to slowly crawl along the length of the building. And then the building began to shake as projectiles from the alien guns ripped into it. Pieces of the roof began to fall and something inside the building burst into flames and then, just as suddenly, there was a high-pitched whirring followed by the roar of guns.

The wall turrets.

"Sergeant, get moving!"

It was Henning. Sigurdsson looked up and saw the gates of Fort Hathaway were open just enough for her to squeeze through. She jumped to her feet and began running, Jaeger four steps ahead of her. Behind her, she could hear the soft, wet thumping of heavy weapons fire pounding through flesh, but still pod-guns fired.

As the Sergeant followed Jaeger through the small gap in the gates, she heard the order given to close them and mere seconds later heard the clang of the gates snapping shut and the thunk of the locking mechanism engaging.

Sigurdsson dropped to one knee, trying to control her breathing.

When she looked up, she saw a crowd of terrified civilians staring at her. She forced herself to stand. To walk. To not let these people see how worried she really was.

Khaifa stepped out of the crowd and approached, slowly at first, then quickly, and threw her arms around Sigurdsson's neck. The Sergeant returned the embrace, somewhat reluctantly.

"I thought I'd lost you," said the doctor.

"Nasrin... this isn't the place or time..."

"I know, I know," said Khaifa, relaxing her grip on the soldier, but not releasing her entirely. "I just... maybe we should talk. Later."

Sigurdsson just nodded and did her best not to think about what that meant. The very last thing she needed was to be distracted when-

"Sergeant! They're preparing for another assault!"

Pulling herself free, Sigurdsson gave the doctor a half-apologetic look before turning and running to the stairway that would take her to the top of the defensive wall. Taking the steps two at a time, she reached the top in seconds and slamming the stock of the 33A1 against her shoulder, joined the defenders peering over the wall.

Staring down the rifle's sights, her barrel dipped momentarily as Sigurdsson felt her heart drop into her stomach. There were hundreds, possibly thousands of the manta-headed things marching on Fort Hathaway. She had thirty soldiers.

But they had walls, she reminded herself. They had high, ten-foot-thick walls.

Gritting her teeth, Sigurdsson raised her rifle, picked her target and double-tapped an alien who had been preparing to fire its pod-guns. It was still falling when she picked and tagged her next target.

"Conserve your ammo," she yelled to anyone and everyone. "Make every shot count!"

If the Vimy Ridge didn't bring relief soon, there was a very real possibility that the Fort Hathaway garrison would run out of ammunition.

One of the wall turrets whirred to life, its mag drum spinning up to speed, enabling it to create the magnetic field needed to launch its projectiles. Sigurdsson didn't fully understand the technology, other than that it was similar in basic theory to a rail gun, but based on reverse-engineered icaran technology. The standard issue sidearm she had strapped to her thigh in a drop holster, the Trondheim REV1, was based on the same technology. The problem with the turrets was that they were rapid-fire units, eating through an ammo canister in minutes when fired continuously. She watched as the turret gunner laid down a blanket of fire that flattened a dozen attackers.

The remaining aliens took a step backward.

Tossing aside her assault rifle, Sigurdsson unslung Vidar and switched on her targeting and image enhancement optics.

"Sergeant?," said Kenwick, his voice coming in clearly through the earpiece despite the gunfire.

"Hold on."

Tracking one of the aliens as it took cover from the turret, Sigurdsson watched it trying to work its way around for a pot-shot at the turret gunner. Sigurdsson squeezed her trigger and the alien dropped to the snowy ground, dead.

"Go ahead."

"I have not had any luck reaching Erindale Station or... hell, or anyone else."

"But we can still reach the Vimy Ridge?"

There was a pause before Kenwick responded.

"Affirmative, Sarge."

His tone told Sigurdsson that Kenwick understood what she herself had realised. If they could still talk to Radko's people, as far away as the Vimy Ridge was, then it wasn't a simple case of these aliens having taken out Commonwealth communications relays. It meant there was no one to reach.

She exhaled and took out another hostile.

If there was no one to reach, that meant there was no one to help. Everything was riding on Radko.

It wasn't until the soldiers on the wall began cheering that Sigurdsson realized the horde was retreating. She forced a smile as she slung the sniper rifle over her shoulder, but she didn't feel at all relieved. She'd seen how many of those things were out there and she knew this wasn't a retreat, but a regrouping. They needed to find any advantage that could help their small garrison survive until help arrived.

Thirty soldiers to hold off an army.

She looked down at her coat, still spattered with Frenchie's blood, and she swore.

Twenty-nine soldiers. And that was assuming no one else was killed in the attack.

"Casualties?"

"Just Frenchie, Sarge," said Henning, appearing out of nowhere.

"The turret gunners have to be more selective," she said. "They can't run those things like they're in a fucking video game. They use up what ammo we have, we're all dead. Everyone needs to make every goddamned shot count, Henning."

"Understood," he said, then paused. "Are... you all right, Sarge?"

"Are you fucking serious?"

She unzipped her parka and tossed it aside. It wouldn't do anyone any good to see her walking around Fort Hathaway wearing parts of a former colleague.

"Henning, none of us are all right," she said. "The men on the wall, don't have them out too long. Make sure we keep fresh eyes up there. Draft a group of civilians to bring them food and water."

The Corporal nodded and walked toward the wall, barking orders into the comm line.

"Kenwick."

"I'm here, Sarge."

She held up her hand, as if scratching her nose, so her voice wouldn't carry to the civilians.

"Some of the colonists have service history in the armed forces, right?"

"I believe so."

"Go through the files, find out who and find out their service history. Anything that could be useful – soldier, medic, whatever – you let me know."

"To what end, Sarge?"

"We're instituting a draft, Private. We're instituting a draft."

Cutting the call short, Sigurdsson waved over Khaifa, who was doing her best to comfort some very frightened civilians.

"They're terrified," she said.

"Not my problem right now," said Sigurdsson, drawing Khaifa away. "The MediCorps treatment centre is still operational, right? You have everything you need?"

"I have basic medical supplies, yes," said Khaifa, nodding slowly. "But we aren't a hospital, Freyja. We're not equipped to... Brill and I are the only doctors."

"But you have nurses. You have a couple medics."

"Freyja, I'm not a combat doctor! If you're asking me to-."

Grabbing the woman by the shoulder, Sigurdsson spun her around and looked Khaifa in the eye.

"Nasrin, does it sound like I'm asking you to do anything? You are our doctor. You will prepare the MediCorps centre to receive casualties and you will set up a triage. I'm sure there are a couple of civilians with first aid experience – you'd know that better than me, so if there are, take them."

"Yes. Yes, of course," said Khaifa, shaking her head as if to clear it. "I'm sorry, I just... I don't know."

"You're out of your element. Don't worry, I get it. Just make sure we can help the casualties, because I guarantee you they will come."

With a nod, Khaifa set off at a jog toward the MediCorps building.

"Sarge," said Kenwick. "I have seven names for you."

"Go ahead."

As she walked back to the crowd of civilians, Kenwick read her the names as well as the basic military history of each person. Some would be more help than others, she figured, but every extra bit of help would be welcome.

"Your attention, please," she said as she stopped in front of the crowd. "Is there a Gerhard Kurtz here. Gerhard Kurtz?"

A small, thin man with glasses stepped forward.

"I am Gerhard Kurtz."

"Mister Kurtz, please proceed to the MediCorps facility to assist Doctor Khaifa."

The man looked slightly confused, but didn't hesitate to do as she asked.

"I'm also looking for Oswald Chanz, Melody Hartwood, Ranjit Sabeena, Terrence Smith, Agatha Ustorf and Uwe Mutombo."

A surprisingly tiny, elf-like woman with short red hair stepped forward.

"I'm Agatha Ustorf. What's this about?"

The rest of the assembled civilians, most of whom would be too afraid to open their mouths otherwise, suddenly found enough courage to voice their concern as well. Had Ustorf not asked, none of them would have said a word, but now they could just be the "me too" chorus.

Fucking civilians.

"You, in particular, Ms. Ustorf, were a sniper with the 168th, correct?"

The woman nodded.

"That's correct Sergeant. I left the army seven years ago."

"Congratulations on rejoining it today. We need you on the wall."

There was a moment where Sigurdsson was sure the tiny woman was going to object, to put up some kind of argument about having left the world of guns and killing behind... but to her credit, Ustorf just nodded.

Not all were quite so understanding.

"So, what, we're just supposed to do whatever you want?," said Oswald Chanz, his sullen-looking wife at his side.

Sigurdsson tried very hard not to let her feelings show through. Chanz had been the wild card in Kenwick's findings. Unlike the others she'd called out, he didn't have any experience with the Commonwealth Armed Forces, but he'd served in the army of the American Free States and after that as an operator for ATC Castle for six years. In Sigurdsson's mind, neither one of those factors made him worth a damn in ordinary circumstances. However, these were absolutely not ordinary circumstances.

"Mister Chanz," she said. "This fort is under attack. We have just experienced the first wave-."

"I thought you said we needed to get inside the fort because of a storm? But you knew this attack was coming all along, didn't you?"

"Yes, I wanted to avoid a panic. To avoid people acting like assholes. I guess I failed in both attempts, didn't I?," said Sigurdsson. "Now. We need people to help defend this fort. You have the skills to help us do that – everyone whose name I called has skills we can use to keep this fort strong, to keep ourselves alive."

She looked into the eyes of those she'd called.

"I'm sorry if I gave anyone the impression that I was asking. I am telling you that you will help defend Fort Hathaway. Consider yourself drafted."

Chanz snorted.

"I thought the Commonwealth abolished the draft. Said it was a contravention of human rights or some shit."

"You can take me to court when we get off this planet."

"That's it? That's your response? What if we just refuse to help?"

Closing her eyes for a moment, Sigurdsson took a deep breath.

"Is this your wife?," she said, nodding toward the woman beside Chanz.

"Yes..."

In one smooth motion, Sigurdsson drew her REV1 sidearm and shot the woman straight through the thigh.

"This isn't a democracy. Get her to medical then report to Corporal Henning for orders."

"You-!"

"Or the next one is through her fucking head, soldier!"

As Chanz scurried away toward the MediCorps building, supporting his limping, whimpering wife, Sigurdsson holstered her pistol and cleared her throat.

"Those of you whose names I've called, report to Corporal Henning immediately. Dismissed."

"You are the Commander Radko?"

Stepping into the shuttle bay a moment earlier, Radko had immediately been approached by one of the icarans, apparently their leader. He held up a hand and tapped his temple.

"Without the bucket."

The icaran tilted its head, not understanding.

"Your helmet," said Radko. "Take it off. I want to speak with an actual face. I want to see your primary eyes."

There was a moment's hesitation where Radko thought he might have had to explain again, but then the icaran reached up and tapped an unseen button on the side of its helmet. There was a hiss as the seal released and the icaran slowly removed his helmet.

The icarans were a contradictory species. They were tall, but not bulky. They were fierce warriors with an impressive military, but it was the arts – song in particular – that were most valued by their society. Their history, in fact, was not told through books and documents like human history, but through songs and epic poetry. It was said that the greatest honour any icaran could dream of was that at death, when his family began singing the song of his life, non-relatives would also take up the song and add their own verses. They found human death rituals, such as burials and long periods of sadness, to be strange and even insulting to the lost.

In addition to the spiritual and philosophical differences between humans and icarans, the physical differences were striking. Radko remembered reading accounts of first contact and how shocked the humans had been at the colouration of the aliens' skin. With their own bland skin tones, humans had always expected alien life would be similar and had always portrayed them that way in all forms of entertainment. No matter what spin the racist groups of Earth's past — and, sadly, its present — had tried to put on it, every human skin tone was more or less a varying shade of brown. But the icarans were anything but bland. With skin tones from the purest white to the deepest of greens and everything in between, icarans also featured bright colouration patterns across their bodies – most commonly on the hadrosaur-like head crest that was more prominent in the males than females. The large male that stood before Radko had white skin, his deep blue and vibrant orange markings looking like warpaint.

One feature where humans had greater variation than icarans was in the eyes. Whether the large primary pair of eyes, or the smaller, rarely used secondaries, icaran eyes were pink. Sometimes pale, sometimes vibrant, but always pink.

"Thank you. Yes, I'm Lieutenant Commander Fin Radko, acting commanding officer of the HMCS Vimy Ridge," he said, pausing slightly. "Formerly of the HMCS Queenston Heights."

As he expected, the icaran – all of the icarans – stiffened slightly in their posture. The leader recovered more quickly than his subordinates.

"Then your decision to assist us is even more deserving of our thanks than I had initially thought," said the icaran. "I am Brigadier-General Locaris, commander of the Venator ICA Commandos."

The translation of alien speech had always been unsettling for Radko. Having a stilted voice in his ear speaking English, the voice not matching even slightly the lip movements of the actual speaker had taken some getting used to. Though he clearly hadn't gotten used to it at all.

And though he badly wanted to ask why an icaran strike team was inside Commonwealth borders, he knew the General would not be giving him the answer.

"Colonel," said Radko. "General Locaris and his team have been disarmed?"

"Affirmative."

Radko looked over the group of icarans. Nine males and two females and not one of them looked happy. Not that Radko knew what a happy icaran looked like.

"General, I'm going to ask for your cooperation here. We're in the middle of a crisis and frankly I don't have time to deal with the political ramifications of your presence. I need you and your commandos to sit tight for now."

"For how long are we expected to... sit tight?"

"I'm not sure. This situation is... fluid."

"Perhaps I can be of assistance, Commander. Do not forget that this 'fluid situation' has swept up my commandos and I in its flow as well."

"I'll take it under advisement," said Radko before turning to leave.

"My people were exploring the galaxy while yours were still developing artificial light, Commander Radko," said Locaris. "There are things out in the deep that you have not yet encountered, but with which we are already acquainted."

Radko turned slowly.

"Are you telling me, General, that you know what attacked us?"

"This is possible. I do not make you any promises, as I was in our barracks aboard the Vestrial Guar when we were attacked, but icaran knowledge of space far outstrips that of your own kind," said the icaran General. "I mean no offense by that, Commander, but surely you see the value in my offer of assistance."

He had a point, but Radko had more pressing matters to deal with.

"As I said, I'll take it under advisement. Colonel Gray, I need a word with you."

The pair stepped out of the shuttle bay and Radko waited until the hatch closed behind them before speaking.

"I want your Rangers prepared to repel boarders, just in case, Colonel. The Leonid Gorshkov is sitting on our doorstep."

Gray looked up sharply.

"What?"

"They showed up mid-battle. They engaged the swarm ships alongside us."

"They aren't allies, Radko."

"I never said they were, Colonel. But they're also not making any hostile moves. I'm waiting to speak with their commanding officer -- my bet is the Soviets have been hit by the swarm as well."

"Sir," said Cortez, her voice coming through Radko's earpiece. "I have a response from the Leonid Gorshkov."

"All right, put them through."

"Um, it's just a message, Commander, not a direct linkup," she said. "Captain First Rank Vladislav Kovalenko requests your presence for a summit aboard the Leonid Gorshkov. And sir, he's adamant that he will not allow armed Commonwealth or ATC Castle personnel aboard his ship."

"Of course he won't," said Radko with a sigh. "Tell him I'll be joining him shortly, under a flag of truce."

After Cortez confirmed, Radko explained the exchange to Gray, who shook his head.

"I don't like this, Radko. Going over to that beast of a ship unarmed would... wait," said the Colonel. "He said no armed Commonwealth or ATC Castle personnel? He said that specifically?"

"That's certainly what it sounded like."

"Two things, then. One, how the living fuck did he know we had ATC Castle people aboard? And two... I can't believe I'm going to say this... he didn't say you couldn't bring any armed icaran commandos with you."

Radko just stared at the man for a moment.

"Considering how you felt about my releasing Quon-."

"I still think that was a horrible idea. We know nothing about her, we have no idea if she's trustworthy. The icarans - while I don't like them and I'm usually exchanging gunfire with them – have a fairly well-documented sense of honour. You gave the order to save their lives. My bet is they'd be willing to serve as your honour guard aboard the Gorshkov."

"It's worth a shot. And I'll take Quon as well," said Radko, holding up a hand to stop the objection Gray was no doubt preparing. "She can get into their heads. She can find out if this is a trap or if they're planning to attack – or what they know about the swarm."

Within thirty minutes, Radko found himself stepping off a shuttle and into the immense hangar bay of the Soviet carrier Leonid Gorshkov, Quon Li-Chen at his side and two icarans – Locaris himself and a commando named Elgrapharr – flanking them. The commandos had had their weapons returned, bulky side arms and heavy-looking assault rifles. When the Soviet soldiers who had been sent as escorts raised their weapons, the two icarans immediately raised theirs, the horizontal cylinders spinning to life, creating the kinetic force that would propel a super-heated disc-like projectile at rail gun speeds. Anyone who had ever faced the icarans knew that being hit by one of those discs was often fatal. Even if it wasn't fatal, the pain was debilitating – it wasn't the kind of wound that let you walk away from the battlefield under your own power.

The Soviets clearly knew this. They hesitated.

"We're here at the invitation of your commanding officer," said Radko. "Under a flag of truce. I had always been under the impression that the Soviets had honour."

"And you were told to come unarmed."

The voice was deep and gravelly and the Soviet soldiers parted to reveal a barrel-chested and beer-gutted man with a bushy beard shot through with grey.

"To be precise," said Radko, with a slight smile. "I was told that armed Commonwealth and ATC Castle personnel would not be permitted."

He spread his hands.

"I am the only member of the Commonwealth Armed Forces present and I am, as you can see, unarmed."

The bearded man glared for several moments, then grinned a toothy grin.

"I like this one! He has brains!," he said, speaking in thickly Russian-accented English.

The Soviet soldiers visibly relaxed, lowering their rifles and Radko motioned for Locaris and Elgrapharr to do the same.

"Captain Kovalenko, I presume?"

"Yes, that is me. And you are commanding officer of Vimy Ridge?"

Radko nodded.

"Lieutenant Commander Fin Radko, acting commanding officer of the HMCS Vimy Ridge. This is my associate, Quon Li-Chen, and my friends from the Venator ICA Commandos, Brigadier-General Locaris and Staff Captain Elgrapharr."

Quon barely glanced at the Russian, while the two icarans offered very human nods of acknowledgement.

"Welcome to aboard the K-773 Leonid Gorshkov, jewel of Soviet Navy," said Kovalenko, waving the group over to the side bulkhead where a table had been folded out from the wall and several chairs placed around it. It seemed that they weren't going to be leaving the hangar. "Please, sit."

As Radko approached the table, he locked eyes with Quon, but she almost imperceptibly shook her head. She wasn't picking up anything about this being a trap. Radko wasn't sure if that was a good thing or not. If the Soviets weren't planning a trap, their actions were even more confusing. He took his seat and folded his hands upon the tabletop. Directly across from him, Kovalenko did the same.

"I have questions, Commander Radko," said the Russian.

"I'm sure you do, but I'm going to ask mine first," said Radko. "How did you know we had ATC Castle personnel aboard?"

Kovalenko shrugged.

"Was educated guess. Your government likes employing these people."

"Having them aboard an active-service Naval frigate is rare, Captain."

"You asked question. I answered question. But you seem to have answer in mind already, Commander. Please. You will share?"

Radko forced a smile.

"First off, you were within Commonwealth space, which in itself is a violation of the latest treaty our governments have signed. But I don't think you or I are stupid enough to think that either side has any intention of actually keeping to the terms of that treaty. Why start now, right?"

The Captain laughed, but said nothing.

"However, my guess is that you had specific orders regarding an interception. You were given intelligence, I suspect, regarding a Commonwealth frigate and a very specific piece of cargo being carried within it, guarded by ATC Castle operators. You wouldn't have been told exactly what the cargo was, of course," said Radko, leaning forward and meeting Kovalenko's unwavering gaze. "We're never high enough clearance to be told just what we're putting our lives on the line for, are we? But even with our course changes over the past several hours, you found us. The problem for you now, though, is that you've seen the swarm. Maybe even lost a station or a ship or even a colony to them, and you're wondering if my 'special cargo' is a weapon that can be used against them."

He leaned back in his chair. An image suddenly popped into his head, an image of Soviet Marines securing their gear on a transport ship of some sort. The image had a certain feel to it and certain... almost a certain smell, and he knew that it was being placed in his mind by Quon, having been lifted by her from someone at that table. Maybe even Kovalenko himself.

"Which is why," said Radko. "You have a team of Marines preparing to launch a boarding action against my ship right now."

The smile that had remained on Kovalenko's face, a forced, fixed smile, slowly disappeared.

"You should know, Captain, that in addition to the ATC Castle personnel guarding that cargo, I have the other members of General Locaris's commando team as well as Lieutenant Colonel Harlan Gray and the 15th Commonwealth Rangers. To attempt a boarding action against the Vimy Ridge would be, to put it mildly, a mistake."

Kovalenko leaned back in his chair and regarded Radko for a moment through narrowed eyes.

"He thinks you're bluffing," said Quon.

"I'm sure he does."

Suddenly, Quon stood.

"And the assault has already launched," she said.

One of the Soviet soldiers, a young Chinese man, swung his Strelkov AK551 assault rifle into firing position, drawing a bead on Quon and then suddenly he was thrown back, hitting the bulkhead with a wet thump, a fist-sized hole in his chest. Before anyone understood what had happened, Locaris has primed his assault rifle again, a Schlieren effect distorting the air around its cylinder. Elgrapharr's weapon was also primed, and aimed directly at the head of Vladislav Kovalenko.

"I would recommend ordering your men, both here and on the assault team, to stand down," said Locaris. "As I can assure you, they will not survive their mission."

"I am not so convinced," said Kovalenko.

"Vimy Ridge, did you copy all that?," said Radko.

"Affirmative," said Gray through Radko's earpiece. "They've already got a hard seal on one of our airlocks – I'm redeploying now."

"Give the icarans back their weapons, Colonel."

There was a pause – Radko knew the Colonel was against the idea of re-arming former enemies – but after a moment, the old soldier agreed and they ended the call.

"General Locaris…"

"The order to support Colonel Gray's defense of the ship has already been given, Commander."

"Thank you General."

The icaran inclined his head slightly, a visual cue that Radko was beginning to understand as their equivalent of a nod.

A tense few minutes of silence followed, neither Radko's team nor Kovalenko's men moving from their positions and neither group lowering their weapons. Then, finally, a communication came through to Kovalenko. It was in Russian, but the translation matrix in the Commonwealth comm devices translated it.

"Captain, we have secured the cargo hold with little resistance."

Kovalenko smiled broadly at Radko.

"You see, Commander, my-."

"But Captain," the Marine continued. "The container is empty and..."

As the voice trailed off an intense exchange of gunfire could be heard over the open comm line. It lasted for several minutes before an intelligible voice came through.

It was Colonel Gray.

"Commander Radko, the Soviet boarding party has been subdued."

"Understood. Thank you, Colonel," said Radko then turned to Kovalenko. "How about the truth now, Captain?"

Smiling, Kovalenko spread his hands wide.

"You understand I had to try."

"The cargo in question is no longer aboard the Vimy Ridge, so your assault was going to fail whether your men made it back here or not. So," said Radko. "The truth."

"You are correct. My orders were to intercept your ship and retrieve cargo. I don't know this cargo, what it is, what it does, but I'm told is powerful weapon."

"It is," said Quon.

"If used properly," added Radko. "But the USSR will not be getting it back. As I said, it's no longer on the ship. The weapon... has been deployed."

"Then I hope it has done what you needed it to do. And our business here is done," said Kovalenko, standing. "Return the bodies of my men and the Leonid Gorshkov will return to Soviet space. No further hostilities between Vimy Ridge and Leonid Gorshkov."

Though anything was possible – especially these days – Kovalenko was being far more accepting of the situation than a Soviet naval captain would normally be. There was something else going on, just as there had been when he'd launched the assault team.

"Very generous of you, Captain. And surprising, given the size mismatch between our two ships."

Kovalenko waved a hand dismissively.

"Vimy Ridge is Brock Class frigate. Have fought Brock Class frigates before. Small, but have fight in them. Tough son of bitch, as you Commonwealth would say. Leonid Gorshkov cannot afford too much damage in petty squabble."

Out of the corner of his eye, Radko saw Quon nodding, confirming his suspicion.

"They hit you too, didn't they?," he said.

Kovalenko regarded Radko in silence for a moment then began to walk away, motioning for Radko to follow. The pair, shadowed by both of their entourages, walked for a short distance down industrial-looking corridors to what Radko assumed was the officer's lounge. It was sparsely furnished, but there were tables and – of course – a bar.

"Come," said Kovalenko. "Drink vodka with me."

They approached the bar and Kovalenko turned and waved away the others. It was just he and Radko at the bar – Radko settling onto a bar stool and Kovalenko heading behind the bar and opening the locked cabinet of his own private stock. He retrieved two glasses and a bottle engraved with Cyrillic lettering and half-full of clear liquid. As he poured the glasses, he leaned over and lowered his voice so only Radko could hear.

"Is not vodka. Is water. Wife made me give up drink one year ago – now drink water, eat salad and shit. Healthy eating is for long life, she says."

The Russian snorted.

"I fly in space in tin can getting shot at. Is fucking vodka makes my life unhealthy? Wife is shithead."

Radko chuckled and held up his glass of water.

"Here's to your wife."

The Russian grunted and they each took a gulp.

"Voloshev Station," said Kovalenko. "Six hours ago. Then contact lost with mining colony on border of No Man's Land. We are recalled by emergency – this is only reason we found you. Is short cut to Naval base at Arkangelsk."

"Any survivors?"

Kovalenko shook his head.

"But you know these… things? You have seen them before?"

"Not before…"

Radko trailed off, frowning.

Not before today? He wasn't sure how many hours it had been since Echo was lost. It could have been four hours or twenty four – he'd lost all concept of time.

"Not before the strike on Echo Station," said Radko. "But yeah, we were docked there when the swarm came through."

"Echo Station," said the Russian, frowning. "Is different direction."

"What do you mean?"

"Here is Voloshev," said Kovalenko, setting a bottle on the bar, close to Radko. He followed it with his own glass, setting it on the far edge of the bar. "Here is Echo. They are far apart, but attacked close together in time. Is only possible if... is fucking flanking maneuver."

"They're attacking from two different angles."

"But what is goal? What is to gain from attack?"

"We projected the flight path of the swarm that attacked Echo Station," said Radko. "It leads straight to Earth."

Standing up straight, Kovalenko looked away at the bulkhead for a few moments before turning back to Radko.

"You will share this information?"

"I can give you a full briefing aboard the Vimy Ridge. We have video playback of the assault as well as video of a ground assault happening right now on one of our colonies."

"I will come to your ship," said Kovalenko, nodding. "Is not Commonwealth. Is not Soviet Union. Is about human now, no politics."

He extended a meaty hand which Radko accepted.

"This is how the attack started," said Radko.

Back aboard the Vimy Ridge, they'd gathered in the logistics centre – Radko, Owens, Gray and Cortez, along with Quon, Locaris and Elgrapharr, and a three-man delegation from the Leonid Gorshkov. The logistics centre had been Owens's idea and had been heartily backed by Gray. There was a sand table there and it would keep the Soviets off the Vimy Ridge command deck.

Several holographic windows were hovering above the surface of the table, displaying the video feeds recorded by the Vimy Ridge hull-cams, but also the footage downloaded from Echo Station before its reactor detonated.

"You had not seen them before the attack? No early detection?," said Kovalenko.

Owens shook his head.

"Possibly due to the materials from which they're constructed, the swarm ships do not register as vessels on our LiDAR system. Our technicians are currently working on recalibrating to make the detection algorithms more sensitive."

"If I may interject," said Locaris. "I would suggest that the inability to detect these ships properly may have less to do with their construction than with energy discharge – possibly the 'exhaust' from their propulsion system. Icaran detection technology is more advanced than the LiDAR systems used by your people and yet we too were without advanced warning."

"If Hamelin – our senior LiDAR tech – can increase the sensitivity of our system, we can combine it with another avenue of detection we have at our disposal," said Radko. "And it does enable us to have some early warning of the swarm's approach."

"What other avenue?," said Kovalenko.

"That's classified. Mister Owens, the projected path, if you please."

With a nod, Owens slid the video feeds upward, the holographic star chart showing the path they'd projected for the swarm showing it sweeping through Commonwealth space – and parts of Soviet and icaran territory – before driving through the heart of the Commonwealth right to Earth.

Kovalenko swore in Russian.

"And I've added an additional layer to this projection based on information provided by Captain Kovalenko," said Owens, tapping another quick command into the control panel. A second projection appeared, overlaid on the first, showing the path of the second swarm, the swarm that attacked the Soviet space station and then the colony.

There was complete silence in the room for nearly a full minute.

The second swarm was following a similar path, straight to Earth, but from a second angle.

"They're flanking us," said Gray.

"The Second Naval Fleet of the Commonwealth is headquartered here," said Radko, pointing to an open point in the centre of the V formed by the two projected flight paths. "If we can get to them, warn them, set up some kind of defensive line, we can prevent the swarm from reaching Earth."

He turned to Kovalenko. No matter what differences might exist between the Commonwealth and the USSR, politically, ideologically, culturally, Earth was their common ground. Earth was the home base of both governments, the entire planet declared neutral ground in what was likely the only treaty between the two remaining superpowers of the human race that would remain intact and unbroken over the years.

"We have a fleet not far from this place," said Kovalenko after a short pause. "But is commanded by Admiral Zhang."

Sighing, Radko rubbed his eyes. He was suddenly reminded of how tired he was.

Admiral Zhang Jianjun was one of the Union of Soviet Socialist Republic's hardest of hardliners. His ship, the Tianlong, was a destroyer, one of the fastest in the Soviet fleet, but also one of its most powerful. The name popped up in report after report from Commonwealth Intelligence, usually in conjunction with a report of a Commonwealth vessel being lost in combat.

"I need your help, Captain."

The big Russian nodded.

"As I said, is not politics now. I will help. We will go to your Second Fleet, then I will go to Admiral Zhang."

"Will he listen to you?," said Colonel Gray.

Kovalenko smiled.

"Vladislav Kovalenko is not commander of largest ship in Soviet fleet by accident, Colonel," he said. "Have reputation. People know am not... how you say, in habit of bullshit?"

Quon snorted.

"Is problem?," said Kovalenko.

"Not in the habit of bullshitting? You have the nerve to tell us that after inviting us to your ship under a flag of truce and then launching a strike team against the Vimy Ridge?"

Kovalenko narrowed his eyes at the woman.

"You are Chinese."

"Yes."

"You are from Soviet Republic of China. Yet you are here, on Commonwealth ship."

"Unlike many, I have not let an accident of birth determine the course of my life."

Though Radko picked up on the irony of that statement, he said nothing.

"Why are you aboard Vimy Ridge?," asked the big Russian.

"Ms. Quon is a special advisor," said Radko. "She's here at my request, Captain Kovalenko, and frankly since this my ship, that's the only answer you're going to get. I expect you'd have a similar response were it me questioning the presence of one of your people aboard the Leonid Gorshkov. Now. I believe we have more important matters to attend to...?"

After another two seconds of glaring at Quon, Kovalenko turned to Radko and nodded, holding up a hand in apology.

"You are right, you are right," he said. "Am old sailor, Radko. As they say, old habits die hard."

"This is a new situation for all of us," said Radko, looking first at Kovalenko then Locaris. "We're far more used to making demands and shooting at each other than trying to work together... but the fact remains that we've all been hit by this swarm, this hostile force, and we need to – to put it bluntly – grow the fuck up and deal with it."

"So poetic," said Quon.

"But entirely true," said Locaris. "Shall we proceed?"

With a nod, Radko tapped his console, causing the location of Von Daniken's Landing on the star map to pulse.

"Von Daniken's Landing. Captain Kovalenko, you no doubt know the name."

Kovalenko nodded, but said nothing as Radko had expected. And Radko himself chose not to elaborate on the comment. No one needed to be aware that the Russian commanded a vessel involved in one of the last significant space battles over Von Daniken's Landing. Especially since the battle had been a resounding defeat for the Soviet Navy.

"There is currently a garrison on Von Daniken's Landing, commanded by a Sergeant named Freyja Sigurdsson. The colony has been attacked by the swarm, but Sigurdsson has kept the colonists safe – for the time being – by holing up inside the walls of Fort Hathaway."

There was a grunt of recognition from Kovalenko. He had no doubt seen reports on Fort Hathway from the ground troops. Though he had known of the fort, Radko hadn't been much aware of any of its details until he'd pulled them up on his tablet after his first discussion with Sigurdsson. It was a well-placed and well-designed fort. Wedged between two sheer cliff faces and with a large lake at its rear, the only traversable ground approach was to march directly to its gates, which would help the garrison immensely in their defense of the place, but left them with no avenue of escape should things turn nasty.

"Which tells us," said Gray. "That whatever these things are, they're not just equipped for ship-to-ship combat, but to fight planet-based wars."

"We've been sharing information and video files with the garrison at Fort Hathaway. Sergeant Sigurdsson uploaded the following videos to us."

Playback began first of Sigurdsson's impressive headshot kill, then of the Fort's defense against the first wave of the swarm ground assault. As everyone else watched the defense video,

Radko saw Locaris reach out and enlarge the holographic window displaying the looped headshot.

"General, do you-."

"They are called ril-galas."

Every head in the room turned toward him.

"Excuse me?," said Gray. "You know what these things are?"

"The ril-galas," repeated Locaris. "They are... very old."

"And why are you just telling us this now?"

"Their space vessels were unknown to me, but this," he said, poking a finger into the holographic alien just as its head exploded. "This I have seen."

"You've fought them?," said Cortez, speaking up for the first time.

The icaran turned to her, looking down at the young woman as if seeing her for the first time. Likely he was. He blinked all four of his eyes and Cortez swallowed heavily, but met his gaze without wavering.

"No. The ril-galas have not been seen in my lifetime. Nor the lifetime of my father," said Locaris. "Or even his father's father."

Most of the humans present understood what that meant. The average lifespan of an icaran was just over three hundred years, so it was entirely possible that the ril-galas had not been seen for over a thousand years.

"General," said Radko. "If there's anything you can tell us that will help fight them..."

Locaris sighed a very human sigh.

"I am afraid, Commander Radko, that there is little to tell. Most of what I know is what I have heard in our songs of history or seen in artworks of icaran societies long past. It would be akin to you looking for military assistance in the stonework of your Earth Pyramids."

"We know nothing, General," said Kovalenko. "Nothing at all. Your information will help, even if just small amount."

Gray nodded.

"He's right. Anything you can tell us will be helpful."

"Very well," said Locaris. Clearing his throat, he enlarged the video feed even further and froze the playback on an image of the as-yet undamaged ril-galas. "It is said that the ril-galas came from beyond the stars, which modern scholars take to mean they came from the very edge of our galaxy. They were great conquerors, ruling a vast empire of many worlds, many species."

"Their army was said to number in the trillions," said Elgrapharr.

"They would occupy a planet and, if it held no strategic value, strip it of its resources and leave it barren. When the ril-galas stripped a world, nothing survived."

Radko and Gray exchanged a look. It certainly explained the presence of a ril-galas army on resource-rich Von Daniken's Landing.

"All right," said Radko. "They obviously, at some point, retreated. Their empire must have fallen apart or some of us –– more likely your people – would have at least heard of them moving about in the intervening years."

"Our scholars have differing views on the disappearance of the ril-galas. Some believe the empire became fractured and dissolved into civil war that decimated the ril-galas. This allowed their subservient species to rise up and destroy their oppressors. Others believe a plague tore through the empire, much like the one that nearly rendered the oodnam extinct. Another theory is that the ril-galas are ruled by strict codes and, much like the udukiin, only carry out certain actions according to very specific timetables. Imperial expansion is thought to be one such action."

"There is also some evidence discovered by our scholars that the ril-galas became embroiled in a war with the udukiin," said Elgrapharr.

"What do you believe?"

"The evidence put forth for all these theories seems sound, Commander," said Locaris. "I am inclined to believe that all were factors in the disappearance of the ril-galas. Empires over-extend themselves and collapse – it is almost a given. Plagues can and do occur, far more frequently than any of us would like. And there are many species in this galaxy – and, one would presume, other galaxies – entirely governed by cultural or religious impetus that does not always conform to logic. And the udukiin are savage fighters who I believe fully capable of toppling empires, should the right leadership arise. It is all plausible. However, the actual reason may have no relation whatever to any of those theories."

Radko listened intently to the icaran's story. To say that it unsettled him that this swarm – the ril-galas – had suddenly decided to reappear and cut a swath through the Commonwealth... and Soviet and icaran space as well... in an apparent drive toward Earth would be a significant understatement.

"Will the icaran government offer any assistance?," said Radko.

"I do not have an answer to that question. My... instinct says no. Not unless an icaran world has been attacked as well," said Locaris. "The enmity and mistrust between our peoples is great and while I have a certain amount of influence, I do not see myself being able to convince our leaders to commit significant military resources to defend your world."

Unnoticed by the rest of the group, Cortez had zoomed out the star map significantly. Earth was highlighted and the territories of the three major powers – the Commonwealth, the USSR and the Icaran Central Alliance – colour-coded. There were other areas coded with a fourth colour, representing the remaining powers – the Udukiin Priex, the Ota of Krellin, the brill home system and the small swath of space awarded the kriasi after the recognition of their independence.

"We're in the middle," she said.

Everyone turned to face her and she looked taken aback by it. Radko thought he may have seen a blush creeping into her cheeks.

"Beg your pardon, Cadet?," said Gray, a little more harshly than Radko would have liked.

"Sir," said Cortez, pointing to the map and looking at Radko rather than Gray. "Earth. It's central to everything."

"Typical human viewpoint," said Elgrapharr. "Overstating your own importance in the universe."

Locaris held up a hand to silence his subordinate.

"That's not what I meant," said Cortez, seeming to find a little courage in the face of the icaran's scorn. "I meant literally – we're actually, physically central to everything. At least every major centre of possible resistance to an invasion."

Everyone remained silent, staring intently at either Cortez or the map she'd brought up.

"Earth is home base for both the Commonwealth and the Soviet Union," she said. "Which makes it a good target to cripple our defenses, but look at the map. The closest civilization to where they came from – or where it looks like they came from – is the Ota of Krellin, but the krellin, as far as we know, haven't been hit. The ril-galas are punching their way straight through to Earth. If these ril-galas are conquerors, why aren't they conquering?"

It was Locaris who broke the moment of slience.

"Well done," he said, speaking very softly. "Well done, human. What do they call you?"

"Um. Cortez. Anna Cortez. Cadet First Class."

"You have the mind of an officer, Anna Cortez," said Locaris. "And you are right. Conquering the krellin would still leave them at the edge of what we all call core space."

Cortez nodded and so did Radko as he began to understand what Cortez and Locaris had seen. The others were still looking confused.

"Look at the map," urged Cortez and they all did. "Krellin space, icaran space, even udukiin or kriasi space – it's all relatively far apart. Weeks of travel time."

"But from Earth, you can reach any of their borders within days," said Radko.

"Oslayob," said Kovalenko, rubbing his temples as the point became clear to him. "Is perfect beachhead. Take Earth, and ril-galas have staging ground to attack everyone else."

A long silence was finally broken by the click of the ship-wide comms coming online.

"Commander Radko to the command deck immediately!"

There was something in Hamelin's voice, a note of borderline panic that sent Radko off at a run toward the command deck. He heard footsteps following, but wasn't sure who it was. Bursting through the command deck hatch, he slowed, seeing everyone staring up at the observation dome. Hamelin was up there and Radko quickly climbed the ladder to join him. There was debris floating past, but nothing to indicate an attack.

"The Second Fleet, sir," said Hamelin, his voice barely a whisper.

"What about them?"

Hamelin pointed out into space.

Radko just stared at the man in confusion for a moment, then looked back out into the debris field. And saw a piece of starship hull float past, turning in a leisurely spin. He could just make out the letters "HMCS" stenciled on the fragment. The more Radko looked at the debris field, the more pieces he recognized as parts of Commonwealth design ships. Pieces of hull, bits of engine. And he thought he even saw a few bodies.

The debris field, now that he was really looking at it, was massive. It stretched for kilometers in every direction.

It was the Second Fleet of the Commonwealth Navy.

The tower was the best view Fort Hathaway had to offer. Standing another nine metres above the wall on which it was mounted, a set of metal switchback stairs led to a three metre square box from which a lookout would have a clear view of the colony and the plains approaching the fort's gates. In times of peace, when the fort wasn't facing any threats, the tower was a favourite place for the garrison's soldiers to unwind, have a drink, play some cards. It had even been used more than once for late-night sexual encounters, if a sympathetic guard was on wall duty. However, in times when there had been threats to the security of the colony – usually from the Soviets – the tower became a sniper position.

Sigurdsson leaned her head back against the cold concrete wall, her sniper rifle Vidar laying across her lap. With the temperatures dropping as they were with the fall of night, she had to change positions frequently to avoid the cold stiffening her muscles. She'd be no good to anyone if she couldn't move when they needed her, so she'd be relying primarily on the sentries posted to

the wall below to let her know if and when targets were presenting themselves. But in between rests and walking in circles in the
small hut and jumping up and down to keep herself loose, Sigurdsson was at one of the tower's viewports, switching between
Vidar's scope and her own multi-layered optics to scan the plains,
trying to keep her own tabs on their attackers. Because though
she was uncertain of a great many things, there was one thing of
which Sigurdsson was absolutely certain: there would be more attacks.

Standing, she stretched her arms and back, rotated her shoulders a few times and winced, swearing softly under her breath.
Whatever she'd done to her shoulder in the mad dash to the gates
of the fort had been worse than she'd thought. The range of motion was still good enough to get by and to not affect her shooting,
but Sigurdsson wasn't sure how much longer she'd be able to say
that, with the dropping temperatures and the cold starting to seep
into her muscles.

Sitting at her side, Jaeger looked up at her and chuffed.

"I know, I should go to the infirmary. And I will, once my watch
is done."

It may have just been her imagination or her weariness or more
likely a combination of both, but Jaeger looked skeptical.

"I promise, okay?"

Picking up Vidar, she turned to the viewport, flipping down the
rifle's bipod. As she set up and began another scan of the snow-
covered plains – this time with her night-vision overlay to compensate for the negligible natural light – Jaeger stretched and
yawned and laid down beside her. His back pressed against Sigurdsson's leg and he faced the only entrance to the tower. It was

something she'd noticed about him in the time they'd spent together, that no matter where they were, when Jaeger lay down he always faced the door. Always on guard duty, always ready to protect.

"If I had a hundred soldiers as smart as you, I'd have no problem holding this place," she said quietly.

Glancing down, she saw the dog looking up at her intently.

"We could be up shit creek, buddy. Not going to lie to you, I have no idea what's going to happen here."

Jaeger's only response was a single swish of the tail and a twitch of the right ear.

"If it comes down to it, you just hide, okay? Get yourself somewhere safe and don't come out until you see more humans," she said, scanning the horizon through the rifle scope and, unsettlingly, seeing the now ever-present shadows lurking on the horizon. "I kind of want to do the same."

As she began a third scan of the area, Sigurdsson heard footsteps clanking up the metal staircase.

Jaeger stood and trotted over to the opening in the floor that served as the hut's entrance and Doctor Khaifa's head poked through a moment later and she entered Sigurdsson's fortress of solitude.

"Hello Jaeger."

The doctor was bundled up against the cold, a toque pulled down to her eyebrows and a fluffy woollen scarf wrapped around her neck in addition to the parka she'd been wearing earlier. The Doctor held an insulated mug in each mitten-clad hand.

"I thought you might like a cup of tea," she said, offering one of the mugs to Sigurdsson.

The Sergeant smiled slightly and set Vidar on the floor of the tower before accepting the mug. Despite the mug's insulation, she could feel the warmth of the tea through her gloves and her smile became a little more genuine.

"Thank you."

Khaifa nodded.

"Your men say you've been up here for much longer than your designated shift. Do you think that's wise?"

"Doctor, I don't need you questioning my-."

"Please, Freyja," said Khaifa, placing a hand on the Sergeant's forearm. "Don't misunderstand me. I'm asking out of genuine concern – for you and for Fort Hathaway as a whole. I don't doubt that you're the best person for this job, but..."

Khaifa looked away for a moment, as if to plan her next statement. Sigurdsson took a sip of tea and waited patiently. That was what snipers did best.

"We need you operating at peak efficiency, Sergeant, and that means making sure you get rest when you can. I'm telling you this both as a medical professional and as... a friend."

Sigurdsson took another sip of tea and glanced out across the plains. There were shapes moving just at the edge of her vision. There were always shapes moving out there.

"I appreciate your concern, Doctor. But do you honestly think I could sleep right now even if I tried?"

"Would you like to talk about it?"

There was the briefest of hesitations before Sigurdsson responded, shrugging.

"Nothing to talk about. I just have to do my job."

And even if she wanted to talk about it, she would rather do so with Jaeger than with one of the other humans in Fort Hathaway.

"I see."

It was then Khaifa's turn to hesitate before continuing.

"I treated a woman in our medical centre, a Sharon Chanz," she said, watching Sigurdsson for some sort of reaction. None was forthcoming. "Is it true?"

"Is what true?," said Sigurdsson, taking a long, fortifying sip of tea.

"She and her husband... they claim you shot her. Did you shoot her, Freyja?"

"Yes."

Still staring out into the distance, Sigurdsson took another sip of tea. She didn't have to look at Khaifa to know the conflicting emotions that would be playing across her face. Revulsion at the violence of course, maybe even some discomfort at how easily it came to Sigurdsson. And then there would be admiration of her ability to take decisive action, to do what was necessary and then, of course, the doctor would be feeling some disgust at herself for those feelings. Other feelings may be intermingled with those, Sigurdsson knew — the feelings that seemed to keep coming back, at least for Khaifa.

The Sergeant just let her think. It was better with civilians, she knew, to let them have their moments of grappling with morality and standards of behaviour than to try to convince them that sometimes none of it fucking mattered.

"Why?," said Khaifa finally.

"It's complicated," said Sigurdsson, turning to face her again. "Chanz has military training. He wasn't willing to help defend the fort and I didn't have the time to play politician."

"So you shot his wife."

"So I made him understand that failing to take up arms was not going to protect him or his family."

"They said you threatened to kill her if he didn't do what you ask."

"And I would have."

They stood in silence for a moment, just watching each other drink their tea, listening to the wind beginning to howl outside.

"Do you think I'm a monster Nasrin?"

"No," said Khaifa without hesitation. "I think you're a woman under enormous pressure, doing what you feel needs to be done. I think you've done the wrong thing, but for the right reason. I think that it's more important whether you think you're a monster, Freyja."

Sigurdsson forced a smile.

"I think we're going to find that out soon enough."

"Just... just be careful. All right?," said Khaifa. "I don't want to see you get hurt and I don't think Chanz is the type of man to forgive and forget. He'll come after you."

"Let him. I can handle myself."

"Of that I have no doubt."

"Sergeant?"

It was Kenwick, his voice filtering through the comm lines.

"Yeah, go ahead Private," said Sigurdsson, holding up a hand asking Khaifa to wait.

"Sarge, I have an incoming call from Lieutenant Commander Radko aboard the Vimy Ridge. He's requesting a secure line with you."

"Give me a second," she said, then muted her earpiece as she turned back to Khaifa. "Sorry Doctor, I need to take this. Thanks again for the tea. You should go warm up and get some rest."

Khaifa smiled slightly.

"Advice you should follow yourself, Freyja."

"You know that's not a promise I can make."

After the slightest hesitation, the doctor nodded and headed back down the metal staircase.

"Okay Kenwick, put him through," she said, reaching down to scratch Jaeger behind the ears.

"Sergeant Sigurdsson?"

"Yes Commander, I'm here. It's good to hear your voice."

"Likewise," said Radko. "Have you had any further contact with the aliens?"

She found herself shaking her head before she remembered that the Commander couldn't see her. Maybe Khaifa had been right about her needing some sleep.

Just to be sure, she scooped up Vidar and sighted through the scope, scanning the horizon again. Still the shadows danced, but still they were no closer.

"No, not yet. We can see them just beyond our perimeter, but so far they haven't tried another assault. It's just a matter of time, though. What about you?"

"Yeah, we've encountered more of their ships. Two battleships, for lack of a better term, and a wing of fighters. We managed to destroy them all with assistance from a Soviet carrier."

"The fuck? The Soviets helped?"

"It's been... an eventful few hours, Sigurdsson. We've struck a deal with the commanding officer of the Leonid Gorshkov, a kind of mutual defense agreement. I also have a team of icaran commandos aboard the Vimy Ridge."

Sigurdsson was silent for a moment as she processed the new information. While she'd always understood the situation both with the Vimy Ridge and on Von Daniken's Landing to be serious, the apparent truce amongst three traditionally combative militaries sent a shiver down her spine that had little to do with the rapidly-dropping temperatures. If even the icarans felt these things were enough of a threat to set aside their considerable dislike for humans...

"Are we fucked, Radko?"

The silence that followed gave her the answer.

"Sigurdsson, the Second Fleet has been decimated," he said finally. "At this point, I have to assume the entire fleet is gone, just like the Third. Thus far, we've had no response to our emergency broadcasts."

"They... they could just be maintaining radio silence. Preparing for an assault. You don't know for certain that-."

"I'm staring at a debris field that extends for hundreds of kilometres, Freyja. We've identified parts of nine vessels so far, including the HMS Rhodri Mawr, the Second Fleet's flagship."

"Fucking hell," she said, resting her forehead against the cold concrete of the tower. "So what now? Where does that leave us? If there's no Second Fleet, then your original plan is done."

"Yeah, it is. But I have new info for you. I don't know if it will help you or not, but I wanted to make sure you have every bit of intelligence we have."

"I appreciate that, sir."

"Stop calling me sir. As far as I'm concerned, you and I are equals, Sigurdsson."

It made her smile just a little.

"Thanks, Radko."

"These aliens. The icarans have encountered them before, but it was so long ago that the strike team we have aboard thought they were legends – or extinct at the least. They call them the ril-galas."

Sigurdsson listened intently as Radko relayed the information given him by Locaris – the nature of the ril-galas, their empire, possible causes of their downfall – as well as the theory put forward by Cortez about the rationale behind their seeming single-minded drive toward Earth.

"Shit," said Sigurdsson once he'd finished. "That would explain why they're here, too. Resources. Same reason we fought the Soviets over this rock for so long. You can't fight a war without resources. There must be something here they need."

"Or they may know that there's something there we need."

"And they want to cut off the supply chain," she said, nodding to herself. "Radko, one of our biggest exports here is a mineral that I can't even pronounce. It's a major component in the hull plate armour on ships like yours."

There was a momentary pause, during which she assumed Radko was updating his own intel.

"Sigurdsson... how are you holding up?"

Rubbing at her weary eyes, she almost laughed.

"I'm okay," she said, even convincing herself it was true. "I've had to draft a few civilians with military service to bolster my garrison – that went over really well, I'm sure you can imagine."

"I'm not one to judge the use of unconventional assets. Between the icarans, the communists and the psychic, I think Colonel Gray might have a heart attack."

She was about to question the comment about a psychic, but decided against it. Her head was already spinning and she figured that if it was something she needed to know, Radko would explain.

"Sigurdsson... with the Second and Third Fleets gone, we may be the only ones left who can reach the First Fleet. If they haven't already been hit."

He paused and Sigurdsson closed her eyes. The First Fleet, she knew, was headquartered in the Sol system, just outside the Kuiper belt. Which meant, given the current position of the Vimy Ridge, the First Fleet was in almost entirely the opposite direction from Von Daniken's Landing.

The HMCS Vimy Ridge would not be coming to Fort Hathaway.

Her garrison was on its own.

"Freyja..."

She hefted Vidar and felt some comfort in its weight.

"I understand, Fin. It's okay."

"I gave you my word that we'd come for you."

"Your responsibility is to the people of the Commonwealth. Just like mine. Even if you were still planning to come here first, I wouldn't let you – you have to warn Earth. You have to do whatever it takes, whatever hard, horrible decisions you have to make to end these fuckers."

"I will, Sigurdsson. Believe me, I will."

"I barely know you, Radko," she said. "But I don't doubt that for a second."

There was another pause, but it occurred to Sigurdsson that none of the pauses in their conversations were awkward. Though they didn't know each other, she and Radko were two of a kind, two people who found themselves with far more responsibility than expected, two equally screwed people.

"How are you holding up?," she said.

Radko chuckled softly and sighed before replying.

"I don't know, to be honest. I've been too occupied to think much about my own mental state."

"No shit. Probably better that way, huh?"

"Probably."

"People keep telling me I need to sleep."

"Same here. But every time I close my eyes, I just see Echo Station exploding over and over and over."

Leaning against the concrete wall of the tower, Sigurdsson sagged a little as an unexpected feeling of relief washed over her. The weight of command, of being the strong one and not showing the others how scared she was, was a heavy one and to hear someone else give voice to her own issues...

"One of my team was blown to bits right beside me," she said. "That's what I see."

"I need to have a glass of Scotch at my parents' cottage, my feet in the sand as I watch the sun set over the lake," he said.

Staring off into the greys and blues of the blowing snow, Sigurdsson smiled.

"That sounds perfect."

"When this shit is done with, Sigurdsson, I'll bring the Scotch, you bring some thick fucking steaks."

"I'll be there."

As the connection to Von Daniken's Landing closed, Radko leaned forward, resting his head against the transparent observation dome. Out in front of him lay the remains of the Commonwealth Second Fleet. Far behind him lay the remains of the Commonwealth Third Fleet. And he may well have just spoken to the Forth Hathaway garrison for the last time.

"Sir."

Taking a deep breath, Radko straightened up and turned, forcing a smile as he did so. Owens forced a smile of his own.

"First off, Commander, I want to apologise," said the Lieutenant, his voice low. "I acted... when this crisis began, I didn't act like an officer. I am sorry."

"Thank you, Owens. I appreciate it."

The lieutenant nodded.

"We also have a problem, sir. Our supplies. We were only equipped for the trip from Echo Station to Duster's Range, which means if we're heading all the way to Earth, we'll run out of supplies – food and water – before we get there. Long before we get there," he said. "And there's also the matter of our ammunition. We've used up a full one third of our ammunition stores."

Radko grunted and rubbed at his eyes.

"We need to re-supply."

"I don't see how we can do this otherwise."

"Commander, if I may?," said Tangaroa.

Radko glanced up sharply at the sound of his voice. He hadn't seen or heard the big man approach, which didn't speak well of his level of alertness considering Tangaroa was all but a giant. He nodded for the Maori to proceed.

"There's an ATC Castle R&D station not far from here. Also serves as a training facility. Plenty of supplies, plenty of weapons, plenty of ammo. With what's happening, I think they'd help out."

It was probably the longest statement Radko had heard from Tangaroa.

"Assuming they didn't get hit, too," said Owens.

"Doubt they would have," said Tangaroa, shaking his head. "Not the kind of place we've seen the ril-galas hit. Besides, it's in the middle of nowhere. Have to be looking for it to find it."

"Thank you, Mister Tangaroa. Can you give Cortez their secure comm channel? I'll place the call immediately."

The PMC nodded and headed down the ladder to speak with Cortez. Owens followed, but Radko wasn't alone for long as Colonel Gray headed up the ladder to join him.

"Captain Kovalenko has returned to the Leonid Gorshkov. He's awaiting your decision as to what we're doing next," he said. "But it sounded like he was thinking of heading back to Soviet space, meeting up with some of his own fleet. Which is probably for the best."

Radko looked up at the Ranger, raising a brow.

"How do you figure?"

"Frankly, Radko, we can't trust the Soviets. We know we can't trust the Soviets. I think it was a mistake trusting them as far as we have -- they have a long, long history of breaking treaties."

"So does the Commonwealth, Colonel."

"The fact remains, Commander-."

"The fact remains, Colonel, that the Vimy Ridge is one ship. One ship. We are all that is left of the Second and Third Fleets of the Commonwealth Navy, and if we are going to take any meaningful action against the invaders who have decimated our armed forces, we need resources. We need assets. If that means making unconventional and even unpopular alliances, whether with the Soviets or the icarans, so be it. Hell, I'd even take the udukiin right now."

"Sir," said Cortez, calling from below. "I have a channel to the ATC Castle facility."

"Just be careful," said Gray. "Situations like we're facing are ripe for backstabbing and with Kovalenko, Locaris and especially that Quon woman, you're passing out knives."

Without responding, Radko descended the ladder to the main command deck and headed over to the sand table where Cortez stood, a standby communications window hovering front of her. Tangaroa stood to her left and Radko took up position on her right.

"Do we have video as well as audio?"

"Yes Commander," said Cortez.

"All right, link us up."

As Cortez tapped in the commands, the screen above her blinked to life, a middle-aged man in an ATC Castle polo shirt appearing within.

"This is John Phelps, director of this facility. To whom am I speaking?"

"Lieutenant Commander Fin Radko, acting commanding officer of the HMCS Vimy Ridge."

"And you," said Phelps, frowning at Tangaroa. "You realise you've violated the non-disclosure portion of your employment contract by providing information about this facility? That's grounds for not just termination of your contract, but legal action."

"Mister Phelps," said Radko, his incredulity sneaking into his tone. "Are you aware of what's happening right now? Are you aware that a hostile fleet is cutting through Commonwealth and Soviet space, destroying everything in its path?"

"We'd heard rumours of the attacks, yes."

"They aren't rumours," said Tangaroa.

Phelps continued to look only at Radko.

"Mister Radko-."

"Commander Radko," said Cortez.

"Commander Radko," said Phelps, forcing a smile that wasn't fooling anyone. "I'm sure you'll understand if I prefer to have this discussion without a contract-breaking soon-to-be former ATC Castle employee present."

"Phelps, we need to dock with your facility for re-supplying. I am formally requesting, on behalf of the Commonwealth, that you assist us by providing food and water, as well as ammunition. My understanding is that your facility doubles as a training centre for security personnel, so you should be well-stocked."

"We're not really in the business of supplying Commonwealth vessels, Commander."

"Mister Phelps, we are attempting to reach the First Fleet to warn them about what's about to land on their doorstep. We need to be prepared for whatever we may encounter and right now our ammunition stores are at sixty percent and our food and water stores are at forty percent."

"That seems more like an internal management issue with your quartermaster, doesn't it?"

Looking down at the sand table for a moment, Radko drew a deep breath, trying desperately to keep his cool.

"This is war, Phelps. We are fighting a war. We are fighting a war in which the enemy is punching through our lines and we are the only ship who can get the word out," he said. "Please. We need those supplies, we need that ammunition."

"I understand your situation, Commander, I really do," said Phelps. "But ATC Castle has always had a policy of neutrality in conflicts for which we have not been contracted. I'm afraid I can't help you."

And with that, the connection was closed.

"Is he serious?," said Cortez.

"Get him back on the line."

"Yes, Commander."

A few moments later, an exasperated Phelps re-appeared.

"Mister Phelps-."

"Commander, I've already given you my answer."

"I understand that," said Radko. "But I need to impress upon you the seriousness of the situation. This alien fleet –– the ril-galas as they're called – is heading straight toward Earth. We are look-ing at large-scale invasion and we need your supplies in order to stop it."

"And as I said, our resources are not available at present. Thank you, Commander."

Again, the connection was closed. Radko slammed a palm down on the console, making Cortez jump.

"That son of a bitch."

Tangaroa turned to Radko.

"I'm sorry. I thought this would be a solution."

"Not your fault, Tangaroa," said Radko, waving a hand as if to swat away the man's guilt.

"I'll start looking for alternative supply sources," said Owens. "It's possible one of our supply stations is intact."

"Or a colony," said Cortez. "For the food and water, at least."

Owens nodded his agreement and began bringing up lists on the nearest stations and colonies, popping them onto large floating windows above the sand table. It took the two of them less than five minutes to plot out the stations, facilities and colonies nearest the current position of the Vimy Ridge and another ten to deter-mine the closest of them that may still have been intact or at least in condition to be salvaged.

Shaking his head, Owens sighed as he tapped a command into his tablet. The lists hovering above the sand table were immedi-ately replaced by a star map, a red sphere at the centre to represent the Vimy Ridge and seven small yellow triangles to represent col-onies or facilities.

"We're in for a bit of a trip," he said, pointing to the nearest tri-angle. "That's Rutherford Hill Station, a small refuelling depot.

They don't generally stock much in the way of supplies and they carry zero ammunition."

"Our next closest option is here," said Cortez, pointing to another triangle. "Lassetter Point — an agricultural colony."

"Food and water should be in abundance, assuming the colony hasn't been destroyed," said Owens. "But it's a four-hour trip from here."

"We don't have time for that. We need supplies and we need them now, so we can get underway," said Radko. "Tangaroa, do you know anything about this facility's defenses?"

There was a moment of silence through the whole command deck.

"You can't be serious," said Gray.

"Standard anti-ship batteries," said Tangaroa. "Canons, not rail guns. Small fighter wing – about twenty planes."

"And once we're inside?," said Radko.

"Lot of PMC trainees. Some with military service, some not. Well-equipped, though. Caliburn SMGs, mostly, but assault rifles too. No room for snipers."

"Do you know the layout?"

Tangaroa nodded and Radko pointed to the sand table, where Owens had just finished pulling up a holographic schematic of the station. Radko and Tangaroa approached, leaning against the edge of the table. Locaris also stepped up, peering intently at the station schematic.

"Radko," said Gray. "This is insane. You can't launch a boarding action against a neutral station."

"I don't enjoy the idea myself Colonel, but those supplies could mean the difference between life and death for a whole lot more people than just this crew."

"You know how I feel about ATC Castle and their mercenaries, but this crosses a line, Commander."

"Under normal circumstances, I'd agree that this would cross a line that shouldn't be crossed," Radko said, pausing for a moment, taking a deep breath. It was true, launching any kind of attack against an ATC Castle facility would be insanity under any other circumstances, and if this type of action had been proposed by anyone a week ago, Radko would have been first in line calling for their arrest. But that was then. "Given what's at stake, Colonel — given what we've been through already and what we're about to go through — I'm not sure those old lines are terribly applicable anymore. At least not for the time being."

"Because you say so? I don't think you get to make those decisions."

"I don't think there's anyone else to make them."

"Radko, I can only say this so many different ways. Launching an attack against ATC Castle-."

Radko stood sharply, facing Gray.

"Fuck ATC Castle, Colonel. Fuck them. I don't give a shit if this pisses them off, I don't care if it pisses off the Commonwealth government. What I care about is there being a Commonwealth to piss off. Do I think an assault on this station is right? No, I don't. But on the balance of the greater good, I can accept doing the wrong thing for the right reasons and I'm willing to face the consequences when this is all over. And you know what? I hope I do have to face some consequences, because that means we will have succeeded in not being completely obliterated by that swarm," said Radko. "You can't make an omelette without breaking a few eggs, Colonel."

Gray stared in silence for a moment, his jaw set, and Radko knew the old soldier wasn't swayed.

"I won't commit my men to this action, Radko."

"I'll commit mine," said Tangaroa.

"As will I," said Locaris. "I believe you are correct, Commander Radko. The good of the many outweighs the good of the few."

"Thank you," said Radko, turning away from Gray. "Cortez, check in with Kovalenko, see if he's willing to lend his fighter squadron to the operation to keep the ATC Castle fighters off our backs. Tangaroa, Locaris, get your men ready. Owens, you'll be in command of the Vimy Ridge until the strike team returns."

Owens looked up, brow furrowed.

"What about you, Sir?"

"I'll be leading the strike team," he said, raising a hand to silence the three or four objections he could hear rising. "We're essentially committing an act of piracy. I can't give an order like that if I'm unwilling to follow it through myself."

"Commander..."

"The decision is made. Everyone begin your preparations."

After Locaris and Tangaroa had given orders to their second in commands to get the teams ready, and Colonel Gray had excused himself from the command deck, the rapid-fire planning of the assault began. With a direct connection to Kovalenko, who had agreed to support the action, an entry point was selected and the framework of a strategy decided upon.

The two teams – the erstwhile ATC Castle squad and the icaran commando unit – assembled in the shuttle bay and were doing final weapons checks when Radko, flanked by Locaris and Tangaroa, strode through the main hatch.

Petty Officer Magendran, the grouchy old Malay in charge of managing the armoury aboard the Vimy Ridge, approached Radko. He carried a Tronheim 33A1 assault rifle and a drop holster containing a REV2 pistol, the slimmer, lighter Navy version of the Army's REV1.

"Commander," he said, handing Radko the REV2 in its holster.

Nodding his thanks, Radko – already having pulled on an armoured vest -- strapped the holster to his right thigh and clipped it over his belt. He took the rifle and tucked the spare magazines into the pockets attached to his vest.

"I'll need a breaching shotgun as well."

Magendran nodded and headed off, disappearing into the local armoury for a moment before returning with a drum mag fed, pump-action shotgun. The drum was not high-capacity, only containing twenty rounds, but those rounds were large, heavy and packed a punch. The particular model of breaching shotgun carried by the Vimy Ridge was an ATC Castle product and had been the subject of numerous debates both within the Commonwealth Senate and with the Soviets. It had come close to being outlawed on three separate occasions.

Slinging the assault rifle over his shoulder, Radko hefted the shotgun.

Without a word, the two teams filed into the shuttle and strapped in, the pilot – one of the few Navy pilots aboard the Vimy

Ridge – going through her pre-flight checks and firing up the engines.

As the shuttle bay doors slid open, Radko could see the Vimy Ridge beginning her bombardment of the ATC Castle facility. It was, as with most of the company's facilities, designed with a greater eye to aesthetics than the standard Commonwealth military installation. Smooth, aerodynamic surfaces were present strictly for their visual appeal, since aerodynamics were irrelevant in space — a fact Commonwealth engineers had embraced long ago. As the shuttle lurched forward, rocketing out into space, he saw the facility's starfighters begin to launch. There was no window to the rear of the shuttle for him to watch, but he heard Cortez confirm the launch of the Leonid Gorshkov's fighter wing.

The strike team all donned their helmets, including the icarans in their eerily blank faceplates.

"Hold on," said their pilot. "We're going for a hard mag-lock."

A heavy jolt ran through the shuttle and Radko heard the groan of overstressed metal and then the familiar buzz of mag-lock clamps engaging.

"We have lock and seal," announced the pilot.

Popping his restraints, Radko stood and met Tangaroa at the airlock door. Locaris was right behind him. They hit the release controls and the shuttle airlock opened, revealing the telescoping airlock seal extending about six feet to the sealed and locked airlock of the ATC Castle facility.

Radko stepped forward and primed the shotgun.

"Do you think your weapon can puncture the hatch?," said Locaris. Even the flat and stilted voice of the translation matrix was able to convey his skepticism.

"This is a breaching shotgun, General," said Radko. "A miniaturized rail gun. It fires seven centimetre long metal spikes containing shaped explosive charges that can be remotely detonated."

Raising the weapon, Radko fired six spikes into the airlock hatch frame – two on each side and one each top and bottom. A tiny green LED light blinked on the end of each spike.

"Take cover."

Back into the shuttle they went, closing the airlock hatch behind them. Leaning against the closed hatch, Radko thumbed the safety cover off a small round button recessed into the shotgun's body. He pressed it and a sharp roar and a violent shudder rippled through the shuttle.

Re-opening the shuttle hatch, the team saw a gaping, smoking hole where the facility hatch had been.

Tangaroa and his team led the way through the breach, moving in pairs, their Caliburn SMGs pressed into their shoulders, the barrels following their eyes. Radko entered the facility next, REV2 drawn in a modified Weaver stance. At his side, Locaris hefted the bulky but deadly icaran assault rifle with a name – aoran – for which the Commonwealth translation software could not come up with an English equivalent. They were followed by the rest of the icaran commandos.

The firefight broke out within seconds, the staccato reports of submachine guns from both sides broken at regular intervals by the booming bursts from the icaran aoran rifles.

16

After ending the call with Radko, Sigurdsson had stayed up in the tower, staring out into the darkness. For part of the time, she had closed her eyes, as if that would somehow mean that when she opened them, she'd wake up to find it had all been a dream. To find out they weren't under attack. To find out that they weren't all likely to die, either at the hands – or tentacles – of the ril-galas, or from exposure or from starvation.

"I thought you were going to get some rest?"

Sigurdsson spun around in surprise.

"Doctor? What are you doing back here?"

"Being a doctor. The well-being of everyone here is my responsibility and that includes you, Freyja," said Khaifa, who looked nearly as tired as Sigurdsson felt. "And you need to get some rest. Don't make me order you."

Rubbing at her eyes, Sigurdsson yawned then sighed.

"You're right. I know you're right. Hold on," she said, activating her comm unit. "Henning, you still awake?"

"Yeah Sarge. What's up?"

"I need to see you up in the tower, please."

"Be right there."

Sigurdsson yawned again. Apparently it had taken the doctor's remonstrations for her to really understand just how tired she was.

"What's going on, Freyja?"

"Just wait for... oh," she said as Henning climbed into the tower. Like Sigurdsson, the old Dane looked exhausted. "Henning, when's the last time you slept?"

He shrugged and Sigurdsson nodded sympathetically.

"All right," she said. "What I'm about to tell you two stays among the three of us until I decide otherwise. Is that clear?"

A pause, and then nods of assent.

The sergeant took a deep breath.

"The Second Fleet is gone."

"The Third Fleet," said Henning. "Yeah, we got that info from Kenwick already."

"No, Corporal, the Second Fleet. The Vimy Ridge found a debris field, a massive debris field, right where the Second Fleet would have been deploying from. It looks like they got caught in the path of the same ril-galas swarm that took out Echo Station and the Third Fleet."

"Two entire fleets?," said Khaifa, her eyes wide.

"Yeah. Two entire fleets. As far as anyone can tell, the Vimy Ridge is the only ship still operational outside the home sector."

Slowly, Henning began to nod.

"I understand," he said.

First glancing at him, then back to Sigurdsson, Khaifa frowned.

"Well I don't," she said. "One of you please explain..."

"If they're the only ship outside home sector, then they're the only ones with a chance to warn Earth about what's coming," said Henning. "And we're in the wrong direction."

"Meaning," said Sigurdsson. "The Vimy Ridge has no choice but to head home."

"Oh my god," said Khaifa as the implication hit her. "They're not coming for us."

Sigurdsson just shook her head.

"But... Freyja, if they don't...," said the doctor, her hands involuntarily clenching into fists. "We're going to-."

"We're going to get some rest," said Sigurdsson, stepping forward and grabbing Khaifa by the shoulders. "Right? We're going to get some rest. Because the three of us are what is going to hold this whole fucking thing together."

She locked eyes with Henning before doing the same with Khaifa.

"Is that clear with everyone?"

Henning grunted his understanding, but Khaifa just stared, wide-eyed.

"Doctor, I need you to understand. Like it or not, the civilians will follow your lead – it's why I dragged you out there to get them inside the fort. So you will keep it together. You will treat the sick and the wounded."

"But," said Khaifa, her voice barely a whisper. "I don't think I can-."

"I didn't ask what you think," said Sigurdsson. "I told you what you're going to do. You're going to be a doctor."

"Yes. I... I'm sorry. I can do this. But Sergeant, I'm not a battle-field medic."

"You are now. Delegate whatever you need to, get rest whenever you can. That's what we're all going to have to do," she said.

There was a long silence before Sigurdsson spoke again.

"Henning, when is your shift up?"

"An hour ago."

Sigurdsson chuckled.

"Delegate. Get some rest – that's an order. Doctor, you do the same and yes, don't worry, I will too," she said, glancing at her watch. "It's closing in on midnight. Henning, meet me in the comm hub with Kenwick at oh five hundred. Doctor, get as much rest as you need, then organize your staff. I'm expecting another assault within the next twenty-four hours."

The doctor and the Corporal nodded. They turned to head down the stairs but stopped when Sigurdsson spoke once more.

"Doctor...," she said, staring out at the perimeter fence. "How's your xenobiology?"

Khaifa frowned.

"Not bad. Brill has more experience with it, obviously. Why?"

"It's nothing. Not yet, anyway – just an idea. Go get some rest."

Sigurdsson yawned again as she listened to Khaifa's footsteps fade away down the stairway. In short order, she followed, Jaeger happily trotting along at her side, heading across the fort to her quarters within the garrison barracks. Shucking her parka and kicking off her boots, Sigurdsson cocooned herself in the heavy wool blankets and chuckled as the big German Shepherd hopped up onto her cot with her and curled himself up against her legs – facing the door, as always.

Sigurdsson was asleep within seconds of her head hitting the pillow.

Jaeger didn't take much longer.

"Sergeant!"

Sigurdsson jolted upright, nearly spilling out of her bed.

"The fuck?!"

Jaeger grunted his annoyance.

"Sorry Sarge," said Eisenhorn from the open doorway. "Two of ours soldiers are gone, along with about twenty civilians."

"Gone?," said Sigurdsson, climbing out of bed and pulling on her boots. She glanced at her watch. 0330h. "What do you mean gone?"

"They left, Sarge. They walked right out of the fort about an hour ago."

Grabbing her parka, Sigurdsson followed Eisenhorn out of the barracks toward the gates of Fort Hathaway.

"Who let them go? Why didn't the gate sentry stop them?"

"The two soldiers who are with them were the ones on gate duty. Rupesh and Danner went to relieve them and they were gone."

"Who was it? Who bailed on us?"

"Privates Lionel Alquist and Lisa Delany. She thinks she knows what happened," he said, pointing toward the small redheaded woman who stood by the gates, a sniper rifle slung over her shoulder.

"Ustorf," said Sigurdsson.

"That guy whose wife you shot," said Ustorf. "Ever since you told us what's really going on, he's been talking up the industrial landing pad over by the mines. Telling everyone that the haulers there can get us off-planet and into the shipping lanes where someone will pick us up."

"And they believed him?"

"He and Delany have been fucking behind his wife's back for months, so she'll believe anything he says. The guy has a way with words and the people are panicked, so yeah, they believe him. They'll believe anything that they think might save their lives."

Eisenhorn turned to Sigurdsson.

"Is he right? About the haulers?"

"No, he's not fucking right, you idiot. Those haulers have been locked down for the winter. Even if they could take off in weather like this, they don't have any fuel."

"On top of that, only the pilot cabin is pressurized," said Ustorf. "So you could fit maybe four people in one hauler. Anyone traveling in the cargo box would be dead by the time you broke atmo."

She smiled slightly.

"It's my job. Hauler maintenance."

"We're going after them. Eisenhorn, get someone to take over for Rupesh and Danner at the gates – the four of us will round up the morons. Ustorf..."

"I'll keep watch from the tower," she said, unslinging her sniper rifle.

Sigurdsson nodded and Ustorf set off at a jog toward the tower access while Eisenhorn headed back to the barracks to pull two soldiers for gate duty. After retrieving an assault rifle and some spare mags from the armoury, Sigurdsson headed to the gates and briefed Rupesh and Danner on the plan. Eisenhorn joined them within minutes and, the four soldiers bracing themselves for the cold, the gates were opened.

It had taken some convincing to get Jaeger to stay behind. The dog was loyal to a fault and as much as Sigurdsson would have loved to have his company, she wasn't sure what they'd find out beyond the walls. She was willing to risk her own life for the wayward civilians, but not Jaeger's.

The wind had died down in those wee hours of the morning, for which Sigurdsson was thankful. Not just because the winds would have made the cold even colder, but because the lower the wind speed, the easier it would be for Ustorf to help them out from her sniper's perch should the whole thing go pear shaped. And Sigurdsson had a bad feeling, from the moment she stepped outside the walls of Fort Hathaway, that pear shaped was exactly where this excursion was heading.

Using hand signals, she ordered Eisenhorn and Rupesh to bring up the rear while she and Danner took point. Though it was still dark, the thick layer of snow reflected enough moonlight to provide a decent range of vision, even without Sigurdsson dropping in a layer of optics.

"Ustorf, you copy?"

"I'm here, Sergeant. Your path seems clear... but I am seeing more movement than normal beyond the perimeter," said the sniper. "In the direction of the landing pad."

Sigurdsson was about to respond when Ustorf spoke again.

"Muzzle flash."

The sound of gunfire was almost immediate. There were short, controlled bursts, but also continued panic firing on full automatic that would eat up a mag in seconds.

The four soldiers set off at a run. They were nearly at the perimeter fence, and beyond that there was a hill about nine metres tall. Beyond that lay the industrial landing pad and the disabled haulers.

Scrambling up the steep hill, Sigurdsson and Danner dropped to one knee as they reached the top, rifles raised, and aimed through the iron sights.

"Holy shit," said Danner.

Sigurdsson said nothing as Rupesh and Eisenhorn came up beside her. The breakaway group had nearly made it to one of the haulers before the ril-galas had noticed them.

Nearly.

Trying desperately to take cover wherever they could, the group was panicking. Alquist and Delany, the two Commonwealth soldiers, were doing their best to hold off the ril-galas as the creatures slowly advanced, their manta-heads waving back and forth, but the civilians were utterly useless. One or more would try running for alternate cover every time one of the ril-galas discharged its gun-pods and Sigurdsson counted five corpses – maybe more – on the landing pad. She silently hoped one of them was Chanz.

The distance between their vantage point on top of the hill and the ril-galas attack was too great for the 33A1 assault rifle to be effective. Keeping low, she led the team down toward the cluster of civilians just as the ril-galas renewed their charge. Rounds from the alien arm pods thumped into the nearest hauler. Had there been any fuel on board, it would have exploded, but regardless it burst into flames, a wave of warmth hitting Sigurdsson as she ducked behind the broad base of a light standard.

With a quick hand signal, Sigurdsson ordered an assault.

Stepping out from behind cover, she put four bullets into the chest of the nearest ril-galas and as a second turned to see the source of gunfire, Sigurdsson heard a burst from her left – Danner – and it went down too, spraying the yellowish green liquid. Rupesh and Eisenhorn had looped around to approach the cowering civilians from the other side and had now engaged the enemy as well. Several more ril-galas fell in the crossfire before they managed to mount a counter-attack.

Blasts from the alien gun pods tore into the concrete and as Sigurdsson made a dash for new cover, she saw the left half of Alquist's head disappear in a cloud of red.

All she could think was that she was now down to twenty-eight soldiers.

Hearing the familiar ka-thunk of the grenade launcher Eisenhorn had mounted beneath the barrel of his rifle, Sigurdsson instinctively ducked as the grenade hit the ril-galas line, tearing three attackers to pieces. As the ril-galas line reeled, Sigurdsson dropped two more attackers but then stopped as she heard... trumpets?

Looking up, she saw movement. Silhouettes wheeled in the night sky above them and she activated her night-vision optics. Whatever they were, there were four of them, shaped like the ril-galas gun pod, but broader, with thick, bat-like wings. Their bodies appeared to be covered in barbs, with four long, forward-facing spines where their heads should be. And one was diving toward the civilians. That was the trumpet sound she'd heard, the screaming of the thing as it tucked its wings close to its body and...

She tried to shoot it down, but it was moving too fast. The thing began to spin as it dove and Sigurdsson realised what was going to happen a split second before it did. Still spinning, the creature plowed through the civilian group, the long spines impaling anything in its path, the barbs shredding anything to its sides. Swooping back up into the air, the thing had carved a bloody swath through the huddled group. Though she couldn't tell how many were dead versus injured, she knew there were seven down.

"Eisenhorn, more grenades!," she yelled. "Danner, cover me so I can take out those fucking bats!"

Danner was at her side in an instant and she could hear Eisenhorn fire another grenade. Crouching low, Sigurdsson engaged her targeting optics and worked to steady her breathing as she took aim at the first of the bats. Her optics gave her the creature's speed and distance and her sniper training gave her the necessary calculations of where and when to take her shot. Squeezing the trigger, she saw the shots hit home and the bat fall from the sky, but she also saw one of the remaining bats begin a dive and heard the trumpeting sound. It took her three attempts, but she managed to bring it down before it reached any of the humans.

"They're charging!," someone yelled.

Sigurdsson spun toward the voice in time to see several ril-galas running straight toward the civilians, firing their gun pods. She watched as Eisenhorn took one out with a few well-placed bullets and saw Rupesh trying to protect a pair of fear-paralyzed civilians only to have his right arm shot off at the shoulder. As he dropped to his knees screaming, Sigurdsson heard something else. She heard trumpets.

"Danner, down!"

As she flattened herself to the ground, she watch as Danner, halfway down himself, was torn to shreds by the spinning, diving bat. As it sped by mere inches above her head, Sigurdsson rolled onto one knee, drew her sidearm and pumped seven rounds into the thing, sending it careening off into its own line. It took out three ril-galas soldiers before crashing to the ground.

And like that it was over. There was silence. The ril-galas were gone, either dead or retreated.

Sigurdsson slowly stood, scanning the area with both her optics and the muzzle of her REV1. She could hear the moans of the dying and knew that most of them would have to be left where they lay. There just weren't enough able bodies left to carry them. Eisenhorn was cauterizing Rupesh's shoulder and most everyone else was staring vacant-eyed at one another. Sigurdsson checked on Danner, but he was in pieces – literally – and even if he'd been alive at that point, she would have put a bullet in his head and called it a kindness.

"Back to the fort," she said. "Now."

Eisenhorn handed off Rupesh to one of the civilians. The Private could walk, but he needed a steadying shoulder. Sigurdsson had to take several deep, calming breaths when she saw Chanz and Delany were among the survivors.

"Delany. Rear guard with Eisenhorn."

Without a word, the woman agreed. Chanz looked ready for a fight.

"I did what I thought was-."

"One more word and I shoot you where you fucking stand, you self-absorbed cocksucker. Give me your weapon."

He shifted his grip on the 33A1 but didn't make a move to hand it over.

The right cross caught him completely off guard and as he stumbled backward, Sigurdsson reached out and snatched the rifle from his hands.

"Fall in line with the rest of the civilians, Mister Chanz."

Glowering at the Sergeant, Chanz nonetheless did what she ordered.

Holstering her sidearm and slinging his rifle over her shoulder, she picked up her own assault rifle from where she'd dropped it diving out of the path of the bat-creature and began to lead the column of civilians on a slow march back to Fort Hathaway.

"Get him to Doctor Khaifa," said Sigurdsson, nodding to Rupesh as the group trudged through the gates. "Get everyone out here."

"The garrison," said Eisenhorn.

"Everyone. Soldier, civilian, even medical, unless they're actively treating a casualty."

It took several minutes – and a great deal of grumbling from the civilian population – but Eisenhorn managed to get everyone into the parade grounds. Chanz and what remained of the breakaway group stood off to one side.

"Twenty of your fellow civilians, led by Mister Chanz and assisted by Private Alquist and Private Delany, decided they would leave Fort Hathaway and attempt to escape Von Daniken's Landing using the cargo haulers left at the industrial landing pad," said Sigurdsson, addressing the assembled group. "Twenty three people left these walls. They were attacked by the alien horde – the ril-galas – and what you see here," she said, pointing to the remnant. "These six people – are all that remain. Of the four-man rescue team I took out to bring them back, one is dead and another is currently in surgery, having lost an arm."

She took a breath, gritting her teeth as she felt her anger rising.

"I don't care whether any of you like me. I don't care whether you like the decisions I'm making. But I am making the decisions for this fort. If we are going to survive this assault, there is no room for splinter groups or political bullshit and I will not tolerate it."

"I thought the Commonwealth was a democracy," said Chanz, the scorn evident in his voice. "I was giving these people a chance to get off this planet and escape the-."

"What you did, Mister Chanz, is cause the needless death of thirteen civilians and two of my soldiers."

"So what are you going to do, put me on trial?"

"No."

Drawing her sidearm, she shot him in the head, his brain matter splattering the wall behind him.

There was a collective gasp from the civilians and as a group they took a single step backward.

"Private Delany, front and centre," said Sigurdsson.

To her credit, the young woman, though shaking like a leaf, stepped forward, her chin held high. A tear rolled down her cheek.

And Sigurdsson pistol-whipped her.

"You're very lucky, Private, that I can't afford to lose another soldier right now. Report to Corporal Henning for duty assignment and do not, do not make me regret this decision."

With a short nod, the woman stepped into line with the Commonwealth soldiers, beside Henning.

"We will survive this," said Sigurdsson, meeting as many eyes as would meet hers. "We've killed many of the attackers. We know it can be done and more importantly, we've proven to them we can do it. And I will keep fighting with everything I have, for as long as I have to, because I am not going to let some fucking aliens come out of nowhere and take my planet."

She was all but yelling now.

"This place, this planet, may be a harsh bitch of a rock, but she's our rock and she's our bitch. We fought long and hard for her. We fought the Soviets and won. We fought the icarans and won. So these ril-galas come here and think they're going to steamroll over us and take whatever the hell they want? Fuck that. They may have been the big kid on the playground a fucking thousand years ago, but the rest of the kids have grown up in that time and we've learned how to fight. And if we have to fight dirty, then that's what we'll do. This is our fucking colony and I will paint Von Daniken's Landing yellow with their blood because the walls of Fort Hathaway will not fucking fall!"

The remaining soldiers of the garrison raised their weapons and cheered – even Delany, Sigurdsson noticed – but the cheer from the civilians was a little more forced. She dismissed everyone back to their duties, but waved over Eisenhorn and Henning.

"Have someone dump that outside the gate," she said, nodding toward the corpse of Chanz. "And then get a couple of ATVs. One with a cargo trailer."

"May I ask why, Sarge?," said Henning.

"I want to know how to kill these things more efficiently. As soon as we have some more daylight, we're going to bring back a body for Doctor Khaifa to autopsy."

Radko aimed his pistol at Phelps. Behind him, the gaping hole where the command centre's 'secure' hatch had been was still smoking, a pair of icaran commandos standing guard just outside. The command team from the ATC Castle facility were on their knees, fingers interlaced behind their heads.

"You're going to order your people to surrender," he said.

"And if I don't?," said Phelps.

"I shoot you and tell your second in command to order the surrender. And if they won't do it, I'll keep moving down the chain of command until I find someone who isn't an idiot."

"I don't believe you."

"Mister Phelps, I just launched an all-out assault on this facility. How many of your people do you think are lying dead or dying in these corridors right now? Do you really think adding one more name to the list of casualties is going to cause me any lost sleep?"

"I'll issue the order," said the woman to Phelps's left.

"Bianca..."

"Just shut up, Phelps," she said. "My name is Bianca Upshaw, I'm training coordinator here, which makes me second in command. You don't have to shoot him, I'll issue the order."

"You are making the correct decision," said Locaris.

Radko nodded to Upshaw, motioning for her to stand and approach the communications controls with him.

"Is it true, about the invasion?," she said quietly.

"Yes. You weren't aware?"

She shook her head.

"Phelps had total control of outside information. The rest of us only heard what he allowed through," she said, then keyed in her personal code to activate comms. "What should I tell them?"

"That you have surrendered the facility and they're ordered to lay down their weapons. Let them know they will neither be harmed nor persecuted, and have them assemble somewhere large enough to accommodate everyone – I want to speak with them all directly, in person."

Upshaw nodded and switched on a facility-wide channel.

"Attention all ATC Castle personnel, this is Commandant Bianca Upshaw. The facility has officially surrendered. You are to lay down your weapons immediately and report to the assembly hall where I will meet with you. There is information you need to have that has been kept from you," she said. "The Commonwealth officers have assured me that no further punitive action will be taken against those who follow this directive."

Closing the channel, she turned to Radko.

"Acceptable?"

"Yes, thank you," he said, nodding.

She glanced over his shoulder toward the hatch and Radko turned to follow her gaze. He frowned as he watched Quon step into the command centre, still clad in her jeans and too-tight tee shirt. And still barefoot.

"He has a gun in an ankle holster," she said, pointing to Phelps. "He's planning to shoot you at the first opportunity."

Phelps looked stricken as Tangaroa roughly searched him and found the concealed weapon. He then hauled the man to his feet and gave orders to secure him in the facility's brig.

Turning back to Quon, Radko offered a small smile.

"Thanks," said Radko. "While you're here, you may as well check out their clothing supplies and see if they have anything that fits. Maybe get some shoes."

"I don't like shoes. I prefer to be barefoot."

"I think you're the first woman I've ever heard say she didn't like shoes."

"Intriguing, aren't I?"

"That's one way of putting it."

"Sorry to interrupt the cute banter," said Upshaw. "But my people are assembling now."

Radko nodded. After asking one of Tangaroa's people to take Quon to the clothing storage, Radko, along with Upshaw, Locaris and three of the icaran commandos headed down to the assembly hall. Tangaroa was left behind to coordinate with Owens aboard the Vimy Ridge to transfer supplies and ammunition from the facility to the ship.

The assembly hall was huge, designed to hold every single individual who could be aboard the training facility at its peak. Though the current compliment was less than half what it could reasonably handle, there were still roughly a hundred ATC Castle trainees standing in uncomfortable silence as Radko and his entourage entered. Upshaw led them to the raised platform from which she would have presided over graduating classes and where Phelps would no doubt have presented many, many overlong speeches. Stepping up to the podium, Upshaw flipped on the microphone.

"As many of you have heard me say in class, one of the most important lessons one can learn in combat situations is when to retreat and regroup," she said, her amplified voice filling the hall. "For this facility, that time is now. No doubt many of you would like to continue fighting, to drive out these invaders, but I urge you to control that impulse. New information has come to light and while there are invaders who need to be driven out, John Phelps had kept it from us. As a result of his deception, I have taken over as commander of this facility."

There were a few murmurs, but no one interrupted. Radko wasn't sure what to think of Upshaw painting her role in this mess as being someone who stood up against a lying Phelps as opposed to someone who stood up to save her own skin, but he was willing to let her run with it for the time being.

"Had this information come to us earlier, this battle and its regrettable loss of life – loss of our friends and colleagues – would have been avoided," she said. "These people are not the enemy today."

She stepped aside and Radko nodded for Locaris to take her place at the podium, knowing how much more impact the words would have coming from him. But he'd also noted that Upshaw had said that they weren't the enemy today. It made him wonder about tomorrow.

"I am Brigadier General Locaris of the Venator ICA Commandos," said Locaris, every single ATC Castle employee in the room paying rapt attention. "I have fought against the Commonwealth on numerous occasions – even once coming into direct conflict with Lieutenant Commander Fin Radko during an ill-advised attack on the HMCS Queenston Heights. And yet I stand before you an ally of Commander Radko, fighting for the survival of not just the Commonwealth, but of its homeworld, Earth."

He paused, allowing the words to sink in before continuing.

"The ril-galas are an ancient race of conquerors. They intend to occupy Earth and use it as a staging ground from which they will expand their empire. They are not benevolent rulers – in fact our histories have shown that they have on many occasions, rendered entire species extinct."

"Anyone wanting to remain here on this facility is free to do so. Once we've re-stocked our supplies and ammunition, we'll be leaving," said Radko. "There are many who would say that our strike against this facility was illegal. Frankly, they're probably right, but when you're fighting for the survival of your species, the line between right and wrong can get a little blurred. We, the crew of the Vimy Ridge, are the only people to have survived the first attack by the ril-galas, we're the lone survivor of the Commonwealth Third Fleet."

On cue, Cortez activated the large wall screen behind him, looping playback of the attack on Echo Station, the Vimy Ridge's defeat of the first ril-galas battleship, the footage provided by Sigurdsson on Von Daniken's Landing and finally, the battle between the ril-galas and the combined strength of the Vimy Ridge and the Leonid Gorshkov.

"But we've done more than survive. We've fought back, we've taken the fight to our attackers and with the help of former adversaries," he nodded toward Locaris and then toward the screen as the Leonid Gorshkov appeared. "We have proven that the ril-galas can be defeated. I don't hold a grudge against any one of you – I needed supplies and Mister Phelps refused my requests for assistance. You will see no further persecution from me, my crew or my allies if you choose to walk away."

He paused for a moment, looking out at the faces gathered before him. Some were old hands, clearly having had experience within a real military, whether Commonwealth or Soviet, or even American, while some looked so, so young. The raw recruits lured in by ATC Castle's promises of high pay. It was a pitch that had been made to Radko himself more than once.

"However, if there are those among you who will stand up, who will take up arms against this alien force carving its way through our sector, who have the courage to stand with us against incredible odds and drive out the ril-galas, then I can promise you this: you will be part of the most critical military action in human history. Right now, you are mercenaries," he said, and he could see several of the ATC Castle types bristle at the name. "That's what everyone calls you. Mercenaries. I am presenting to you the chance to be part of something historic, to play a role in defending not the Commonwealth but all of humanity. Those of you with the courage to join us, report to the main shuttle bay in fifteen minutes."

There was utter silence as Radko, Locaris, Owens and Upshaw filed out of the assembly hall.

"That was ballsy," said Upshaw as they headed down the corridor toward the shuttle bay.

"We need people who can fight. What about you?"

"What about me?"

"Are you coming with us?"

Shaking her head, Upshaw chuckled harshly.

"Not a chance. I have a job and a sizeable mess to clean up if I want to keep it. The Commonwealth had its chance to keep me in the fold and they didn't," she said. "End of story."

It was Radko's turn to shake his head.

"Then go back to work."

With a huff, Upshaw did just that, turning on her heel and heading to the command centre while Radko and his group continued into the shuttle bay. Four cargo shuttles lined one side of the bay, all filled to near capacity with food, water, ammunition and equipment. As Radko strode across the deck, Tangaroa came up to meet him.

"Commander. Got everything on Owens's shopping list," said the big man. "And some extras."

"Extras?"

Tangaroa actually smiled at that and led Radko to the nearest shuttle. It was filled with weapons. Some common items like the Caliburn SMGs and Jericho assault rifles, but also heavy weapons – rocket launchers, machine guns and the like – and...

Radko frowned.

"Is that...," he stepped forward, picking up a long, heavy-looking rifle.

"The X2 Behemoth," said Tangaroa.

"Bloody hell."

"Exactly."

Hearing a large number of footfalls on the shuttle bay deck plates, Radko set the giant rifle down – gently – and stepped back into the bay. Standing in a line in front of Locaris, at rigid attention, were nearly sixty ATC Castle people. Most, Radko noticed, were the ones he had pegged as former soldiers. The kind of hard cases they would need. A particularly rough-looking man with a full beard, still wearing his ballistic armour, stepped forward.

"Reporting for duty, General," he said.

"You are all prepared to join us in this fight?," said Locaris.

A chorus of yessirs followed and Locaris turned to Radko, who nodded.

"Get geared up," said the Commander. "But first, this…"

He stepped forward and tapped the large ATC Castle logo plate fastened to the chest piece of the man's armour.

"This has to go. You're not fighting for a corporate logo anymore, Mister…?"

"Young, sir. Alban Young. And that won't be a problem," said Young, turning to the assembled group. "All right meatheads, get yer armour and grab some cammo paint. Green the fuckin things!"

With Young barking at them, the ATC Castle soldiers quickly grabbed their gear and, as ordered, covered all their logos with heavy-duty camouflage paint.

As he watched Locaris and Young organize the new recruits, Radko frowned and had Cortez connect him with the Leonid Gorshkov.

"Radko," said a cheerful-sounding Kovalenko. "Was good speech you gave. We have recruits I am told."

"We do, Captain. Not as many as I would have hoped, but around sixty."

"Is better than none, yes?"

"It certainly is," he said. "Captain, I have a favour to ask."

"Of course."

"Do you have any of those high-speed blockade runner drones – the cargo carriers – on board?"

There was a pause of several seconds before Kovalenko responded.

"I don't know what-."

"What happened to this not being about politics, Vladislav? What happened to doing what we needed to do to protect Earth? We both know you guys have these things."

"We have two on Leonid Gorshkov," said Kovalenko with a sigh. "Why?"

"I need to borrow one."

"Does not 'borrow' mean you will return?"

"All right, Captain, may I please have one of your blockade runner drones?"

Kovalenko chuckled.

"Consider it gift to new friend."

Radko smiled. After all, that's exactly what he intended it to be.

"Ustorf?"

"Clear from here, Sarge."

"Same here," said Sigurdsson. "You're clear to move forward, Eisenhorn."

Lying prone in the snow, sighting the scenery through the scope of her sniper rifle, Sigurdsson slowly rose to one knee and began scanning the horizon. She switched on her image enhancement optics.

"Preparing to move to next marker."

"Acknowledged," said Ustorf. "I'm on overwatch."

Standing, Sigurdsson set off at a jog for her next waypoint, which just happened to be the top of the hill that looked out on the industrial landing pad. Or what remained of the landing pad. As she neared the top, she dropped to her belly and commando crawled the remaining distance, slowly setting up Vidar.

"In position," she said as she sighted through the scope.

She could see the bullet holes and the scorch marks on the concrete and several dead ril-galas. With a frown, she scanned the entire area again.

"Ustorf, are you in position?"

"Just setting up, give me a second."

"Let me know if you can see any of our dead."

There was a pause during which Sigurdsson kept watch for living ril-galas, before Ustorf responded.

"I see their dead, but none of ours," she said.

It didn't make any sense. The landing pad had been littered with bodies and body parts, but there was nothing there, nothing but the bloodstains. And of course, the ril-galas corpses.

Her thoughts were interrupted as Kenwick came over the comms.

"Sarge, we have an incoming craft."

"What? What kind of craft?"

"I don't really know, Sarge. All I can tell is that it's coming in and coming in quickly," he said. "And it looks like it's headed right for the landing pad."

"Shit. Ustorf, Eisenhorn, you get that?"

They both confirmed.

"I'm on-site," said Eisenhorn. "Should I continue with the mission, or back off?"

"No, get me a body," she said. "But do it quickly. Ustorf, help him – I'll stay on overwatch."

"Understood."

Taking up a position with full view of the entire landing pad, Sigurdsson glanced upward, but could see no sign of an approaching ship. Looking back to the landing pad, she watched Eisenhorn and Ustorf drag a dead ril-galas across the tarmac and heft it into the trailer attached to Eisenhorn's ATV. As they hopped onto the ATV and started to pull away, Sigurdsson began to hear the whine of large engines. She looked up and saw some kind of boxy ship careening directly toward them.

"Eisenhorn, gun it! Get moving!"

She heard the ATV engine growl as Eisenhorn followed her order and then Sigurdsson rolled backward down the hill for protection as the craft slammed hard into the landing pad. After a moment, she crawled back up to the top of the hill and saw that the ship – which bore large yellow letters on its green hull reading CCCP – must have pulled up at the last minute, as it sat on its fat belly.

As she watched, a hatch popped open partway down the ship's flank. Raising her rifle, Sigurdsson took aim at the open doorway, but when she saw what emerged, she hesitated.

"What the hell..."

An icaran commando in full battle armour, carrying one of those deadly icaran assault rifles, stepped out, followed by a second icaran commando. The pair scouted the area, rifles at the ready, before stepping forward and allowing...

Sigurdsson frowned.

Allowing a quartet of Soviet Marines to emerge. And they were followed by a dozen well-armed soldiers in what looked like ATC Castle gear that had been repainted with cammo spray.

"Uhh, Sarge...," said Kenwick. "I'm getting a call for you from someone who says he's a Captain in the icaran army or something?"

"Put it through," she said, staring through her scope at the two icarans. "This is Sergeant Freyja Sigurdsson. To whom am I speaking?"

"I am Staff Captain Elgrapharr of the Venator ICA Commandos. I bring greetings from Lieutenant Commander Radko."

"Radko?"

"Of the HMCS Vimy Ridge," said the icaran. "He regrets that he cannot bring his ship to you as of yet, but wished to provide assistance against the ril-galas onslaught you face. We are that assistance."

Sigurdsson smiled and stood, heading down the hill toward the newcomers.

"Then welcome to Von Daniken's Landing, Captain Elgrapharr."

"We have also brought supplies," said Elgrapharr, leading Sigurdsson to the back of the cargo drone, where crates of weapons and ammunition were strapped to the walls. "And the Commander insisted I personally deliver this to you. I believe his words were 'Sigurdsson will play this like a violin.' I do not know what a violin is."

Lifting the large rifle from its restraints, he handed it to the Sergeant. Her eyes went wide.

"This is an X2 Behemoth... it's... I thought..."

She stopped as she accepted the rifle and hefted it in her arms. It was heavy, but the good kind of heavy. It felt solid, real. And its weight was fitting for the most powerful sniper rifle ever designed by human hands.

"There were only a dozen of these produced," she said. "They were just too expensive per unit – no one would foot the bill for large-scale development. This must be one of the prototypes."

The icaran just stared at her, so she smiled and thanked him.

The X2 was a dream weapon, the kind of sniper rifle she never thought would exist, let alone find its way into her hands. It was a rail gun in sniper rifle form, firing projectiles at speeds of three thousand metres per second with an effective range of twelve kilometres. Its projectiles, six inch long red metal cylinders loaded into six-round magazines, had been nicknamed Devil Cocks as much for their appearance as for the destruction they wrought upon impact.

"Okay," she said, bringing herself back to reality. "Get your men unloading these crates. I'll call in some wheels to haul them back to the fort."

"And I shall set up a perimeter."

Sigurdsson nodded then activated her link to Kenwick.

"I need a truck out here, Kenwick," she said. "That boat that landed here was a care package from Radko. We have gear, guns and ammo, not to mention another thirty soldiers to shore up the garrison."

"Oh shit that's good news," he said. "I'll send something out ASAP, Sarge."

As the connection closed, Sigurdsson hefted the X2 and headed to where Elgrapharr was manning the perimeter he'd set up, though as she approached the icaran, she realised it wasn't Elgrapharr, but the other commando.

"Didn't catch your name," she said, wondering how the translation matrix would butcher the phrase as it translated to icaran.

Apparently it did so without issue.

"Aeltheer," said the icaran, a female. In their full helmet-masks, it was virtually impossible to tell males from females.

"Sigurdsson. So, how bad is it up there?"

"It is quite bad."

Sigurdsson stayed silent for a moment, waiting for the icaran – Aeltheer – to elaborate, but she simply continued scanning the area with her eyes and whatever other sensory input the HUD in her helmet was providing.

"We've been stuck here from the beginning," said Sigurdsson finally. "We know very little about what's going on up in the black."

"People are dying in droves. Your people. My people. Others, too, I suspect."

Nodding, Sigurdsson picked at some dried blood on her sleeve. She thought she'd cleaned it all off, but obviously she'd missed some. She wondered whose blood it was, but then stopped thinking about it. Sigurdsson had a very strong feeling that by the end of this, she'd have lost track of the number of people whose blood she'd had on her. On her hands.

"Maybe if everyone gets hit, everyone fights back."

"General Locaris believes that Radko is the only individual seeing the totality of this situation," said Aeltheer. "It is the nature of most sentient beings to not see beyond their own immediate needs. Radko sees the wider implications of the ril-galas attack. It is rare to see such thinking in a human."

"I'm pretty sure that's kind of an insult."

The icaran bobbed her head slightly. Sigurdsson wasn't sure how to interpret the body language.

"It is more observation than insult. When I said most sentient beings do not see beyond themselves, I was including my own people," she said. "Like your species, we icarans have spent more time fighting amongst ourselves than we have fighting external forces."

"Yeah, I'd heard your civil wars were pretty nasty."

"One of the few things our two species have in common, I think."

"I don't know, I'd say a lot of the species we've encountered have quite a few things in common with humanity," said Sigurdsson. "From what I hear, we've all had empires of the past built on slavery, racism, political persecution, religious fundamentalism and fear mongering."

Aeltheer continued to look off into the distance for a long moment, before turning her blank faceplate toward Sigurdsson.

"I had not considered such connections. Perhaps you are correct – perhaps we are connected through the shame of our past."

"Cheerful thought, ain't it? We should all get along now because we all used to be giant assholes."

"Used to be is perhaps an overly optimistic use of past tense."

Sigurdsson chuckled and nodded a farewell to Aeltheer before heading further along the perimeter. She was about to work her way back toward the cargo craft to check on the progress when one of the other soldiers – one of the ones in the repainted ATC Castle gear – flagged her down.

"Sergeant Sigurdsson, right? I'm Alban Young. Formerly ATC Castle, but a Sergeant in the 23rd Commonwealth Rangers before that."

"Glad to have you here Young. What can I do for you?"

"There were people killed here at this landing zone, yeah?"

"Yes. About a dozen. They were ambushed by the ril-galas last night."

"How were they killed?"

She frowned.

"Weapons fire. Some were impaled by these flying creatures," she said, doing with her hands what she realized too late was an absurd impression of bat wings. "Why do you ask?"

He made an odd face and Sigurdsson immediately disliked the feeling it gave off. He nodded for her to follow him and she did, unconsciously thumbing the safety off the X2 as she went. Young led her around a rock outcropping on the opposite side of the landing pad to Fort Hathaway, the direction the ril-galas had both come from and retreated to, and he squatted down beside a large ice-covered boulder. The snow there was saturated with blood, spread out for three metres. And in the centre of the bloody snow...

"Jesus fuck."

A jumbled pile of human bones, stripped of most of their flesh, black with dried blood.

A single eye stared up at the sky from the socket of a skull.

"Jesus fuck," she repeated.

"Yeah," said Young, obviously unsettled. "You ever been hunting, Sigurdsson?"

"Yes. Yes, I have...," she said, backing up a step, trying very hard not to vomit. It was just pure luck that she hadn't eaten anything.

Closing her eyes, the Sergeant took a deep breath.

"Burn it. Then get Elgrapharr and round up your people to head back to Fort Hathaway."

"Understood, Sergeant."

Without any further acknowledgement, Sigurdsson began heading back at a jog to the cargo ship and the truck that was almost fully loaded. The panic was like a hand closing around her chest, squeezing her until she could barely breathe. Despite the sub-freezing temperatures, Sigurdsson had broken out in a sweat.

She keyed up her comm line.

"Kenwick, get me Radko right fucking now."

With the Vimy Ridge fully re-stocked and re-armed and en route to the Kuiper belt, Radko had retired to his quarters for some much-needed rest. Though he felt he could have used a good twelve hours, he set his alarm for two hours, which would put the ship a third of the way to the First Fleet and hopefully within communication distance. The fact that the Vimy Ridge had not been able to make contact with any other Commonwealth military personnel aside from the garrison at Von Daniken's Landing was worrisome, but the radiation – or something very much like radiation – given off by the ril-galas had caused communications issues and he hoped that was the sole reason for their lack of contact.

If there were other reasons...

He tried to put the thought out of his mind as he drifted off to sleep.

Radko suddenly woke to both the sound of his alarm and the door chime.

With a grunt, he turned off the alarm and swung his legs over the side of the bed. He'd not bothered to take off his uniform, just having tossed his red coat over a chair. Standing, he picked up the coat and began to pull it on as he went to the door and opened it.

"You had said not to let you sleep for more than two hours," said Quon.

Radko grunted and nodded, stepping aside to allow the woman to enter.

"I understand your rationale, but that's likely not enough sleep," she continued, stepping inside and looking around. She was now dressed in a standard-issue black and gold thermal undersuit worn by ATC Castle fighter pilots, skin tight on her slender frame. And she was still barefoot.

"You're probably right," he said, yawning. "But under the present circumstances, I can't afford to be out for too long. Things are changing by the hour. The minute, even."

Quon nodded. She had stepped up to his bookcase and was running a finger along the top of the sixty centimeter long replica of the HMCS Queenston Heights.

"I've heard both you and Locaris mention this ship," she said.

"Yes, you have."

"There's an interesting story to be told, I think."

Crossing his arms, Radko leaned against the bookshelf and stared at Quon for a moment before responding.

"One you probably already know."

She shook her head, continuing to examine the model. It was intricately detailed and was in fact the very design model Cagliari Aerospace had used in their initial presentation to the Commonwealth that landed them the contract to build the Brock Class frigates. It had taken him over a year and more money than he cared to admit to have the replica come into his possession, and he wasn't sure that all of the steps between Cagliari and his bookshelf had been legal.

Quon shook her head again.

"I certainly sense your feelings about it. And to a lesser degree, I sense Locaris's feelings about it. But when I enter someone's mind, I can't see everything, not all at once," she paused, frowning. "I don't know how to explain it."

Her eyes fell back to the Queenston Heights and she raised a brow.

"It's like a ship."

"A ship?"

"Entering a ship. When you stepped onto the Vimy Ridge for the first time, stepped through the airlock and onto her deck plates, you didn't know what was behind every door, what was down each hallway. You may have had some idea of what might be found, because you'd seen deck plans, but maybe the extra engine parts that were supposed to be in storage A had been moved to storage B, or one of the officers' quarters converted to quarters for an NCO with special needs," she said. "You wouldn't know for sure until you walked in and saw it with your own eyes. My... my gift, my curse, whatever you'd like to call it, works much the same way. I know the general shape of the human mind, but everyone keeps things in different places. Everyone has their own filing system. Yours is horribly disorganized, so when I walked in, I only had time to take a quick look at what was, at the time, in the forefront of your mind. And at the time, it was the invasion and how I could be of use."

He nodded.

"I think that sort of makes sense."

"Good. So, I haven't stolen any of your secrets. I haven't written down any youthful indiscretions to use against you later."

"What about all my adult indiscretions?," he said with a small smile.

"Perhaps more interesting stories to be told, Commander?"

"I don't think we have enough alcohol on board to get me to admit to half of them," he said, settling into a chair and nodding for Quon to do the same. She remained standing and he shrugged. "The HMCS Queenston Heights was one of the original Brock Class frigates – in fact, she was second off the line after the HMCS Isaac Brock itself. Sorry, I don't know how much you know about Commonwealth military history."

"Very little."

"Okay. So the Vimy Ridge is a Brock Class. Kind of a Brock Mark II, but there's no official Mark II designation. The Queenston Heights was where I served a significant portion of my career."

Standing again, Radko stepped up to the small refrigerator and retrieved a bottle of water for himself and one for Quon. She accepted with a nod and just waited for him to continue.

"We were assigned to border patrol – the icaran border," he said, taking a sip of water. "We were going slow, because we'd had a small asteroid impact that had buggered our navigation systems. Pilot was flying by eye, which is very difficult in a ship of this size. The thing is, the asteroid impact had been planned by the icarans to cover up the fact that they'd hit us with a Trojan Horse – a pod carrying three commandos that mag-locked itself to our hull."

Tilting her head slightly to the left – something Radko had noticed as a quirk of hers – Quon frowned.

"The icarans launched an asteroid at you?"

"Believe it or not, yeah," he said, taking a sip of water. "The area of space we were patrolling was disputed at that time. Disputed as in we had it, they wanted it. I don't even remember why."

He began pacing the room as he continued.

"An icaran cruiser showed up and started threatening us, firing warning shots, making a big, distracting fuss, while those three commandos cut their way into the Queenston Heights. When the icaran ship launched a shuttle with a boarding party, we started to get ready to repel boarders, but we were already too late. The commandos already on board were cutting our people down before we even knew they were there. And they locked down our shuttle bay, so we couldn't prevent the boarding party from landing."

"But clearly you survived."

"Yeah. We lost over seventy percent of our crew, but I survived."

"I feel I may know the answer to this," said Quon slowly. "But how did you survive?"

"I snapped. I saw the stacks of bodies in the morgue, the dead and dying in the corridors that we had managed to keep under our control. I heard over the comm lines the fear in people's voices on the command deck when the icarans started trying to break down those doors. And I snapped."

He saw Quon glance down at his empty hand, clenched in a white-knuckled fist, and he forced himself to relax.

"We still had control of the armoury, so I rounded up a team and we armed ourselves with everything we could carry, anything we could find – guns, knives, power nailers even – and we started clearing them out. The icarans I mean. I took a fire axe," he said, bringing his left hand downward in a sharp chopping motion. "And we just kept going. I decided I wasn't stopping until they were dead or I was, and like you said, I survived."

"The icarans didn't."

"No. They did not."

"How many?"

"Thirteen. The original three who snuck on board, plus the ten-unit boarding party," he said, then sat down with a sigh. "And however many died when I ordered the nuclear strike on the cruiser, but that was more sending a message than anything else – I wanted the icarans to remember what happened. Wanted that cruiser to have to tell people about the Queenston Heights and what their failure to take us out had cost. That's why Locaris reacts the way he does when the incident is mentioned – we dealt the icarans an embarrassing defeat and made sure everyone knew about it."

Quon was silent for a moment, then nodded slowly.

"You want to do the same to the ril-galas."

It wasn't phrased as a question.

Looking up at the strange young woman who, in the space of days had gone from a naked prisoner in a metal box to someone he actually trusted – to a certain degree – as an advisor, Radko nodded.

"Yes."

"And you think that Locaris will help you?"

"I think we're both realists."

"But considering what happened-."

"I don't hold Locaris responsible for the attack on the Queenston Heights any more than I hold Kovalenko responsible for decisions made by his superiors. Or any more than I hold you responsible for being part of Project Nightwatch. Sometimes we're caught in decisions made by others and get carried along with the tide. It happens. Even if I was inclined to hold a grudge against the icarans, only an idiot would hold on to it so tightly that they'd put it ahead of the survival of mankind. The enemy of my enemy is my friend, as the saying goes, and you know what? Maybe after this is all done, we'll discover that we've actually become friends."

Turning toward Radko, Quon simply looked at him for a long moment, head tilted to one side.

"Even after having touched your mind, I don't understand you Fin," she said. "Despite everything, you still have... optimism."

Despite himself, Radko chuckled.

"It may be all I have, but yeah. I can't go through life – especially now – assuming the worst outcome. Prepare for it, certainly, but not assume it's a foregone conclusion. And it's not easy."

"Especially now."

He nodded in agreement.

"Especially now."

"I'm not used to seeing the good in people. With the possible exception of your pet Cadet," she said, then immediately held up a hand to quell the protest forming on Radko's lips. "With the exception of Cadet Cortez, not one person on this ship would think twice about putting a bullet in my head. Some consider doing it every time I walk into the room. But you, you treat me... I don't know."

"Like a person?"

Again she just stared at him for a few moments and Radko wished that he was the mind reader so he could see just what was going on behind those unsettlingly blue eyes. It was both surprising and welcome to see her letting her guard down, letting herself be herself rather than a version of herself crafted in the Night-watch laboratories.

"Yes," she said finally. "It's... a new experience for me."

She smiled at him briefly.

"You continue to surprise, Fin. You continue to surprise. I find myself actually wanting to help you as opposed to just fulfilling my end of our bargain," she said, stepping closer and placing a hand on his chest. "I find you intriguing."

"Miss Quon..."

"Please call me Li."

"Li. I should get to the command deck."

"The command deck will survive without you for a little longer, Fin. I don't need to look into your mind to see your stress levels," she said, moving even closer, their bodies mere centimetres apart. "Let me help you relax."

And Radko burst out laughing.

Stepping back quickly, Quon frowned and Radko could almost see the defenses going back up. He held up his hands in apology, still laughing.

"I'm sorry, I'm sorry, it's just... Li, the leading cause of male performance issues is stress," he said, and when she didn't immediately respond, he spread his arms wide and looked around the room. "As stressful situations go…"

He saw the realization dawn in her eyes and then she too began to laugh.

The first message came through almost exactly one hour later.

"Sigurdsson, say again, you're breaking up," said Radko.

"Resources!," she said, her voice barely audible through the static. "That's why they're here but that's also why they're heading for Earth."

Gray, standing beside Radko, shook his head.

"Earth's resources were depleted years ago, Sergeant," he said. "There isn't enough there to make it worthwhile. I think it's clear they're trying to set up a forward operating base."

"You're not understanding me, Colonel. I agree they're setting up a FOB, and I agree that they're after the resources we have here on Von Daniken's Landing, but what's the most important resource for any army?"

"Food," said Radko.

"Food?," said Gray, frowning at first, then his eyes widening. "Are you…?"

"We found human remains. They'd been butchered, cleaned of all the meat and most organs, Commander. I think they're after Earth because it's a strategic entry point to the surrounding space and because it's a fucking buffet."

"General, does that sound plausible to you?," said Radko.

Locaris stood in silent thought for a moment before nodding.

"Shit. Cortez?," said Radko, tapping his earpiece.

She nodded, understanding what he meant. By the time he'd climbed the ladder to the observation dome, the call to Sigurdsson had been put on a secure channel between just he and the Sergeant.

"How are you holding up, Sigurdsson?"

"I've been better. Thanks for the care package, by the way."

"I wish I could have done more."

"Hey, I've never had a guy send me a gift of commandos and a borderline illegal sniper rifle," she said, her smile evident in her voice. "You sure know the way to a girl's heart, Radko."

He couldn't help but grin.

"Just stay in one piece."

"I'll do my best, but no promises," she said. "How are things up there?"

"I wish I knew, Sigurdsson. I wish I knew. We haven't been able to reach any other Commonwealth military units. We're getting close enough now that we should be able to tap into the local comm channels, so we're hoping that gets us to someone."

There was a period of silence and for a moment, Radko thought the transmission might have failed.

"What if there isn't anyone?," said Sigurdsson.

"They can't have wiped out everyone. The Vimy Ridge survived, your group survived, and there's no way that we're the only ones. It's just not possible."

"So somewhere out there are two other people having this same conversation?"

"But with far less charisma, I'm sure," he said, grinning.

He heard Sigurdsson laugh and it was a good sound to hear.

"When all this shit is done," she said. "I am really looking forward to meeting you. For a Navy guy, you're just fucking nuts enough to be interesting."

"And for a ground-pounder in the Army, you're pretty tolerable yourself, Sigurdsson."

"I bet you say that to all the girls."

"It's my standard opening line. Probably explains why I'm single, eh?"

"Listen, Radko," said Sigurdsson, her tone turning serious. It was a sudden shift, but not unexpected given the circumstances – moments of levity had to be just that. Moments. "We've got a body. One of the ril-galas foot soldiers. I'm having it sent to our MediCorps building for dissection."

He frowned.

"To what end?"

"I want to find their weak points."

"Commander!"

There was something akin to panic in Cortez's voice and Radko looked down on the command deck to see everyone frozen in place.

"I have to go, Sigurdsson."

Closing the connection, he hurried down the ladder and over to Cortez.

"I managed to connect us to the local channels..."

She trailed off and Radko began listening to what he understood to be a looped emergency broadcast.

"...has been attacked by an unknown alien force. Our attempts to fight off the attackers have failed – there were too many of them and they struck too quickly. We have had no choice but to offer surrender," said a shaky male voice. "Earth has fallen. The planet has been attacked by an unknown alien force. Our attempts…"

Radko stabbed his finger into the mute button.

"Owens, what's our current position?"

"Three hours from… from Sol system… just passing the Ishtar Gate, Commander."

"Take us in."

"Sir?"

"Take us inside the Ishtar Gate," said Radko. "Just deep enough to hide. Advise the Leonid Gorshkov and pass along the message about Earth, in the event they haven't heard it yet."

"Yessir."

"Radko," said Gray. "I thought all traffic was supposed to avoid the Ishtar Gate? Something about radiation storms?"

"We can't sit out here in the open, Colonel. We need to lay low and plan our next move."

"Our next move is to hit Earth, Commander. That should be obvious."

"Our next move is to conceal ourselves within the Ishtar Gate and work out a strategy, not to go kicking down doors without knowing what lies beyond," said Radko. "Cortez, use those codes I gave you to access the intel subnet, my personal directories. You're looking for a secure comm code with the codename 'Thor's Hammer.'"

"What is 'Thor's Hammer'?," said Locaris.

"A project that I'm hoping like hell was completed," said Radko. "It was supposed to have been finished a year ago, but it kept being delayed for security reasons – we couldn't let anyone know it was there, so we had to keep construction low-key, which slowed it all down."

"How come you know about this and I don't?," said Gray.

"For starters, you're not part of the Navy. Also, while I was on administrative duty after the Queenston Heights incident, I helped design the security network on the station."

"If you knew this place was there-."

"I don't know if it's there, Colonel. I don't know if it's operational. I don't know if it's been destroyed like every other fucking thing we've gone looking for."

"Entering the Ishtar Gate, sir," said Owens.

An eerie reddish-purple glow began spreading through the command deck. The Ishtar Gate, a relatively new stellar phenomenon at the edge of the Kuiper Belt and just outside the orbit of Neptune, was a seventeen thousand kilometer long cloud of dust and gas. It was essentially a miniature nebula that produced ion and radiation storms of such strength that few ships ventured within a thousand kilometers of the Gate. At one time, it was thought to be the perfect ambush point for pirates, but now the core of the Ishtar Gate was littered with the lifeless husks of pirate vessels, their engines having been damaged beyond repair and the radiation storms cooking their occupants alive.

"The Leonid Gorshkov is following," reported Owens. "Cadet Cortez, set up a dedicated channel to the Gorshkov."

"Yessir," she said and then spoke up again a moment later. "Commander, I have the Thor's Hammer code."

"Good. Where's Li? I want her on alert."

"Who?," said Gray.

"Quon. Get her up here and on look-out. I don't want anything sneaking up on us," said Radko. "Cortez, key in the code on a secure line, using full R7 encryption."

It took several minutes for the line to be open and for the encryption to be verified. No one said a word while they waited. Cortez finally announced the connection and switched it on.

"This is Lieutenant Commander Fin Radko, acting CO of the HMCS Vimy Ridge, calling Thor's Hammer. Do you copy?"

There was a long silence, but just as Radko was about to repeat his message, a response came.

"This is Thor's Hammer. Repeat identification."

Radko resisted the urge to smile, though he couldn't deny the relief at hearing another voice from the Commonwealth.

"Lieutenant Commander Fin Radko. Service number R6055-55890-32765. To whom am I speaking?"

There was a pause, during which Radko knew the people at Thor's Hammer would be accessing personnel records, trying to verify his identity. He'd be doing the same in their place.

"Commander Radko, we've verified your service number, but we have you aboard the HMCS Vimy Ridge based out of Echo Station with the Third Fleet. How have you managed to access our local subnet?"

"To whom am I speaking, please?"

"This is Lieutenant Kumar Majandrapul, chief of communications for the Thor's Hammer project."

"Lieutenant, can you verify the security of this transmission your end?"

"I can and have."

"The Vimy Ridge is currently concealed within the Ishtar Gate."

"The Ishtar...? Where is the rest of the Third Fleet?"

Radko exchanged glances with several of his crew. It seemed that everyone was out of every loop there was.

"Lieutenant, we are the Third Fleet. Echo Station was destroyed – the Third Fleet bore the brunt of the initial ril-galas assault."

"The... the what? Commander, we've been cut off from everything from the beginning of the attack."

"We'll send you an information packet, everything we have," he said, nodding to Cortez to make it happen. "Lieutenant, what's the status of Thor's Hammer?"

Another voice came over the speakers.

"Who is this?"

"I've already provided my credentials," snapped Radko. "How many goddamned times do you want me to do it?"

"As many times as I ask you to. Now who is this?"

Radko closed his eyes and took a deep breath.

"Lieutenant Commander Fin Radko, acting commander of the HMCS Vimy Ridge. And who are you?"

"This is Rear Admiral Phillip Mahoney, Commander."

"What's the status of Thor's Hammer, Admiral?"

"Commander, Thor's Hammer is a highly classified installation and its status is not-."

"With all due respect Sir, are you fucking kidding me? Do have any idea what kind of unholy shitstorm we're up against? Take a look at the information packet we've just sent through to you – watch the vid clips. This is not the time to try to protect secrets and play our hand close to the vest. We're looking at the future of the human race. All of it, whether Commonwealth or Soviet or independent."

"Commander…"

There was a pause, almost like Mahoney was conferring with someone off-mic, before the Admiral continued.

"Thor's Hammer is operational but understaffed. We're being hemmed in behind an alien blockade. We lost one of our corvettes trying to break a hole in their perimeter. Currently, we have four vessels in defensive positions and two in drydock that were undergoing repairs when the attack came."

"How well-armed?"

"Three are battleships – the HMS Sir Walter Raleigh, the INS Godavari and the HMS Edinburgh – and we also have the Ludwigshafen am Rhein, a missile cruiser."

"And the two in drydock?"

"The HMCS Haida Gwaii…"

Radko nodded to himself. He knew the Haida Gwaii. She was a tough old fast-attack gunboat. But he said nothing, as the Admiral paused.

"And," said Mahoney finally. "The HMS Royal Sovereign."

Among the naval officers present, there was a moment of surprised silence. Named after Admiral Collingwood's flagship in the Battle of Trafalgar in 1805, The HMS Royal Sovereign was the largest and most powerful warship ever designed by Commonwealth engineers, and would make even the massive Leonid Gorshkov look small. Possessing more rail guns than the Vimy Ridge and the Gorshkov combined, the Royal Sovereign was designed for one thing and one thing only – to pummel its adversaries into dust.

Which was exactly what humanity needed.

"Sir," said Cortez softly. "We're receiving an info packet from Thor's Hammer about the ril-galas presence in their vicinity."

Acknowledging her with a forced smile and a nod, Radko continued his discussion with the Admiral without missing a beat.

"Sir, how close to being ready for launch is the Sovereign?"

Though the ship itself was a closely guarded secret, at least from the general public, most officers within the Commonwealth Navy were aware of the construction delays that had plagued the ship ever since her construction contract had been taken from Cagliari Aerospace and assigned to ATC Castle. She had missed three projected launch dates already.

"She's at ninety percent, I'm told. How many ships do you have with you, Commander?"

"It's just us, Admiral. And the Leonid Gorshkov."

"What? What did you say?"

"Stand by Admiral," said Radko, motioning for Cortez to cut the line. "Owens, get me a star map on the sand table with us, Earth and Thor's Hammer. And feed it through to the Gorshkov – I want Kovalenko in on this discussion as well."

"Aye sir."

It took a few moments for the holographic map to appear above the table, the three points highlighted by softly pulsing red arrows. As Radko, Gray, Owens, Locaris, Tangaroa and Quon gathered around the map, Radko waved for Cortez to join them – after all, she was the one who hit on the key to the ril-galas strategy.

"Commander," said Locaris. "What exactly is this Thor's Hammer?"

"It's a ship construction and deployment base, but designed to be... I guess 'low profile' would be the best way to put it. It was to be a replacement for the base we mothballed on Makemake, but far more advanced. A space-born drydock, a repair, resupply and deployment facility for launching long-range strikes against the icarans and the Soviets. It's not exactly secret, but it's been designed in such a way that you'd have to be inside it to know what it really was," said Radko before turning to address them all. "All right, you all know what's happening. The ril-galas have taken Earth. At present, it appears that the Vimy Ridge and the Leonid Gorshkov are the only human ships in the sector that have not been either destroyed or trapped behind a blockade."

"And we are a food source," said Gray. "They may have already begun harvesting."

"Very likely," said Radko, staring at the slowly turning holographic orb of the Earth. "Which makes our decision even more difficult."

"How so?," said Gray. "We flank them, us and the Soviets."

He reached forward, drawing an arc with his finger first from the Vimy Ridge to the Earth, then an opposite arc between the Leonid Gorshkov and the Earth.

"We come at their defenses from both sides, we hammer a hole through and then we drop every last one of our troops – my men, Locaris and his, the ATC Castle mercs and all of the Soviets – right onto the ril-galas."

Gray waited for Radko's response, but began to frown when the Commander simply continued to stare at the map for a long, long moment.

"Two ships," he said finally.

"What?"

"We're two ships, Colonel. We had trouble with a pair of ril-galas battleships and a wing of fighters," he said. He tapped a few commands into the sand table console and a larger image of Earth appeared above the star map, showing the planet being orbited by at least a hundred small red arrows. "Those are ril-galas ships, Gray. And just the ones LiDAR can positively identify as ril-galas ships."

Gray narrowed his eyes, anticipating the next statement.

"We're not going to Earth," said Radko.

Every set of eyes on the command deck turned toward Radko.

"Commander," said Kovalenko, his voice layered with static. "Are you suggesting retreat?"

"No, just that we strategize, that we think through our options. We can't rush into anything – there's too much at stake."

"Yes, there is," said Gray. "The lives of everyone on Earth. And they're already dying under this occupation, but we can strike quickly and get some out."

"Some. And how many is some, Colonel?," said Radko. "How many shuttles full of people do you think we can get from Earth to the Vimy Ridge or the Gorshkov without them being shot down? Or without one of our exactly two capital ships being destroyed?"

"So we shouldn't even try?"

"It's not a matter of trying or not trying, it's a matter of making sure that when we do hit Earth, we're giving ourselves and the rest of humanity the best chance of surviving the operation. Right now, if the Vimy Ridge is destroyed, what hope does the Gorshkov have?"

"In other times, I would see that as insult," said Kovalenko's static-riddled voice. "But is also true in present circumstance."

"Commander," said Gray. "We have to go to Earth. You heard Sigurdsson. We're a food source! I read your file, I know you weren't born on Earth, so you wouldn't know what-."

"Colonel if you had actually read my file – all of my file – you'd know that I have a sister on Earth. And two nephews. Twins. Turned eight years old earlier this year. I was deployed and couldn't get back for the party. Bought them the full set of Commonwealth Heroes action figures and the HMS Victory command deck playset. Took me forever to track the fucking thing down. So don't tell me I don't know what is at stake here," said Radko. "I know what this decision means, but I also know that this is the right call. Because if we go running off half-cocked and the only two human vessels currently actively engaged in battling the rilgalas are destroyed, then Earth is absolutely, unequivocally, lost. Permanently. Now please go brief your men and get them prepared. You too Locaris, Tangaroa. I want everyone ready to go on a moment's notice. Clear?"

Locaris and Tangaroa nodded immediately and headed out to meet with their respective teams. Gray stared daggers at Radko for a moment longer before turning on his heel and stalking off the command deck. The Commander sighed, looking at the sand table display for several more minutes before climbing the ladder to the observation deck.

Shortly thereafter, he was joined by Quon.

"The Colonel is not happy."

"Did you read his mind?"

She shook her head.

"I gave my word I wouldn't do that and I haven't. Mostly," she said. "I am going to get some rest, but you may call if you need me."

"Thanks."

As her footsteps faded down the ladder, another set came up. Cortez stepped up beside him, hands clasped behind her back. He knew she was doing her best to keep it together and frankly she had been one of the most impressive members of this strange little crew he'd ended up with. Rangers and mercenaries and icarans and Soviets and this one young woman who, somehow, had performed like a seasoned naval officer under near-impossible conditions.

"I'm making you an Acting Sub Lieutenant," he said.

"I beg your pardon, sir?"

"You have exceeded all possible expectations, Cortez. I don't think I could have come this far without your help."

"Thank you, Commander," she said, then paused before continuing. "Sir... my parents are on Earth."

Radko sighed.

"We can't assault Earth," he said, staring out at the glowing, deadly whisps surrounding the ship, hiding it from the ril-galas. "It would be suicide, Anna."

"I know, I wasn't... I'm just worried. Scared, actually. Terrified."

Turning to lean his back on the observation dome, Radko reached out and placed a hand on Cortez's shoulder.

"We all are. No one has ever faced anything like this before, so none of us know how to react," he said. "Gray, for instance. He's scared to be powerless, so he can't think beyond the whole 'kick down the doors' approach. And me. I'm scared to make the wrong decision. I know what decision I have to make, but I'm still scared to make it."

"Because you know it will mean a lot of people will die," she said.

He nodded.

"But...," she said, reaching up and putting her hand over his. "Your plan – what I think your plan is – it increases our chances of saving humanity."

"I think so."

"So do I."

A long silence followed with the two officers – the seasoned Lieutenant Commander and the newly-gazetted Acting Sub Lieutenant, both thrown into their roles through death and destruction – just stood quietly, listening to the thrum of the engines and the buzz of the ship's crew going about their business.

"You've brought us this far, sir," said Cortez, her voice low. "We'll follow you wherever you lead."

"They're coming again!," said Ustorf, her voice filtering through the open line.

Sigurdsson braced herself against the wall beneath Ustorf's sniper perch in the tower and dialed up her targeting optics. The sun was rising, making it much easier to see the approaching ril-galas horde as well as the shapes silhouetted against the sky.

"We've got bats and foot soldiers," she called out. "Henning, Zolnerowich, Petrov and Ustorf, take the air units. Elgrapharr, Aeltheer and I will roam. Everyone else, pound those ground units."

Priming the X2 Behemoth, she didn't bother using the bipod. Instead she held the big gun almost like an assault rifle and aiming through its bulky scope, drew a bead on the first of the approaching ril-galas. Squeezing the trigger, she watched as a hole the size of a basketball was blown through the first one and the projectile continued onward, shearing the leg of the enemy directly behind.

"Freyja, I need to see you right away."

Sigurdsson frowned. It was Doctor Khaifa.

"Doctor, we're under attack. I haven't time for a chat."

"Make time, Sergeant – this could help you."

Sigurdsson swore under her breath.

"Young, take my spot on the wall!"

The big bearded man acknowledged and Sigurdsson hurried down the stairway from the wall and sprinted across to the Med-iCorps building. Weaving her way through triage and asking about Doctor Khaifa's whereabouts, Sigurdsson was directed to one of the three operating suites.

Stepping inside she nearly gagged from the smell.

"Here," said Khaifa, handing Sigurdsson a respirator like her own. "It isn't dangerous, it just smells awful."

As Sigurdsson put on the mask, she nodded a greeting to Brill, but barely noticed his awkward return nod – she was already staring at the operating table. Laid out on the table, its head, neck and chest and one arm splayed open in autopsy, was the ril-galas corpse they'd retrieved.

"Intriguing specimen," said Brill, a little too cheerful to Sigurdsson's mind. "Very interesting, to be the first – as far as we are aware – to dissect-."

"I'll make this quick," said Khaifa. "Look here."

She pointed to the head. The front of the skull had been removed, the thing's eyeballs sitting loosely in the pulpy innards.

"These are the optic nerves that, at least in the anatomy of every alien being we've ever encountered would lead to the brain."

"And?"

"There is no brain in this skull," said Brill.

Khaifa nodded.

"Look."

She trailed her finger along the optic nerve which, rather than connecting to an organ within the skull, was fed down through the long neck and into the chest cavity where it connected to a cartilaginous wall surrounding a large, purplish mass that reminded Sigurdsson of dead jellyfish she'd seen wash up on the beach. The mass had thick veins extending outward in several directions, particularly toward the limbs, and had six horizontal slits arranged in two rows of three across its top.

"So that thing, is that the brain? Or the heart?," she said.

"Freyja... it's everything."

"Nasrin, I'm really not in the mood for riddles."

"Sergeant Sigurdsson, these are not veins," said Brill, using large forceps to peel back a layer on one of the thick 'veins' to reveal a complex musculature. "They are arms. And these..."

It pointed toward the six horizontal slits and Khaifa reached in. Using two fingers, the doctor opened one of the slits and Sigurdsson stepped back involuntarily.

"Fuck me."

It was an eye.

"This right here," said Khaifa, pointing to the tentacled mass. "Is a ril-galas, Freyja. This large creature, the creatures we've been fighting this whole time, they're essentially machines. Biological, to be sure – I've found rudimentary nervous, cardiovascular and even digestive systems – but machines. Everything connects through the..."

She glanced quickly at Brill.

"We have dubbed it 'the pilot," it said. "Our assumption is that the flying creatures are structured in a similar way, though we cannot be certain without a carcass to similarly dissect."

"Even their space vessels may be the same."

Still staring at the ril-galas pilot, Sigurdsson was beginning to work out some alterations to her defense plan for Fort Hathaway. She had been hoping for something of use to come out of this autopsy, and while she hadn't known what to expect, it wasn't this. She'd never heard of anything even close to…

Trailing off, she glanced up at Brill, who, already watching her, simply nodded.

"The similarity occurred to Doctor Khaifa and myself very early in the process," it said. "Though of course my exo-suit is entirely mechanical. Even with the advanced medical technology we brill have, living exo-suits are beyond our reach."

Sigurdsson nodded absently. Her mind had already moved on.

"Have you recorded all of this?," she said.

Khaifa nodded, pointing to a small video recorder mounted to the large bank of lights that hung directly over the operating table.

"Upload the whole thing to Radko."

Then Sigurdsson drew her sidearm and put a bullet through the gelatinous mass that was the true face of the ril-galas. Khaifa jumped, the brill simply cocked the mechanical head of his exo-suit.

Without another word to the doctor, Sigurdsson tore off her respirator and headed out of the MediCorps building, switching on an open comm line as she did so.

"Everyone, this is Sigurdsson. Aim for the chest with every shot, multiple hits if possible. That's where these bastards keep their brains."

As the acknowledgements flowed in, she heard the rate of gunfire increase and heard the tell-tale whine of the wall turrets being fired up. It sounded like the ril-galas assault was ramping up and her garrison and its cobbled together group of reinforcements were ramping up their defense in response. Over the regular bursts of gunfire, Sigurdsson could even distinguish the pop of Ustorf's sniper rifle and the booming of the icaran assault rifles. Whatever problems may have existed between the Commonwealth and the icarans and the Soviets and whatever resentment had festered between the armed forces and the private military contractors, Sigurdsson was happy to have the extra trained guns at her disposal. And to the credit of each and every being manning the walls of Fort Hathaway, all of them had stepped up right in line with the original garrison. Not one complaint, not one hesitation at following the orders of a sergeant – and technically an enemy sergeant for some of them.

Maybe there was some hope for the future, if they could manage to survive the ril-galas. Not just the future of Fort Hathaway and Von Daniken's Landing, but for humanity. For the icarans. For all of them. Maybe when this was all over the Commonwealth, the Soviets and the Icaran Colonial Alliance would be able to sit down and realise that there were bigger problems in the universe than their political posturing and maybe – just maybe – they were all stronger facing those problems together.

Sadly, she realised the people with enough influence to make those decisions weren't the people on her walls fighting together to protect the colony. And they weren't the people on the Vimy Ridge helping Radko fight his battles. The people who could make those decisions were likely safe and sound in some bunker waiting for the dust to settle.

If it were up to the soldiers, the ones putting their lives on the line, the story might have had a different ending.

Humans – Soviet and Commonwealth – and icarans working together. Sigurdsson almost smiled at the thought. The things they'd have been able to achieve if not for the politics of division.

As if on cue, one of the Soviets – a scarred old veteran named Chung – appeared at the top of the wall, waving frantically for her. She took the steps three at a time and joined him where he'd taken up position, again firing down at the ril-galas advance. Raising the X2, Sigurdsson took up a shooting spot between Chung and Elgrapharr and was preparing to fire when she saw why Chung had been waving so frantically.

"Shit."

"Indeed," said Elgrapharr. "It would appear that the ril-galas have heavy ground units."

There were only two of them, hulking monstrosities only slightly shorter than the walls on which the defenders stood. Four thick, stubby legs, bent outward like a Komodo dragon, supported a barrel-like body covered in lumps and spines. Two arms, each ending in a massive claw, protruded from behind the squashed-looking head, with its wide mouth, six eyes and spikes.

There were only two of them, but as they advanced, Sigurdsson could hear the thunder of their footfalls and knew the garrison was in trouble. Briefly, she wondered how many ril-galas blobs it took to pilot one of the... one of the tanks, for lack of a better term.

"Eisenhorn, you copy?"

"Yeah Sarge, go ahead."

"Get one of those grenade launchers from Radko's care package and join Ustorf in the tower," she said. "I want you to target those big things. The tanks."

"On my way."

Sigurdsson turned to Elgrapharr, but he was on the same track already.

"Aeltheer and I shall target the... tanks as well. Our assault rifles can inflict much more damage than yours."

"I'll assign one of the turrets as well, then I'll join you and Aeltheer," she said, targeting an approaching ril-galas bat and blowing it to pieces with a dead-on shot from the X2. "I can do a little damage myself."

She wasn't sure, but she thought she saw the icaran equivalent of a smile flicker across Elgrapharr's face as she slung the rifle over her shoulder and headed toward the Eastern turret. As she gave the turret gunner her orders, word came in from Eisenhorn that he'd reached the tower and was preparing his barrage of grenades.

"All right," said Sigurdsson as she set up at the wall. Activating her targeting optics, she also thumbed on the X2 scope's built-in image enhancer. "All guns designated as anti-tank, target the nearest of the two. Everyone else, you have clearance to lay into the foot soldiers with whatever weapons you have at your disposal... Now!"

As the barrage began, Sigurdsson watched through her scope as the first of Eisenhorn's grenades hit home, blowing a small chunk of flesh from the tank's back. The turret was spraying the creature with standard projectiles, doing some damage but not enough to have much of an effect. Squeezing the trigger, Sigurdsson sent one of the X2's projectiles straight through the thing's left arm, leaving a ragged gaping hole. The arm still seemed functional, so she quickly chambered another round and fired again.

The arm fell to the ground with an audible crunch as it was severed just below the shoulder.

Incendiary rounds from Elgrapharr and Aeltheer's aorans peppered the tank's legs, cutting pieces from them as the grenades from Eisenhorn continued to hammer the beast from above.

Suddenly, the tank opened its broad mouth, its insides glowing, and projectile vomited a stream of glowing orange liquid in a powerful jet that burned through several of its own foot soldiers before impacting the wall of Fort Hathaway with enough force that Sigurdsson felt the vibration through her boots. She also felt the heat of the liquid, whatever it was.

As she lined up another shot, Sigurdsson saw the thing open its mouth again and fired directly down its gullet. The two icarans had the same idea and suddenly the beast was keeling over, falling heavily to the ground, the glowing liquid spilling from its mouth and several holes in its throat. And then, suddenly, the tank's entire front half exploded in a ball of flame so intense that every single defender on the wall ducked down. When they retook their positions, they found the explosion had claimed nearly two-dozen ril-galas who, if not torn to pieces, lay burning in the snow.

There were cheers all around until another orange glow appeared. The second tank's mouth was open wide and a jet of the liquid shot out, straight up into the tower, the heat twisting and melting the metal structure. The metal collapsed and the flesh was incinerated. Sigurdsson hoped that Eisenhorn and Ustorf had died instantly and never felt the skin and muscle melting off their bones.

Overspray from the jet splattered down all around the tower and Sigurdsson watched in horror as the substance splattered across Aeltheer's faceplate, the metal immediately becoming molten. Dropping the X2, Sigurdsson ran over to the icaran woman as she hit the ground, clawing at her melting helmet. The icaran's left hand was a misshapen mass of flesh, having been hit by overspray. Grasping the helmet herself, Sigurdsson quickly drew back her hand, a line of burning, sizzling skin across her palm, but she gritted her teeth, took hold once more and used all her considerable strength to wrench off the helmet.

It was no use.

Sigurdsson stared down into the lifeless eyes of Aeltheer. Her left side eyes. The right side of her face was a mass of burned and mangled flesh and bone mixed with rapidly hardening melted metal. The helmet, she realised, had pulled away so easily because it was so weakened by the heat that it had nearly torn in two.

Standing, Sigurdsson let the mangled helmet drop at her feet.

To her left, Elgrapharr continued to fire into the advancing horde, while to her right, Chung staggered backward, blood spurting from a neck wound as he dropped to the ground unmoving.

"Henning, do you copy?," she said. "What's the status of the gates? Can they withstand that kind of heat?"

There was a several second delay before a response was forthcoming.

"Sergeant, this is Delany. Henning's been taken to medical."

"Fuck! How bad, Delany?"

"I... had to hold his intestines in."

"Goddammit. The gates. Status?"

"They should hold, but if that level of heat is sustained for an extended period..."

She didn't need to finish the sentence.

"Delany, go to the civilians. Every single healthy adult not tasked with medical duties is to be armed."

"If they object-."

"There are no passengers on this bus anymore! If we don't fight these fucking things off they will eat us, Delany. Do you understand me? I'm not being figurative or dramatic or exaggerating. We are part of the food chain."

She could almost hear Delany's mind processing the information. The girl was young and had made some bad decisions and would pay for them later, but one thing she wasn't was a moron.

"Understood, Sergeant."

"Kenwick, how much fuel do we have for the ATVs?"

"Uh, we have... we have plenty, Sarge," he said, his voice as unsteady as Sigurdsson herself felt.

"Get someone to bring it all out. Hook it up to our fire pump and get the hoses to the top of the wall."

"I don't understand-."

"I don't give a shit if you understand, just fucking do it, Private!"

Her lip curled in a snarl, Sigurdsson tore off her parka and grabbed Aeltheer's aoran assault rifle. It was a slightly awkward grip, being designed for the three-fingered icaran hand, but she forced herself to adjust. Priming the rifle, Sigurdsson felt the buzz of kinetic energy building up as the cylinder ramped up to speed and she ran to the wall, taking up position between Elgrapharr and the ex-Castle man, Alban Young.

Her palm stung fiercely, but it was a good pain, she decided. If she was in pain, she was still alive, and if she was still alive then she could still fight.

As she began firing the powerful, booming icaran rounds into the extant tank creature, she could hear Elgrapharr speaking. In low tones, clearly intended for no ears but his, Sigurdsson realised he wasn't speaking at all, but singing.

He was singing the history of his fallen comrade, Aeltheer. He was singing...

Sigurdsson's steady firing pace faltered momentarily as the translation matrix picked up a few additional words.

He was singing the history of his fallen wife.

Gritting her teeth, Sigurdsson increased the barrage from the muzzle of her aoran.

"I'm sorry to say it, Commander, but it sounds like they're in serious trouble," said Owens as the latest update from Fort Hathaway faded from the screen.

Radko couldn't bring himself to do anything but grunt. Though he knew, logically, he'd done everything he could have done for Sigurdsson and her garrison – resupplying them, providing reinforcements – it still ate away at him that his first promise to the Sergeant, to get her and her people off Von Daniken's Landing, had fallen to pieces so completely.

"I recommend a wide-dispersal broadcast of the autopsy footage," continued the Lieutenant. "As soon as we're clear of the Ishtar Gate, that is. The information may help whatever pockets of resistance may still be out there."

"Agreed, Lieutenant," said Radko, looking up as Locaris entered with the icaran who had taken Elgrapharr's place as his second in command. Radko wasn't sure of the newcomer's name.

Tangaroa was already present, as was Quon, hanging back in the shadows as was her tendency. A moment later, Colonel Gray marched onto the command deck, three of his senior NCOs with him, including Vossek.

"All right," said Radko. "We've had some new developments."

He began by having Owens replay the autopsy video recorded in Fort Hathaway by the MediCorps personnel. When the doctor performing the autopsy finished explaining everything she had found, summarizing her discoveries by directly addressing the camera, Colonel Gray became noticeably agitated.

"The doctor in this video," he said. "Is Nasrin Khaifa."

"I believe so," said Owens.

"She's his wife," said Quon.

Radko glanced to Quon, then back to Gray, who simply nodded.

"I'm sorry, Colonel. I had no idea she was there."

"Neither did I. She was supposed to be aboard the MCV Seraphim," he said. "It doesn't matter now. I assume you've called us all here to discuss strategy?"

"Yeah. Yeah, I have. Owens?"

The Lieutenant closed the hovering video display windows and brought up the star map that had previously been on display, showing their current position alongside the Leonid Gorshkov as well as the relative positions of Earth and Thor's Hammer.

"You've all seen this before," said Radko. "Captain Kovalenko, is this coming through on your end?"

"Yes, we have the map, Commander," came Kovalenko's still static-riddled reply.

"All right. Based on our own knowledge, plus the info packet Cortez has decrypted from Thor's Hammer, we're now able to add to this map with some degree of accuracy the ril-galas deployment. As you can see," he said as an overlay appeared on the map. "The news is not good."

The overlay, on which components of the ril-galas space fleet were marked in purple, painted a dire picture. Huge blotches of purple appeared in several different spots in or near Earth's orbit. A thin semi-circle of purple marked the blockade hemming in the ships at Thor's hammer and various smaller purple patches could be seen throughout the space in between.

After a moment of silence in which everyone looked over the map in detail, it was Kovalenko who broke the silence.

"There is no easy approach," he said. "Looks like most of swarm is here."

"It does indeed," agreed Locaris.

"There are holes in their deployment, here and here," said Gray, pointing toward two open spots between the purple blotches orbiting Earth. "My plan still stands. We hammer our way through one of these holes and land ground troops to take out any command and control centres planetside while the Vimy Ridge and the Leonid Gorshkov continue the naval battle."

For several moments, Radko stared at the map as everyone else waited for his response.

"We're not going to Earth, Colonel," he said finally.

"Excuse me?," said Gray, staring daggers at Radko from across the sand table.

There was dead silence from around the command deck as the other humans aboard heard the news. No doubt more than a handful felt as Gray did, so Radko pushed on to outline his plan, hoping to allay any fears.

"We'll continue on through the Ishtar Gate in the direction of Thor's Hammer-."

"Commander Radko, an entire planet – our entire home world of over eight billion people – is under attack and its population is being looked at as food and we're not going to help them?"

Radko could see a vein throbbing the Gray's forehead, his jaw muscles clenching.

"Colonel, this wasn't an easy decision to make, but it's the right decision. If we..."

"You need to reconsider your decision."

"Gray," said Radko, trying his best to remain calm and diplomatic. "I realise this isn't the decision you were hoping for, but the decision is made. I'm sorry, but the Vimy Ridge will not be launching an assault against Earth. If you'll listen to my..."

"No," said Gray, quickly drawing his sidearm and pointing it directly at Radko's head. The three NCO Rangers behind him did the same, pointing their weapons at the icaran commandos and ATC Castle personnel. "I'm not going to let you abandon Earth. I went along with your plan to set Quon free, I went along with your use of the icarans, hell I even accepted that we could use the Soviets. But then Quon somehow became your right hand, putting who knows what kind of thoughts into your mind, and then you felt it was justifiable to launch an all-out assault on an ATC Castle facility. And now you want to walk away from Earth? No, Radko. No. You are going to give the order to begin the assault on Earth, Commander. Or I will put you down and give the order myself."

Radko swallowed heavily, staring down the barrel of Gray's REV1 pistol, and tried to prevent his inner fear from showing outwardly. It was strange how clearly he was seeing everything in those few seconds. The five o'clock shadow Gray was sporting, the deep gouge just under the barrel of his pistol, the scars on the man's knuckles.

"I'm sorry, Gray," Radko said, slowly. "I won't be giving that order."

"Fine. You had your chance."

Gray's finger twitched on the trigger, almost in slow motion as he began to squeeze. A shot rang out and despite flinching at the sound, Radko saw clearly a spray of blood and bone and brain matter spatter across the sand table as Gray dropped to the deck plates.

To one side of the command deck, forgotten in the short-lived power struggle, Anna Cortez stood, REV2 pistol still clutched in her shaking hands, her eyes wide, her face drained of colour.

Vossek immediately swung his own weapon around toward Cortez.

"Stop," said Locaris.

It wasn't the order that caused Vossek and the two remaining Rangers to freeze, but the buzz of the aoran assault rifles springing to life. In the moment of confusion caused by Gray's death, the two icarans as well as Tangaroa and his second had armed themselves.

Taking a couple of deep breaths, Radko stepped over to Cortez and took the pistol from her shaking hands. The girl looked completely stunned. Tucking the pistol into his belt, Radko gave Cortez's hands a quick squeeze of thanks.

"Vossek," he said. "I need you and your men to stand down."

The Ranger gritted his teeth and adjusted his stance, but did not lower his weapon.

"Commander, I can't do that. She killed Colonel Gray."

"No, she didn't," said Quon, stepping up to the sand table. "I did."

Everyone simply stared at her for a moment until Vossek spoke again.

"What? We all fucking saw her! She shot him in the fucking head!"

"When you shoot an enemy, do you say that your gun killed him? Do you give the credit for the kill to the tool you've used to accomplish your goal?," she said, tapping a finger on her temple. "You have no idea what I'm capable of, Vossek. No idea."

"You shut up," he said, swinging his gun around to aim at Quon.

It was just the opening Locaris needed. He stepped forward, pressed the barrel of his rifle into Vossek's chest.

"I will pull the trigger in three seconds unless you surrender your weapon."

One of the other NCOs took an aggressive step forward, but found herself taking a bullet in the shoulder from Tangaroa's pistol.

"We're done," he said, the barrel of his pistol not wavering an inch. "Don't make this any worse."

The Rangers, after the briefest of hesitations, lowered their weapons.

"Everyone just take a moment to get your shit together," said Radko, then motioned toward the small office at the rear of the command deck that was assigned to Owens. "Quon, Cortez, come with me."

He said nothing else until the three of them were inside the office with the hatch shut behind them. Taking Cortez's head in his heads, he forced her to meet his gaze.

"Are you all right?"

She nodded, but said nothing. Radko released her and spun angrily toward Quon.

"How could you do this? After all the trust I put in you, you go and turn one of my officers into your puppet?"

"I didn't do anything," she said.

"She didn't," said Cortez in a small voice. "It was me. Just me."

Radko stared intently into Quon's unsettling blue eyes and she stared back unflinchingly.

"I swear to you Fin, I did not do anything to Miss Cortez."

"Then why-."

Quon chuckled humourlessly.

"Because Gray and his mindless robots all wanted to see me shot from the moment I stepped out of my prison cell. What's the harm in taking the blame for the death of their leader if they already want me dead? If they hold me responsible, maybe they'll leave Cortez alone."

Radko stood for a moment looking at Quon. When they'd first made their bargain, he never would have imagined they'd be in this position, her putting herself on the line for one of his people. He turned to Cortez.

"Anna..."

"He was... I had to. He was going to kill you. I had to shoot him," she said, her eyes welling up with tears.

"I know. I know, it's okay," he said as she buried her face in his chest and cried. He turned to Quon. "Li, as much as I'd like you to stay, if my plan works…"

She nodded. If she was taken into custody by the Commonwealth, she'd likely be shipped off to Duster's Range to become an ATC Castle science project. Neither she nor Radko could imagine the Commonwealth hierarchy giving a free pass to a Nightwatch subject under any circumstances – and especially since a peace offering might be required to placate ATC Castle.

Just where she would go? That was another matter entirely. In days past, before humanity's conception of the universe changed, there were any number of independent colonies on which she could have disappeared. Any number of pirate havens on which she could have started a new life. There was no way for her or Radko to know whether any of those place still existed, but they both knew she had no alternative but to try.

"You'll have to get through the Ishtar Gate as soon as possible. The shuttles aren't as well-shielded against radiation as the Vimy Ridge," he said. "And take one of the Ospreys, not a Flamingo. They're faster and more maneuverable. And it's easier for a single operator to be both pilot and gunner."

As Cortez released her grip on him, Radko patted the small of her back then turned to Quon and extended his hand.

"The shuttle should be small enough that the ril-galas will leave you alone, but don't take any chances – find a safe haven as quickly as you can."

Glancing at Radko's outstretched hand, Quon smiled and pushed it aside, embracing him instead. She tilted her head closer to his and whispered in his ear.

"Thank you for treating me like a person."

Releasing him from the embrace, Quon turned and left without another word, closing the office hatch behind her. Radko turned back to Cortez.

"I have to get back out there, but if you need a few minutes..."

"No," she said firmly. "I'm okay."

The young woman forced a smile.

"You need me out there."

"Yes I do."

As the pair re-entered the command deck, Quon was already gone. Vossek was tending to the bullet wound sustained by the female NCO and while both Tangaroa and Locaris still held their weapons, some of the tension had gone out of the air.

"If we're all done waving our cocks around, maybe we can start fighting the actual enemy," said Radko, sharply. "If that's all right with everyone?"

With the exception of Vossek, the Rangers had the good sense to look sheepish.

"Are we still linked with the Gorshkov?"

"You are," came Kovalenko's static-riddled confirmation. "You have experienced... issue, Commander?"

"Personnel malfunction, Captain. It's been rectified."

"Glad to hear."

Radko resisted the urge to say 'me too' and instead turned to Owens.

"Pipe this through the whole ship and through to Thor's Hammer. I want everyone to hear the plan directly from me. And send it to Fort Hathaway as well -- maybe it will give them a little hope."

Once Owens had nodded that the channels had been set up, Radko cleared his throat and took a deep breath.

"Attention everyone, this is Lieutenant Commander Radko. As you know, Earth has been invaded and occupied by the ril-galas. We have no idea what current conditions are on the planet and while I know most if not all of you have friends or family living on Earth – myself included –– I have made the decision not to attempt to break the enemy line around Earth. This was not an easy decision, nor do I expect it to be a popular one, but given the strength in numbers the ril-galas possess on and around Earth, it would be utter suicide for two ships, even two ships with the kind of spectacular crews we have on the Vimy Ridge and the Leonid Gorshkov, to take on an armada. However," he said pausing dramatically. "If we can obtain six more ships, including the HMS Royal Sovereign..."

Several people on the command deck – and he assumed elsewhere on the ship – began to stand a little straighter as it dawned on them what Radko had been planning.

"I have asked a lot of you over the past...," he faltered as it occurred to him he really had no idea how long it had been since the fall of Echo Station. "Since we lost Commodore Edwards and so many of our fellow sailors in the Third Fleet. But we, the few, the survivors, have carried the banner of the Third Fleet through hell and while we have our scars and we've suffered our losses, we are still here. Against incredible odds, we have survived, we have fought, we have won every battle. The HMCS Vimy Ridge has accomplished what no Commonwealth politician has ever dreamed of accomplishing."

He glanced at Locaris and half smiled as the large icaran nodded and then he himself nodded to Tangaroa.

"We have joined together with the icarans. We have joined forces with the Soviets. ATC Castle personnel have tossed aside their contracts and joined our crew. The Vimy Ridge and the fearsome Leonid Gorshkov have become a unified battle group, a joint task force against the ril-galas invaders and now we intend to add to that task force."

Hitting the controls on the sand table, Radko brought up a close up of the blockade surrounding Thor's Hammer. A similar image would be popping up on the Gorshkov for Kovalenko as well as on multiple terminals throughout the Vimy Ridge.

"Thor's Hammer. A disguised ship-building and repair facility. The ril-galas clearly don't understand its importance or they would have destroyed it already," he said. "Behind this blockade is a base of operations. Behind this blockade are supplies, ammunition, trained personnel. Behind this blockade is what I intend to make the First Fleet of Joint Task Force One…"

As he began to list the ship names, holographic representations of the vessels materialized to one side of the holographic Thor's Hammer.

"The HMS Sir Walter Raleigh. The INS Godavari. The Ludwigshafen am Rhein. The HMS Edinburgh. The HMCS Haida Gwaii," he said and then paused for dramatic effect. "And the HMS Royal Sovereign."

He outlined the plan. With support from the Gorshkov's fighter wing, the two vessels would smash their way through the blockade while the ships trapped within the blockade were harassing the ril-galas to keep them off-balance. Joint Task Force One would then secure Thor's Hammer, scatter the blockade and regroup, re-arm and re-supply while planning the next move – the move to Earth.

A risky operation, without a doubt, and failure meant much the same outcome as a failed assault on Earth: the end of the war and the perhaps inevitable end of the human race. The difference, in Radko's mind, was that this operation, the liberation of Thor's Hammer, actually had a chance of success.

"If we are not successful," said Kovalenko. "Our enemy will strike major blow against Thor's Hammer."

"That's true," said Radko, nodding though the captain of the Leonid Gorshkov couldn't see him. "If we fail, or frankly even if we succeed, we will be met with harsh reprisals."

"But success means additional ships at our disposal," said Locaris.

Owens, staring thoughtfully at the sand table, slowly nodded.

"War assets," he said. "Which we'll need if we have a hope in hell of turning this thing around."

"And maybe," said Cortez, then stopped and cleared her throat. "Maybe if word of it gets out – word of a victory at Thor's Hammer, of Joint Task Force One – others who've gone into hiding might join us."

Unlike during her first contribution at the sand table, what seemed like forever ago, this time when all attention turned to her, Cortez neither flinched nor paused.

"We have to assume other ships have found places to lay low. Commonwealth, Soviet, and especially pirates – it's what they do, right? When we take back Thor's Hammer, we give them all a place to go."

"A rallying point," said Tangaroa.

"Agreed," said Kovalenko.

"Good," said Radko. "Everyone make whatever preparations you need. We launch the operation in sixty minutes."

Weapon racks had been brought up to the top of the wall by some of the civilians. It had become necessary for some of the defenders to swap out their rifles in order to prevent the weapons from over-heating and possibly exploding in their hands. Buckets of magazines sat at various points for easy access and the civilians unable to wield weapons of their own – the elderly, the wounded, the children – had been put to work re-filling empty magazines.

Sigurdsson glanced up as she heard her name and saw Young dragging one of the three fire hoses toward her, its other end snaking down over the wall back into the main compound of Fort Hathaway, where it was connected to a fire pump, which in turn was connected to a fuel supply. The other two hoses were being taken to strategic points along the wall.

"Hose teams in position," yelled Young as he aimed the hose out over the wall, toward the ril-galas.

"Fire up the pump! Grenadiers at the ready!"

A second later, the foul-smelling fuel began to spray out of the fire hoses, falling like rain on the alien attackers and the ground around them. The sudden onslaught of liquid seemed to confuse the ril-galas, as their forward momentum slowed to almost nothing. Still the rain of fuel continued until all three hose streams petered out.

Sigurdsson scooped up the grenade launcher at her feet and aimed toward the enemy line.

"Grenadiers fire on my mark," she said. "Two... one...... mark."

All along the wall, Sigurdsson heard the now-familiar whump of the launchers as the grenades arced out from the walls of the Fort toward the enemy line. When they impacted, the entire ril-galas line erupted in a single, elongated ball of flame. Cheers went up down the length of the wall and even Sigurdsson smiled a little. It was a huge blow to the enemy to be sure, but there were still many more of them out there still alive and untouched by the flames. And there was still the tank.

As if it knew what she was thinking, a stream of the fiery liquid shot through the flames that were engulfing so many of the tank's fellow ril-galas and hammered into the gates of Fort Hathaway. She could see the thing beyond the wall of flame and she could see others on the wall firing at it with both bullets and grenades, but the creature had learned well from the fate of its compatriot. It was staying outside the range of standard weaponry.

Tossing aside the grenade launcher, Sigurdsson picked up the X2, chambered a round and took careful aim, Behemoth versus behemoth. Even as she fired and watched the round slam into the tank, she knew it wasn't going to be enough. They had just the one X2 rifle and it would take far too long-

Her thought process was interrupted as another blast from the creature's mouth slammed into the gates, causing the entire wall to shake. At her side, Jaeger crouched low to the ground, growling softly.

"Sergeant," said Delany through the comm lines. "That last hit caused some buckling in the left side gate. I'm not sure we'll be able to withstand more than one or two more hits like that."

"Understood. Try to reinforce with whatever you have handy – I'll think of something."

As she looked out at the tank, Elgrapharr and Young stepped up beside her.

"You have a plan?," said Young.

"Well... it's hanging back, out of range of our weapons. If the fucker is too far away for us to fight from here..."

"We take the fight to it," said Elgrapharr.

Sigurdsson nodded.

"A small strike team, heavily armed. There's enough confusion down there with the fire and we can have the wall defense keep pressing to occupy most of the ril-galas foot soldiers," she said. "We bring a shit tonne of grenades and whatever other explosives we have on hand and we hammer the thing at close range."

"Probably a one-way trip," said Young.

"It's been a long time since I had any belief I was ever going to leave this planet alive, Young," she said with a shrug. "I'll be leading the strike."

"And I will be by your side," said Elgrapharr, looking out across the battlefield.

Sigurdsson simply nodded. She knew his reasons and didn't feel the need to question them.

"Yeah, me too," said Young.

With a nod, Sigurdsson led the pair down the stairs to the armoury. Jaeger, of course, following close behind. As much as she loved the X2, a sniper rifle wasn't going to do her any favours in close-quarters combat. For a CQC operation, she needed the old standby. She took off her heavy sweater and tossed it aside, leaving her in just her standard-issue grey tee shirt. She might feel the cold -- though that was debatable given the fires raging outside the walls – but she wanted as much speed and maneuverability as she could have. In place of her sweater, she strapped on a tactical vest and stuffed spare mags for the 33A1 into the pockets. Young, who was already well-stocked with weapons and ammo, filled a backpack with explosives while Elgrapharr ensured that both his own assault rifle and the one formerly belonging to Aeltheer were primed and ready, as was his boxy sidearm.

For good measure, Sigurdsson clipped a Caliburn submachine gun to her tactical vest.

She looked up as Delany entered. The woman was sweating profusely.

"Sergeant, it's no good," she said. "The hinges are starting to melt. Another couple hits and those gates are coming down."

"We're going to deal with it, Private," said Sigurdsson.

"You're going out there, aren't you? Into the field to attack the tank."

Sigurdsson nodded.

"Three of you?"

Again, Sigurdsson nodded as she checked her sidearm.

Delany set down her rifle, took off her parka and pulled on a tac vest like Sigurdsson's. She slung a drum-fed grenade launcher over her shoulder and checked the mag in her rifle.

"What are you doing, Delany?"

"Always work in two-man teams. That was what you told us when we first got here. Work in pairs at all times. You can't work in pairs if you have a team of three, so I'm going with you."

The young Private held up a hand, cutting off Sigurdsson's objection.

"I helped get a whole bunch of people killed for no good reason, Sarge. Let me do this."

There was a moment's hesitation, but Sigurdsson nodded.

"You stick to me at all times."

She looked down at Jaeger, sitting and watching the preparations, his head tilted slightly to the left, then turned back to her team.

"I need a minute. I'll meet you on the wall."

With nods all around, they gathered their gear and headed out, leaving Sigurdsson and Jaeger alone in the armoury.

She knelt down beside him and began rubbing behind his right ear. He pressed his head into her hand.

"Okay buddy, here's the thing. I need to go do something now, and... I'm not certain I'll be able to come back. Remember what I told you, all right? Shit here goes sideways, you find somewhere to hide and you stay hidden until it's safe."

She stopped rubbing his ear and Jaeger looked at her for a second, then inched closer and chuffed.

With a genuine smile, Sigurdsson rubbed the sides of his muzzle with both hands, trying to fight the tears that were forming in her eyes.

"You're such a good boy. Just please stay safe," she said, her voice starting to fail her. "I love you, Jaeger."

His tongue immediately flicked out, catching her right across the lips and nose and she reached out and gave him a hug and then stood. She headed out to the wall without looking back, knowing that if she did, she wouldn't be able to hold back the tears any longer.

When she reached the top of the wall, Young looked at her, frowning.

"Everything cool?"

She glanced at him, then looked out onto the battlefield.

"I need to go kill something," she said.

With the gates sealed, the four soldiers had to go over the wall, rappelling down until their boots hit the ground. Where there had been snow not so long ago, there was now mud, the snow and ice having melted in the heat of the fires still burning.

Keeping low to the ground, Delany right behind her, Sigurdsson held her assault rifle at the ready as they weaved through the burning corpses of the ril-galas. Anything that moved, they double-tapped in the chest and moved on, not stopping to confirm the kill. Shots whizzed over their heads as the soldiers manning the wall did their best to provide covering fire. The closer the team got to the tank, the more living and largely functional ril-galas they encountered. Elgrapharr was merciless in taking them down, blowing bits and pieces off the aliens as he continued to sing the history of his late wife. Young, like Sigurdsson and Delany, was doing his best to put bullets through the chest of the foot soldiers in the hopes he was killing the actual ril-galas.

Sigurdsson ducked behind the perimeter fence and Delany took cover beside her. Peeking out, she saw Young and Elgrapharr taking cover behind the half-fallen wall of one of the older colony buildings. The tank was just ahead, a sprint of maybe four hundred metres. As she watched Young lean out and fire a salvo of grenades at the tank, Sigurdsson heard trumpets.

"Young! Air units incoming!"

It was too late. The bat struck him full on, tearing him in half before Elgrapharr turned the thing into a bloody mess with a shot from his rifle.

"Cover me!," said Sigurdsson.

As Delany began her own grenade salvo and the icaran laid down covering fire from his assault rifle, Sigurdsson dove over to what remained of Young and yanked the bag of explosives from his shredded corpse before ducking behind cover.

"Sergeant, this isn't working," said Delany, continuing to hammer the thing with grenades. "It's not enough, we don't have enough firepower!"

"The girl is right," said Elgrapharr. "Even with the explosives in Young's pack, we would need a perfectly-placed blast to take the creature down."

"The mouth!," yelled Delaney. "The last one exploded from the inside – we have to get the explosives down its throat!"

Breaking cover, she headed toward Sigurdsson, firing grenades up at the tank as she went. Sigurdsson glanced up to see the creature's massive head turn downward, its mouth agape.

"Delaney!"

The soldier continued to fire even as the stream of burning bile engulfed her.

And then the tank unleashed another jet toward Fort Hathaway. Engaging her optics, Sigurdsson zoomed in and watched the gates shudder but thankfully hold. For the time being, at least. She swore under her breath. She had a bag full of explosives that she needed to launch into the creature's mouth, but no means with which to actually launch them.

She briefly closed her eyes.

"Elgrapharr. I need you to lay down covering fire," she said as she tossed aside her assault rifle and slung the explosives-laden pack over one shoulder. She unclipped the Caliburn from her vest and held it in her right hand while drawing her combat knife with her left.

She was relieved when Elgrapharr simply nodded and set up a defensive position behind a pile of rubble. Had he asked her to explain her plan, hearing herself say it aloud might have given her the chance to realise how insane it was.

She resisted the urge to have Kenwick connect her to Radko.

As soon as she began to hear the sustained booming of the aoran rifle, Sigurdsson broke cover at an all-out run, directly toward the tank. Anything in her path that moved and didn't go down under the icaran's fire, she tagged with a burst from the SMG. She didn't care at that point whether her shots were fatal, she just needed them to slow down the enemy, prevent them from catching her or stopping her.

The Caliburn clicked empty and she tossed it aside, less than a hundred metres from the right foreleg of the tank. Somehow, she found an extra burst of energy. She ran hard, so hard her chest was burning. A few metres from the thing's leg, a ril-galas foot soldier, downed by Elgrapharr's weapon, began to rise again. Sigurdsson used it as a step, launching herself from its back toward the tank's leg.

She slammed hard into the creature, stabbing her knife deep into its muscle with her left hand while gripping tightly to one of its lumpy protrusions with her right. And she climbed. Climbed up to the tank's elbow and along its upper leg to its neck, using her knife as a secure handhold, focusing only on putting one hand after the other as she listened to the music of Elgrapharr's steady barrage. If the thing felt the pain of her knife, it showed no outward indicator, which in Sigurdsson's mind just reinforced the fact that it was more biological machine, more vehicle, than creature.

The amount of heat it generated was enormous. Her wounded palm burned. Her shirt already soaked through with sweat, Sigurdsson could feel welts beginning to form on her hands and bare arms as she climbed ever closer to the tank's gaping maw.

Gaping...

"Fuck!"

She turned her face away and flattened herself against the tank's neck as a stream of liquid shot from its mouth. The wave of heat that washed over her nearly made the Sergeant pass out, but she knew she had to move quickly. With its mouth already open, Sigurdsson would hardly have a better opportunity to get her explosives in where they could do the most damage. But she needed to be closer.

She climbed further along, until she was practically on the thing's face and found herself looking directly into one of its eyes.

"Surprise, you piece of shit."

Dropping down, she gripped the spikes on the tank's lower jaw and swung the bag of explosives into the beast's mouth. Allowing herself a small smile and a fleeting thought that she might survive this insane mission after all, Sigurdsson prepared to drop to the ground. But as she took one last glance, she saw the bag caught on something inside the creature's mouth. It was nowhere near deep enough to cause the kind of damage that would save Fort Hathaway.

Residue from the thing's bile burning into her hands, she hauled herself up, hooking her left arm inside the tank's jaw, screaming in agony as she felt her skin bubbling and melting, and with her right arm shoved the explosives deeper into the thing's throat. As she did so, her entire arm became slick with the liquid and she saw – she actually saw – her skin start to slough away and the underlying muscle burst into flame.

As she screamed, she somehow held on long enough to see the bag slide down the tank's throat and then the strength left her burning, melting arms entirely and Freyja Sigurdsson began to fall.

On the walls of Fort Hathaway, Private Rupesh, manning one of the turrets with his remaining arm, called out a warning.

"The tank is preparing for another burst!"

Everyone on the wall hesitated for a moment. They all knew that the fort's gates were just barely hanging on. One more shot from the tank and the gates would crumble.

And the ril-galas would swarm inside the walls.

And the humans would all be dead.

"Prepare for CQC!," yelled Petrov, who had assumed command of the garrison in the absence of the three highest-ranking Commonwealth soldiers – Sigurdsson, Henning and Eisenhorn. "Turrets, sustained fire on the ground forces! Snipers watch the skies!"

"Here it comes," said Rupesh.

They watched in horror as the thing opened its mouth and took several steps forward, joining the rear ranks of the ril-galas foot soldiers. The orange glow began to building the tank's throat but then suddenly the thing lurched and instead of sending a controlled jet into the gates of Fort Hathaway, the tank's head burst, spraying the caustic substance in a wide arc across half the ril-galas line.

As the ril-galas foot soldiers fell, burning, the tank keeled over and a secondary explosion ripped through its gut.

Their numbers decimated in the explosion, the ril-galas began to retreat.

As cheering broke out across the wall, Petrov ran to the edge of the wall and threw a rope over the side, waving for a team to join him.

"Come on! Take back your colony!"

As he went over the edge, a dozen soldiers followed as well as a handful of the now-armed civilians.

They ran through the burning corpses of the ril-galas, chasing those who retreated, gunning down those who stood to fight.

It was Melody Hartwood, one of the civilians drafted into service by Sigurdsson, who called out first.

"Hey! It's one of ours!," she yelled, lowering her Caliburn.

Out of the smoke and the ashes and the waves of heat from the four-plus metre high flames, came Elgrapharr. He was battered and bruised and black icaran blood coursed down one side of his face, but he was upright and walking.

And carrying the limp form of Freyja Sigurdsson over his shoulder.

Like sharks cruising just below the ocean surface, the Vimy Ridge and the Leonid Gorshkov slid silently along inside the tail of the Ishtar Gate. The route through the Gate would take the two ships right up beside the centre of the ril-galas blockade force, the radiation and distortion fields within the phenomenon keeping them hidden until the last possible moment.

At least, that was the assumption on which the entire plan was based.

Though he had great confidence in the science behind it, Radko couldn't help but feel a kernel of doubt settle into the back of his mind. After all, everything they'd discovered about the ril-galas had been unusual, so there was the possibility, however slim, that whatever passed as sensor equipment for the invaders was advanced enough to see right through the Ishtar Gate.

But if that were the case, he reminded himself yet again, there was no chance at all the Vimy Ridge and the Gorshkov would have been allowed to get so close to the enemy position without being attacked.

"We're coming up on the edge of the Ishtar Gate, Commander," said Owens. He spoke at a lower volume than normal, as if he were worried the enemy might hear him.

"Ril-galas presence still focused on Thor's Hammer," said Hamelin. "LiDAR shows no alteration in movement patterns."

So the plan, thus far, was working.

"Ready port batteries. I'll want to fire immediately as we leave the Gate."

"Aye sir," said Owens. "Which port batteries, Commander?"

"All of them. Ready a full and repeated broadside. Leonid Gorshkov, confirm readiness."

"Leonid Gorshkov is ready with full broadside, Commander," said Kovalenko.

Radko took a deep breath.

The Vimy Ridge was in position. The Leonid Gorshkov was in position. The Soviet fighter wing was ready to launch the second Kovalenko barked the order. Gunnery crews on both ships were standing by.

Releasing the breath, Radko closed his eyes for a moment, and took two more deep breaths. One aspect of the tale of the Queenstons Heights he'd omitted for Quon was the counselling he'd undergone afterward – some mandated by the Commonwealth Navy and some that he'd requested himself. In the early days post-trauma, he'd experienced anxiety attacks, not of the crippling variety – he'd have been shocked if anyone not inside his mind would have noticed much difference in his behaviour – but combined with the usual stresses of military life, he had known he was on a downward spiral. The technique of deep breathing, of closing his eyes and centring himself, had got him through and even now, having not suffered an anxiety attack in over two years, the act helped calm his nerves.

Two years without an anxiety attack.

He smiled slightly to himself and thought that it must have been a testament to his therapists that even during a time when the fate of the world quite literally rested on his plan, his decisions, the old symptoms of anxiety remained a distant memory.

Or perhaps he'd developed some kind of dissociative disorder.

The multi-coloured swirls of the Ishtar Gate drifted past the observation dome, reminding Radko that lingering much longer within the cloud would increase the risk of radiation poisoning or cancer in his crew. Some may have already received enough low-level radiation to develop tumours, maybe even Radko himself, but it wasn't something any of them could spare time to worry about – not until they'd succeeded in breaking the ril-galas blockade. If they didn't break the blockade, he didn't expect any of them to live long enough for cancer to be a concern.

"Sir," said Cortez, approaching quietly. "We're all ready."

The young Sub-Lieutenant wasn't speaking strictly about duty stations or weapon batteries or systems statuses, Radko knew. The crew itself, the lifeblood of the Vimy Ridge, was prepared to face whatever came next. That they were, if that was to be the outcome, ready to die. Many would have written letters to loved ones to be delivered in the event of their death – letters to people who may themselves already be dead – and those who believed in some form of deity or higher power or spiritual force or imaginary friend had made peace in whatever manner they needed, knowing that this day could be their last. Radko wished that they hadn't had to prepare themselves for that potential outcome, but there were a great many things that he wished they hadn't had to do.

Sometimes we're caught in decisions made by others and get carried along with the tide.

Though this time, it was a tide of his own making. If, like some of the crew, Radko had been religious – even in the slightest – facing the coming battle and the weight of its responsibility may have been easier. It would have allowed him to sit back and use the "god's will" excuse to justify inaction, to sit and pray and wait on an invisible hand to sweep in and save humanity rather than forcing himself – forcing his crew – to push on, beyond what any reasonable man could expect of them.

He hoped the crew understood the rationale behind it, the necessity of it...

"Thank you, Cortez."

"Thank you, sir. For having so much faith in me."

"Faith is just another word for hopeful guesswork," he said, waving his hand dismissively as if the word were a fly buzzing around him. "What I had was an understanding of your capabilities."

"Then thank you," she said with a small smile. "For understanding my capabilities better than me."

That made him chuckle.

"You're welcome. Now," he said, becoming serious. "I'm about to give the order that commits us to the assault. No second-guesses, no second chances. We only have two possible outcomes here, Anna: we win, or we're destroyed. There won't be any middle ground."

He paused, glancing out at the fading swirls of the Ishtar Gate.

"I don't intend on dying today," he said. "So let's get this victory underway."

"Yes, sir."

Taking a deep breath, Radko stepped up to the second level sand table, where he could view all of the data for the coming battle while still able to watch first-hand, through the transparent observation dome.

No stirring speech was to be made, no words to be said that hadn't already been said a dozen or more times. The crew of the Vimy Ridge knew what was at stake, as did the crew of the Leonid Gorshkov. As did the icaran commandos – while Locaris had remained on the command deck, the remainder of his team were in the shuttle bay, geared up and on standby should their skills be required. At that moment, there was really nothing left for Radko to say even if he had felt inclined to launch into a speech, and anything he'd said would simply have distracted the crew, broken the concentration they all knew was so crucial. So he said the only thing that mattered at that moment.

"Begin the attack run."

Almost immediately, he felt a slight change in the thrum of the engines through the deck plates as the Vimy Ridge accelerated sharply. For a moment, there was silence, and in that silence, Radko imagined he could hear the whir of the gun ports opening and the metallic thunk of rail guns deploying and the heavy clang of the missile launchers locking into place and then the moment was broken.

"Exiting the Ishtar Gate!," said the pilot.

"All gunnery stations report ready to fire on your order, Commander," said Owens. "Gorshkov confirms same."

Radko didn't respond. He didn't need to. The multi-coloured gasses of the Ishtar Gate were sliding away from the observation dome with an almost liquid consistency as the Vimy Ridge and the Leonid Gorshkov broke the surface of the quasi-nebula.

The sharks had risen for their attack.

"Enemy battleship directly-."

The pilot's exclamation was drowned out by a proximity alarm, which someone mercifully shut off immediately. It was no secret to anyone what had caused it.

Less than a kilometre to port sat a motionless ril-galas ship, its stern turned slightly toward the Ishtar Gate. Exposed. Unaware. Directly beside it – in fact tethered to it with some kind of thick, organic cabling – was one of the centipede-like carriers, fully stocked with swarm fighters.

There were four other ships in the blockade, but for the moment, it was only those two that mattered.

"Full broadside on my mark, then gunnery teams are free to fire at will," said Radko.

As Owens relayed the order and Kovalenko did the same, Radko almost smiled.

"Fire."

A low rumble shivered its way up through the ship as every port-side weapon array – cannon, rail gun, missile battery – fired as one. A full broadside. It was a battle strategy almost unheard of in modern warfare, with vessels most frequently trading salvos at great distances, but the old school naval broadside was a devastating attack even when launched from an ancient ocean-going vessel of twenty hand-loaded, gunpowder-fed iron cannons. The Vimy Ridge had sixty weapon emplacements, thirty per side, with more power in a single shot than the entirety of the old British Royal Navy's ten best ships of the line.

It was true the British Royal Navy had never faced an adversary like the ril-galas – the British Empire had been facing fellow humans who, more or less, thought as they did and had access to the same technologies they did – but it was also true that the ril-galas had become complacent in remarkably short order, settling in to a blockade as if they thought the war was over.

As the ordinance of the Vimy Ridge and Leonid Gorshkov tore through the enemy battleship and then hammered into the carrier, Radko was certain that the invaders had received the message: this isn't over.

"Gorshkov is deploying fighters," said Cortez.

Radko said nothing, just nodding his acknowledgement. The ril-galas battleship disintegrated into a short-lived ball of blue flame and as the carrier began launching its fighters, something burst along its spine and a chain reaction of explosions rippled backward down the length of the ship. Within seconds, its entire rear half was gone, nothing but a cloud of debris, and the majority of its fighters, having still been locked by their docking clamps, were reduced to slag.

"Battleship confirmed destroyed," said Owens, just as another set of internal explosions ripped apart what remained of the carrier. "And I think we can consider that one confirmed, too."

There were some tense chuckles and Radko even smiled slightly.

"Pilot," he said. "Thirty degrees to port, full speed."

The four remaining ril-galas ships – all battleships – were beginning to turn toward them and the closest of the four was charging its powerful energy cannon.

"We cannot allow them to use those weapons against us," said Locaris.

Radko looked up at the icaran. He hadn't even noticed his approach.

"Four cannons with firepower of that magnitude will tear your vessel apart."

"Agreed. We need to," he paused as the ship shook from a swarm fighter strafing run. "We need to focus-fire on one at a time if we're going to take them out quickly."

Instead of responding, Locaris narrowed all four eyes and stepped closer to the observation dome. Reaching out he activated a magnification window and enlarged the farthest of the ril-galas battleships. There were small explosions occurring all along one side.

"Cortez," said Radko.

"I see it, sir. Thor's Hammer confirms that the INS Godavari and the HMS Sir Walter Raleigh have joined the battle."

Though he simply nodded, it took a great deal of control to not allow the immensity of his relief to show through. And when Locaris turned back and caught Radko's eye, he knew the icaran understood and felt the same. Four against four, now. Their odds of success, of survival, had increased significantly.

And then Hamelin cried out.

"Commander! Swarm battleship-."

The ship suddenly lurched under heavy impact, Radko stumbling and only managing to stay upright by gripping the rail of the catwalk. Locaris staggered against the dome.

"Owens?"

"We've been hit by one of the ril-galas energy weapons," said Owens. "Damage report in a moment."

"They came up on our stern, sir," said Cortez.

Radko cursed.

"Commander, we've lost three of our starboard cannons. No rail guns affected. One engine offline. No word yet on how quickly any of it can be repaired."

"Casualties?"

"Injury reports are coming in now, though it's too soon to know exact numbers. There are a lot, Sir. Gunnery crews seventeen and eighteen are not responding."

"Battleship is priming its weapon again!," someone shouted.

"Bring us around, hard starboard! Ready another broadside. Kovalenko?"

"Am here, Radko," came the static-riddled response. "Enemy must have been hidden by Ishtar, like us."

"Looks that way. We're more maneuverable, so we'll deal with it – you keep hammering the ones caught between us and Thor's Hammer."

"Agreed. Will re-assign one-third fighters to support Vimy Ridge."

"Much appreciated, Captain."

"Is my pleasure, Radko," said Kovalenko, the predatory undertone evident even through the interference. "Is my pleasure."

As a wing of Soviet fighters streaked overhead, Radko gave the order to k-turn – Navy slang for firing the fore and aft maneuvering thrusters in opposite directions, causing the ship to spin on its axis. It was rarely done, as it could be a very dangerous maneuver, but neither Radko nor his crew were where they were in order to play it safe.

Nor could they afford to.

The thrusters fired at full power and the Vimy Ridge spun so quickly that Radko could feel the tug of the additional gravitational forces. No one lost their balance, but a few crew members gripped their consoles a little tighter.

The ril-galas battleship slid into view.

It was the closest the Vimy Ridge had ever been to one of the enemy ships and Radko could see every detail – the series of spines dotting its mottled green hull, the ports along its ventral line that he now knew were connectors for some sort of inter-ship tethering system, and the large opening in its bow that was the muzzle of its powerful energy cannon. A cannon which was already glowing brightly.

The beam lanced out, the brightness causing spots to dance in front of Radko's eyes, but the k-turn had taken the Vimy Ridge out of the ril-galas firing arc. The Soviet fighters weren't as lucky. When the beam faded, two friendly fighters had all but disintegrated.

Radko hoped that for the pilots, it had been as painless as it had been quick.

"Fire at will."

Repeating the order for all the gunnery crews to hear, Owens waited for confirmation, then looked up at Radko on the catwalk above, frowning.

"Commander, half of our gunnery crews can't get a clear shot. We need to reposition."

"Enemy beam weapon is charging!," said Cortez.

Through the dome, Radko saw the ril-galas ship was repositioning itself dead ahead of the Vimy Ridge, turning to bring its most powerful weapon to bear. The Soviet fighters were doing their best to harass the battle ship and deal what damage they could, but whoever or whatever was controlling the battleship was focused on the bigger threat.

The armour of the Vimy Ridge wasn't designed to protect against beam weapons. Even the most technologically advanced of human adversaries, the icarans, still fired projectiles. Radko had no idea what an energy weapon discharging point blank into her hull would do to the Vimy Ridge or her crew. He watched the glow become brighter, its light reflecting off the hull spikes of the...

Hull spikes. Rigid hull spikes.

Possibly rigid enough to penetrate the first layer of the Vimy Ridge's Electromagnetic Reactive Armour.

"Full station lockdown," he said sharply. "And give me ramming speed."

There was hardly a second of hesitation before the order was repeated, carried through the ship and the main engines brought up to cruising speed quicker than was, accordingly to all the rules and regulations, advisable for a ship of her age.

"Impact in twenty seconds," said Owens, his voice echoing through the ship-wide comm system.

Radko gripped the rail of the catwalk.

He was gambling with the lives of his crew and possibly with the lives of those aboard the Gorshkov, Thor's Hammer and the handful of Commonwealth ships that remained. But, he reminded himself, that's exactly what he'd been doing all along. Gambling. He's just have to hope that his lucky streak wasn't about to run out.

"Ten seconds," said Owens. "Nine. Eight."

The Commander braced himself and saw others doing the same.

"Seven. Six."

Cortez was looking up at him he knew, but he stared straight ahead, into the ril-galas ship that was filling his field of vision at an alarming rate.

"Five. Four. Three."

Their enemy had realized what was happening, started to turn and fired whatever passed as maneuvering thrusters in their technology in an effort to avoid impact, but they had been too slow to understand and too slow to react – which made Radko smile.

"Two," said Owens, strain creeping into his voice for the first time. "One."

"Surprise, you piece of shit," said Radko softly.

Sirens wailed as the blunt prow of the Vimy Ridge hammered into the exposed side of the ril-galas ship, crushing the alien hull inward.

Radko tore his eyes away from the live display to look at the sand table and slapped his palm on the rail in his only outward show of emotion.

All across the bow of the holographic Vimy Ridge, small yellow spheres were pulsing. The ERA indicators.

He glanced up again and saw arcs of electricity coursing across the battered hull of the enemy and then heard the low excited murmur of the crew below him who had just realised what he hadn't had time to explain: the spines on the ril-galas hull had punctured the first layer of ERA plates, unleashing the tremendous voltage that was now reducing portions of the enemy hull to slag.

"Engines and thrusters full reverse!," he said, not wanting to linger too closely to admire their handiwork, given the explosions beginning to bubble up from inside the ril-galas ship. "Get us to a safe distance. Rail guns, fire at will."

As the Vimy Ridge pulled away, Radko watched with a grim smile as his rail gunners began to fire, their projectiles tearing chunks out of the crippled battleship and then, in one sudden, brilliant fireball, the ril-galas ship vanished.

"Bring us about," he said, before anyone let themselves start cheering. "Get us back in position with the Gorshkov."

After confirming the order, Owens changed the sand table display to show current positions of all combatants. The remaining ril-galas ships appeared to be converging on the Leonid Gorshkov.

"Damage report, Owens."

"Minor, Commander" said Owens, the surprise clear in his voice. "We don't look as pretty as we used to, but no structural damage and no hull breaches."

Nodding to Owens, Radko quickly turned his attention back to the sand table.

"Captain Kovalenko," he said. "We're on our way back."

"Is good, Radko. Leonid Gorshkov is about to be hit very hard."

Frowning, Radko stepped up to the observation dome and activated a magnification window. On either side of the Gorshkov was a ril-galas battleship, their energy canons beginning to glow.

When Private Kenwick had burst into the MediCorps building and gasped the words "It's Sigurdsson," Khaifa had felt a knot immediately form in her guts. She'd abandoned the patient upon whom she had been performing first aid, grabbed the nearest of their makeshift medical supply bags and run after the private faster than she thought possible.

The Sergeant had been laid out in the open space behind the gates of Fort Hathaway, an empty weapons crate having been converted into a makeshift bed for her, as had been done for many of the badly wounded. The dog – Jaeger – sat stock still, vigilant, beside the crate, facing the gates of the fort. The doctor stumbled slightly, her legs weakening as she saw the mangled and charred remains of the woman's arms. All that remained of Sigurdsson's left hand was the thumb – everything else having been so badly and deeply burned, it had likely broken off in pieces as she'd been carried back to the fort. That the right arm was in better condition was no comfort. It too was burned black. Flakes of charred skin and muscle floated to the ground as Khaifa watched, horrified.

There was no chance Freyja Sigurdsson would ever use her arms again.

"She came into direct contact with the incendiary fluid from the large creatures," said Elgrapharr.

Khaifa just nodded, not trusting herself with a verbal response. Stooping over the patient, she reached out to gently touch Sigurdsson's left arm, but drew back in shock. There was still an alarming amount of heat coming off the burned limbs. Almost as if they were still burning.

The doctor removed her coat and tossed it aside. Kneeling down beside the crate, she swallowed heavily and tried to focus on the injuries and not the person. Khaifa found herself sweating and she wasn't certain if it was from the waves of heat coming off her patient or from her own near-panic at the situation before her.

Kenwick leaned in beside her.

"Is she...?"

"Shut up, Kenwick," she said, then looked up at the cluster of soldiers and civilians alike crowding the area. "I need snow. Clean snow. Pack it around her – not the arms, leave those clear – but legs, torso. We need to stop her from overheating."

Thankfully, no one questioned the order – they just went and found whatever they could, be it a bucket or cardboard box or a helmet, and started filling it with the cleanest snow they could find. When Brill stepped up beside her and began to do his own examination of Sigurdsson's wounds, Khaifa barely glanced up.

"It is unsettling to see this much heat being generated by her wounds," it said.

And indeed it was. Such was the heat remaining in Sigurdsson's arms that tiny glowing ribbons of red flickered throughout, like embers in a fire. They flowed up what remained of her biceps and into the deltoid and...

Khaifa drew back and she heard a small sound of surprise from the brill.

Slowly but surely, the embers continued to climb higher, into the less damaged flesh and then into undamaged areas.

"She's still burning," said Khaifa, a look of horror on her face.

She pressed a finger into the previously undamaged area and yanked away in pain.

"It's so hot," she said. "This is going to spread until her whole body is nothing but ash."

Turning to the brill, Khaifa knew what she had to do and she knew the brill knew it as well. She felt a tear roll down her cheek and she wiped it away roughly with the back of her hand.

"We have to amputate."

The brill bobbed its head in agreement.

"I would suggest we proceed immediately," it said. "Before the incendiary fluid enters her bloodstream."

Doing her best to remain calm, Khaifa forced herself to nod.

There was no time to do it properly. There was no time to do it cleanly. Climbing atop the container, Khaifa straddled Sigurdsson's waist.

"You and you," she said, pointing to Elgrapharr and one of the former ATC Castle commandos whose name she couldn't remember – if she'd ever known it in the first place. "Hold her still."

As they moved to comply, Khaifa held out her hand to the ATC Castle commando.

"Give me that."

He looked confused for a moment, but quickly understood. Unstrapping the tactical tomahawk from his chest rig, he handed it over before taking a mirroring position to Elgrapharr and getting a grip on Sigurdsson.

Taking the tomahawk in her hand, Khaifa adjusted her grip once, twice, three times, before briefly closing her eyes and swearing under her breath. As she opened her eyes, she looked down into Sigurdsson's face, etched with pain and sweating profusely, then the doctor clenched her teeth and put all of her strength into a downward swing of the hatchet. The blade struck with a wet thunk and the cracking of bone and a small spray of blood spattered across Khaifa's cheek. The heat of it nearly scalded her, but she ignored the pain, quickly wiping the blood away and swinging the tomahawk once more.

It took Khaifa three strikes with the blade to sever each of Sigurdsson's arms.

"Take those," she said to the ATC Castle soldier. Sliding off the crate, Khaifa pointed with a shaking hand to what was left of the Sergeant's amputated arms. "Throw them over the wall. Wear heavy gloves or you'll burn yourself."

She was about to ask Brill to take over, to dress the wounds, but she realized it was already doing so, quickly and efficiently as it always did. So instead, she let the tomahawk slide from her grasp.

Jaeger still sat at Sigurdsson's side, never having moved a muscle or disrupted his vigil for a second during all the commotion. Protecting his master, thought Khaifa, just as his master had protected everyone inside the walls of Fort Hathaway. Standing guard, come what may.

"When the brill is done, pack more snow around her," she said to no one in particular. As she sank to her knees in the snow, she saw that several people were rushing to gather more clean snow and she leaned her forehead against the cold metal of the crate and began to cry.

"Missiles away!"

Radko watched intently, as if by force of will he could make the warheads fly faster, hit harder. If the Vimy Ridge couldn't at the very least get the attention of one of the ril-galas battleships, the Leonid Gorshkov was all but lost. Though he didn't doubt the Soviet ship could withstand a blast from one of the alien energy weapons, rolling the dice on the survivability of two simultaneous blasts was not something they could afford.

"Closing within rail gun range in five," said Owens. "Four..."

"Rail gunners will fire at will," said Radko, involuntarily clenching the rail a little tighter as he watched their missiles strike home. The ril-galas ship began a slow turn toward the Vimy Ridge and Radko slapped the rail with his left hand in relief.

"Areas damaged by our missile batteries are priority one targets," he said. "Order our wing of Soviet fighters to support the Gorshkov."

The fighters streaked overhead, aiming directly for the second, undamaged enemy vessel while Radko felt the vibrations in the Ridge's deck plates that told him his rail gunners were active.

However, whatever relief he'd felt at drawing an enemy away from the Gorshkov was short-lived. The battleship's beam weapon was primed and ready and would be pointing at the Vimy Ridge in seconds.

"Brace for impact!"

It struck the lower port bow and the deck plates vibrated violently under Radko's boots. He saw pieces of hull plating twisted and spinning off into space.

Alarms were sounding – three of them – only two of which he could even identify.

"Damage report!"

"Two more rail guns offline," said Owens. "I'm getting no data at all from missile batteries one through three and we have a hull breach on deck six."

"Get it sealed," said Radko through gritted teeth. He knew the order was unnecessary – Owens had likely dispatched crews before Radko even knew the breach existed – but he felt the need to do something, anything.

"Enemy weapon charging again!"

He didn't know who it was that had called out and Radko felt himself losing his grip on his calm. It occurred to him that his calm may have been an act all along, one that he'd bought into himself. Clenching and unclenching his fists, he turned to see Locaris suddenly at his side.

"We have a very old saying in the icaran military," he said softly. "That the battle is not lost until the commander is."

The icaran was probably a hundred years his senior. Maybe more.

The wisdom of age.

Radko couldn't lose it now, he wouldn't lose it now. His crew was depending on him to see them through; the crew of the Gorshkov were looking to him to see them through. Even the people on Thor's Hammer, the crews of the other ships...

His upper lip curling into a sneer, his eyes narrowing, Radko pointed at the approaching ril-galas ship.

"It doesn't end like this."

He spun toward the upper level sand table, to the holographic Vimy Ridge.

"Owens! Status of starboard batteries?"

"One rail gun offline, one missile battery offline, Commander."

"Pilot," yelled Radko, not even trying to keep the anger out of his voice. There was a time to project calm, he figured, and a time to let everyone know he was done strategizing a ready to unleash hell. "Half k-turn on my mark. Owens, direct a full broadside of starboard weapons on my mark!"

Owens and the pilot confirmed and Radko looked over to Locaris and was positive he saw the commando smile.

"Half k-turn now," said Radko, his voice slightly more controlled.

As the pilot hit the thrusters, the back end of the Brock Class frigate swung outward, exposing its starboard flank to the oncoming battleship.

"Ready broadside!"

"All starboard batteries are go," confirmed Owens.

"Fire!"

The deck plates shook once more as every functioning starboard battery on the Vimy Ridge opened fire.

"Continuous fire," said Radko. "Until I order otherwise."

He watched as flames bloomed and vanished on the battleship and as the projectiles fired by his rail guns tore through its hull, sending detritus cartwheeling off into the black. Just as with their very first encounter with a ril-galas vessel, Radko could see the glow of its energy weapon beginning to fluctuate, the weapon's containment losing stability in the face of increasing damage. Out of the corner of his eye, he saw the Gorshkov unleash a broadside into its own adversary, but Radko remained focused on the now-reeling ship off his starboard. The gunnery crews continued to pummel it.

And then something inside it seemed to crack.

The damaged battleship erupted in a sphere of fire and debris.

"Do we have a targeting solution on the second ship?," said Radko, immediately changing focus to the remaining vessel attacking the Gorshkov. It had just unleashed a blast from its beam weapon that struck a glancing blow off the stern of the Soviet vessel. One of the Gorshkov's four engines winked out.

"Missile batteries confirm targeting solution, Commander. Rail gunners report no arc."

"Fire missiles, then get us into rail gun territory."

"Aye, sir."

As the Gorshkov's broadside continued to tear into the alien ship, a dozen missiles from the Vimy Ridge's batteries slammed into its aft section, opening a gaping hole in its hull.

Seconds later, the battleship – the final vessel in the ril-galas blockade of Thor's Hammer – ruptured internally and exploded.

Glancing down into the command deck, Radko saw a crew about to cheer and felt himself ready to join them, so he spoke quickly.

"We need status reports on damage – us and the Gorshkov. Same for the ships from Thor's Hammer that joined the fight."

"On it, sir," said Owens.

Both his ship and Kovalenko's had taken damage. Time would tell how serious the damage was, but they couldn't allow the rilgalas to take advantage of the weakness -- no matter how minor or how temporary.

"Cortez, contact the station. We need immediate and continual patrols. We didn't break one blockade just to give them time to set up another."

"Yes, Commander."

"And please set up a ship-wide broadcast. Pipe it through to the Gorshkov and... you know what? Give me a full broadcast. All Commonwealth channels that are still active."

The young woman looked up at him and he met her gaze and smiled. While he didn't want anyone to get carried away, maybe it wouldn't be so bad to let them know they'd scored a significant victory. He watched as Cortez tapped out a few commands into her tablet and then she looked up again and nodded.

A green light was blinking on the secondary sand table console. He tapped it to activate the channel.

"This is Lieutenant Commander Fin Radko of the HMCS Vimy Ridge. The blockade around Thor's Hammer has been broken, the enemy destroyed. We have struck back against the invaders and while we can't become complacent in this victory, make no mistake – it is a victory. With that said, we still have work to do. Continue to man your stations."

Closing the connection, he stepped up to the observation dome and looked out toward Thor's Hammer. Toward the last bastion on the Commonwealth.

It had taken a great deal of talking and some borderline insubordinate remarks before Admiral Mahoney had been convinced that evacuating the civilians and the wounded from Van Daniken's Landing was something to which assets should be committed. In the end, that was the argument Radko had been forced to make – preservation of assets. The colony itself and the mines around which it were built were in little danger of ril-galas occupation due to the severity of the impending winter, but the Commonwealth – such as it was at that moment – could not afford to lose the assets represented by the civilian and military personnel stranded at Fort Hathaway. Miners could work in dark, enclosed spaces, he had argued; mechanics could be re-trained to work with the starship repair and maintenance teams on Thor's Hammer. Soldiers were needed to fight any war, and soldiers with combat experience against an otherwise unknown enemy were more valuable than gold.

In the end, the HMS Edinburgh had been dispatched.

Radko, sitting in his office for a rare moment of peace while crews from the Vimy Ridge and Thor's Hammer went over every inch of the ship to catalogue repair requirements, re-opened the communications link to Fort Hathaway.

"Vimy Ridge, this is Von Daniken's Landing," said Kenwick. "Good to hear you again."

"Likewise, Fort Hathaway. How's the situation there?"

"Stable," said the Private, not even trying to conceal his surprise. "We... we managed to beat them. I mean, for now. It's been hours since we've seen any movement beyond the walls."

"That's good news," said Radko, meaning every word. "I need to speak with Sergeant Sigurdsson."

There was a long pause and Radko was about to repeat the request, assuming their troubled connection had been interrupted, when another voice came on the line.

"Vimy Ridge, this is Doctor Nasrin Khaifa."

Radko nodded to himself. The doctor from the autopsy video.

Then he paused and rubbed at his tired eyes with one hand.

The doctor who was married to Colonel Harlan Gray. The late Colonel Gray.

He pushed the thoughts aside. It wasn't the time to have that discussion – not while he was so bone tired and not over a poor audio connection during an ongoing crisis.

"Doctor, thank you for your work regarding the ril-galas autopsy," he said. "I was hoping to speak with Sigurdsson. Is she otherwise occupied?"

"Freyja was... badly injured in the last attack."

He waited for her to elaborate, feeling something uncomfortable develop in the pit of his stomach.

"Is she all right, Doctor?," he said once it became clear nothing further was forthcoming.

"She'll survive."

"That isn't what I asked, Doctor Khaifa. Will she be all right?"

"I... I don't know. I don't think so."

"But she'll live?"

"Yes."

Small victories. It wasn't the way he had been hoping this conversation would go, but Radko was becoming accustomed to finding the small victories.

He explained to Khaifa that the Edinburgh was currently en route to Von Daniken's Landing to evacuate Fort Hathaway and provided her with a direct comm channel to the ship so she could advise of any resurgent ril-galas activity.

When the channel closed, Radko leaned back and rubbed his eyes and then swore and threw his tablet across the small room. It broke into two pieces and clattered to the floor just as his door buzzer sounded.

Taking two calming breaths, he tapped the button that would signal the all-clear to enter.

Stepping inside the office, Cortez first set down a pile of paper reports and then, beside them, a steaming mug of tea.

Radko stared at the mug for a moment.

"That's tea."

"Yes sir."

"If I could promote you to Captain right now, I would," he said, picking up the mug and taking a long sip. "I need this more than I need scotch. And I thought I needed scotch pretty badly."

"Are things not going well at the Fort?," she said, the concern evident in her young face.

With a sigh, Radko recounted his discussion with Khaifa, noticing Cortez flinch at the mention of the doctor's name. She'd of course heard Quon's statement and Gray's acknowledgement that Khaifa was his wife. The battle had pushed the young woman's feelings about Grey's death – be they guilt or something else – into that same little black compartment in her head like the one Radko had made such liberal use of in his own head after the Queenston Heights. The vault where he kept the things that would have driven him crazy if they'd been sitting out in the open. They were feelings that Cortez would need to deal with, but as with telling Doctor Khaifa about her husband's death, Radko was simply not in the frame of mind to play counsellor to Cortez, no matter how much he might have liked to do just that. Counselling would have to be left to someone more qualified.

"So what do we do now?," said Cortez.

"We rebuild our fleet. We rebuild our alliances," he said, tapping the reports she'd brought in – after-action reports from the Leonid Gorshkov and Brigadier General Locaris. "We find any other ships like us, ships that survived the onslaught, and we bring them here. Mahoney has already started an emergency regrouping broadcast, so has Kovalenko. We find places like Fort Hathaway, where our armed forces have held out, and we get them support."

"And then... we take the war to the ril-galas?"

Radko nodded.

"And then we show them that this war isn't over. We show them that it's only just begun."

About the author:

David Whale lives in Stoney Creek, Ontario Canada, with his spouse Crazy, his step-daughter Lil Crazy, their dog Mundungus. He has been telling stories in various forms since he was a kid, from writing and drawing his own comic books to creating photo-stories using his old Kenner Star Wars action figures to script doctoring on a televised sports show to novels.
When not writing, Whale enjoys reading, drawing, creating custom action figures, and trying like hell to finish the Stormtrooper costume he's been working on intermittently for a year.

He also spends time writing a blog at his website, Whale-Writer.com, though probably not as often as he should.

Website: WhaleWriter.com

Facebook: facebook.com/davidwhalewriter

Twitter: @davidwhale

Instagram: whale.david